final cut

by Daniel Stern

final cut

cut

a

novel

by

daniel

stern

a richard seaver book

the viking press

new york

Copyright © 1975 by Daniel Stern
All rights reserved
A Richard Seaver Book/The Viking Press
First published in 1975 by The Viking Press, Inc.
625 Madison Avenue, New York, N.Y. 10022
Published simultaneously in Canada by
The Macmillan Company of Canada Limited
Printed in U.S.A.

Library of Congress Cataloging in Publication Data
Stern, Daniel, 1928-
    Final cut.
    "A Richard Seaver book."
    I.   Title.
PZ4.S838Fi   [PS3569.T3887]   813'.5'4   74-4799
ISBN 0-670-31333-5

For Andy . . . for friendship and integrity.
And in memory of Richard Stuchiner: 1947–1969.

In fact, the life of a private citizen would be preferable to that of a King at the expense of the ruin of so many human beings. Nevertheless, whoever is unwilling to adopt the first and humane course must, if he wishes to maintain his power, follow the latter evil course. But men generally decide upon a middle course which is most hazardous; for they know neither how to be wholly good nor wholly bad, and so lose both worlds.

—The Prince, by
Nicolo Machiavelli

final cut

This is the hottest spring in the history of New Mexico. Or so Juan, the guide furnished by the hotel, tells me. It has been a year of extremes—the coldest New York, the wettest London, the sultriest Rome, the smoggiest Hollywood. Perhaps these were simply the usual tales told by natives to the naïve visitor. In many ways that is precisely what I have been in all these places, in all the lives I have visited this year, this sabbatical of celluloid and blood. A tourist in the lands of power, and now a convalescent under this inverted cup of blue sky, its blazing circle of sun.

I had done two Indian reservations, squatted on a massive mesa peering into shaky horizons I could barely grasp with sun-blasted eyes; had bought the appropriate souvenirs, the postcards (though I have no desire to write to anyone except Kim, and she must write to me first), the native dolls, the obligatory sandals. Certain signs did point to the extremeness of my retreat. Like the unopened telegram I was certain was from Kleinholz. I was proud of that sealed flap. Telegrams test the will. Or is it the absence of will?

Yesterday Juan and I were touring the Taos Pueblo and suddenly, from nowhere or from behind a little pile of rocks, there appeared a twisting, whirling cone of dust, rocks, air: all accompanied by an awful clattering and whistling. The two or three Indians who had been sitting somberly wrapped in their Sears, Roebuck blankets, in spite of the intense heat, jumped up and vanished behind one of the two- and three-story muddy brown buildings. Juan too, was gone in a second. And so was the heavy, lethargic inner mood I'd been carrying with me since I'd left New York. I hit the ground and rolled toward a low, smoking chimney, then crawled the last few feet on my stomach, to complete cover.

In the aftermath of quickened breath and adrenalin I realized how foggy I'd been; how much in need of solitude, even of self-indulgent apathy. And so I've sought it again. I sleep a great deal. The telegram remains unopened. And I'm not likely to encounter another mini-twister. Devil Dusters they're called, Juan told me on the way up to the shrine of D. H. Lawrence.

We'd begun the dramatic climb back at Albuquerque, then drove up to Santa Fe, about two thousand feet higher. My heart had been beating faster and faster in the two days I'd been in Albuquerque, but the clerk, an Indian who wore a blanket in and out of the air-conditioned lobby, told me it was the altitude. By the time Juan and I passed Arroyoseco and made the upward turn toward Taos it was a sensation I could take for granted.

"Should have come on horses," Juan said. He shifted into low gear for the steep climb. "Movie people sometimes come on horses."

"Not this one," I said.

"You are movie people ... ?"

"I was," I said. "But I was never much on horses. I'm from New York."

That seemed to settle the horse question, and Juan was silent. He was very strong on "movie people." Many of them had been his clients, some doing research on the local Indians for film projects; others had been tourists who told him as many tales of the film world as he'd told them about New Mexico history in the pursuit of his work. The Burtons had once tipped him a hundred dollars, he informed me solemnly, and then asked if I would like to meet Russell James. He lived above the Arroyoseco, was quite old but still made sense when he spoke. And he was a great movie person. Everyone said so. I told Juan I knew he was, but that I had no desire to meet Russell James. Juan fell silent again and continued silent as we climbed through the browns and reddish yellows of dust and leaves. Sordino had wanted to take me down to Sicily to visit Greek ruins, along with Nick Bohm and the poor boy with the perfect face: Karol. The browns and reds of Sicily, Sordino had said, were the most beautiful in the world. But events had moved too swiftly.

We passed a sign informing us that the Lawrence shrine was now owned and administered by the University of New Mexico, turned right through a shroud of overhanging leaves, and came to a cottage whose door was open. In the doorway, his back to us, stood a figure who could have been Nick Bohm: the body slouched in a casual curve to the right as he leaned with one hand on a desk, the other hand lightly laid on his hip in one of those Bohm-like attitudes which I later learned—or thought I did—were not so instinctive at all. But that was one of Nick's great and mysterious charms for me. The constant question of how much what he did was studied, how much was spontaneous. Seeing this arc of arm and hand from behind I again became aware of the pounding of my heart.

I got out of the car and walked up to the cottage. The sound of Juan parking made the man turn around. He was much younger than Nick Bohm, with a sunburned skin far less intense than Nick's rich brown—burnished by twenty years of attention from the suns of Hollywood, Las Vegas, Cannes, and Majorca.

"Hello," he said.

"May I have a glass of water," I said. "My chest is pounding."

"The altitude," he said as I drank. "I'm from L.A. myself. It took me months to adjust." He was chatty. (Not many people made the pilgrimage in the heat, I would have guessed.) "I'm a student at the university. A film major."

Juan stood silently behind me, waiting.

"Yes," I said. "I understand film is very big at the colleges these days."

"But I'm doing a paper on Lawrence, so—I work around the place here. . . ."

He stood outside the cottage as Juan and I hiked up the

narrow path leading to the shrine. Birds flushed from bushes as we passed. The sun stood at right angles to the shrine, in the western sector of the sky. It was good to step into the shadows of the shrine for a moment; peaceful and cool, the stillest moment I'd had in a year. It was the kind of place I should have visited with Kim. She would have been quiet, not out of false sanctity but out of the natural sense of the moment. Later she might joke about shrines and the ego of artists. But now she would understand the moment: some instinctive, inbred Southern feel for the external rightness of things; the manner that surrounds the matter.

The shrine was neatly arranged, with Lawrence's wife, Frieda, buried outside, perhaps because she had remarried after Lawrence's death and was being punished. I felt a little foolish for having been oblivious to the banal, unconsicous reason for coming to Taos. I'd spent part of the last year working with Sordino on an extraordinary film based on Lawrence—and then just fell in on Lawrence's tomb, with no awareness of the connection. It had all the sensitivity that marked the lives of Juan's favorite "movie people."

They flew into my mind so quickly—those "sensitivities" —that I could not turn them away or distract myself. The day we heard of the crash during the shooting of a World War I picture, a crash in which a young French director was killed and two others badly hurt. Becker, the Executive V.P., said quickly: "It's all right. It's only a pick-up deal. We can get out." Then, sensing the thick silence all around, added: "What a tragedy!" Or, Kleinholz, the day the brilliant singer Joseph Jack Johnson died with a needle in his arm: "Do you think it'll hurt the stock?"

It was not as if Robinson hadn't warned me. He'd known them all, every horror, every gross insult to the spirit that was in store for me.

"Ezra, buddy," he'd said one night, lyrical with self-contempt, "the people I now spend my daily life with have raised the irrelevance of the universal human element in man to a high style not seen since certain incidents took place in the Doge's Palace in medieval Venice. The movie business is so riddled with dishonesty, cowardice, hatred, lechery, nepotism, and other such virtues that the entire atmosphere is without the element of surprise. No matter what disaster befalls anyone—it is expected. Every rumor is at least partially true; most of them are utterly correct—especially if they carry bad news. The root is an economics raised to the status of a transvaluation of values. It's not like economics in Washington, where values are mixed: money, power, even—God help us—patriotism. Money in the film world eclipses every other value. When that sublime measure becomes mixed with an institution, the result is a unique power system. That institution is called the Studio . . . and every sin done in its name only binds one closer to it, as with the church, and if that institution is threatened (and it is always threatened but never more than now), then no supercrime is out of the question, no action too horrendous to the imagination, if the Studio is to be saved. . . ."

It was a few moments after this speech that he suggested I join the studio: "Think of the challenge!"

I was no stranger to Robbie's challenges. In his class at the Harvard Graduate School of Economics he'd taken special pleasure in singling me out: "Perhaps Mr. Marks will explain to us all how he arrives at the correlation between purchasing habits, age, and class background. Without relying on his namesake Karl, of course."

Over a drink at the Ritz Bar I reminded Professor Robinson that my name was spelled differently from either Karl or Groucho. He, in turn, reminded me that he was no professor: only a guest lecturer in a dubious new discipline: communications.

"Mine is only a little less dubious," I said. "Demographics. What kind of a name is that for a nice little non-science?"

And thus, having played the Harvard game of ironic cool, each of us dropped defenses. Robbie launched into a speech about a new religion called public television. It began with simple fervor and ended—over fish and wine at Lundy's—with unprofessorial passion.

"For Christ's sake, the people of the country don't own much! But at least they own the airways—think what you could do with a public television network that handled birth control or disarmament openly, without worrying about business interests and sponsors. . . . You couldn't have had a Joe McCarthy run wild the way he did if you'd had a real public TV setup in this country."

We sat on a bench in Copley Square, listening to bells chime at 3:00 a.m. while I talked about youth . . . demographic patterns . . . the connection between sexual and voting patterns. . . .

"Once in generations something crazy like the baby boom of World War II sets off a situation when the power shifts—just by weight of numbers—to young people. That's where we are now. And if Jack Kennedy wins in November. . ."

That was almost eleven years ago. September, 1960. My questions were different ones, now. And Robbie's questions, of late, were more like answers. Answers I would have to face, one way or another, in a few days, when I faced Robbie . . . Robbie the cool, who had taken me with him into two worlds; had played Virgil to my Dante guiding me through the subtle twilights of Georgetown and the smoggy dangers of southern California . . . who had finally urged my emigration into that pure air beyond good and evil, where an airplane crash is what jeopardizes a deal and death is what hurts the price of the stock. . . .

But I knew where such thoughts led. I roused myself out of the cool shelter of Lawrence's tomb; and Juan and I sauntered down the grassy hill. The student of film who had looked like Nick Bohm was waiting, framed in a halo of flashing sunbeams.

"Isn't it beautiful?" he said.

"Yes. I've heard about it for years. I'm glad I saw it."

"Have you read *The Plumed Serpent*?" He fell into step beside me as I headed for the car.

"Yes."

"My name is Paul."

"Hello, Paul," I said, not offering my name or my hand. I had no desire to be discourteous, but I had even less desire to get involved with anyone, no matter how slightly.

"I know who you are, Mr. Marks," Paul said. I had reached the car and Juan was sliding into the driver's seat but, naturally, I turned back.

"Oh?"

He smiled quickly. "I read *Variety* and the Sunday *New York Times* and the *Wall Street Journal*. And I read that great interview you gave when you joined King Studio. Where you talked about the need for confidence."

"You read the *Wall Street Journal*?"

"I read everything."

"I thought it was all film, now."

"Don't you believe it. You can love words *and* movies."

"Praise God," I said and smiled for the first time I could remember in weeks.

"Music, too," Paul said, fighting against our departure, against the sound of the motor Juan was patiently idling.

"I was at the festival you filmed in Maine."

"I wasn't," I said. "It was all an afterthought. A magnificent afterthought. Some of the best movies are these days."

The sun was falling fast, the way it does in the Southwest. It was already chilly; in an hour or less it would be dark and cold.

"I read you were with the guy they arrested for the killing. Why do you think he did it?"

"Oh Christ," I said. "So long, Paul."

He was at the window of the car. "Listen, Mr. Marks . . ."

"I'm not forty yet," I said. "If we ever run into each
other again you can call me Ezra."

"Well, listen," he said. 'I'm finished here, now and I'd
love you to meet Russell James. I'm kind of his protégé. I
use his library—he's got everything from silents to video
cassettes. He's a marvelous man. And I'll shut up about that
other stuff. I promise."

Russell James, again. Motiveless fate seemed to have
some motive for having me meet Russell James. But it was
getting late, the wind was picking up speed. . . .

"It's cold," I said.

Paul interpreted my hesitant tone his own way, probably
correctly.

"I've got a terrific sweater. You just wait there for a
second."

He disappeared, returning with a bulky, cable-stitched
sweater made for New Mexico nights; and with the news
that he'd called Russell James, who was delighted at our imminent visit.

If I was expecting some relic—some doddering, sentimental bore with tales of Ramon Novarro and Gloria
Swanson—and I imagine I was, Russell James was not the
man. Tall and thin, like a leaning knife, he welcomed us to
his home. The house was built into the side of a mountain
and high enough for us to be able to make out a great mesa
far below. Half stone, half wood; cool during the day and
comfortable in the evenings. It was sand colored, and during the climb I had been unable to pick it out until we were
almost on top of it.

"It gives privacy. Pleasant after a long, public life."

He must be at least seventy-five, I thought, and wondered how high up we were, as my heart thumped against my chest. The man seemed to have nothing of the Hollywood style about him; he was pure Santa Fe: the elegant tan pants, the shirt with just enough fringe to be Southwest and not enough to be "cowboy," the small mustache.

Back inside we settled in a large living room, full of books and without the usual signed photographs that embalmed a successful career in films.

"Well," James said. "The studios have come a long way."

"How do you mean?"

"You were with Kennedy, weren't you? Worked on research for McNamara?"

First Paul, now James—the magic of the *New York Times*. All the news, fit or unfit.

"Yarmolinsky, actually," I said. "Sociology, research, all that. I ended up doing films on Indians and Chicanos for the Department of the Interior. Not such an unusual background."

"You think not? In my day, do you know what the man who had your job at the studio did?"

I shrugged and deferred to the wisdom of the past.

"He was a pimp. He got girls for the producers. Studios have come a long way."

"That's right," I said. "I had a man on my staff who took care of that."

In the general laughter I became aware that James had been speaking with a German accent. I'd taken it, at first, for a kind of clipped regularity. But there was no mistaking it: it was German. I am no great scholar of films and came into the movie world by chance. Still, somewhere at the edge of recollection I could glimpse something about Russell James. He was one of the early directors who came out of Germany between the two wars: UFA, the company was called, and it gave Hollywood Von Sternberg and Von Stroheim as well as James. This remembrance came to me with a sharp, even a hostile edge—because I was angry at the pimp analogy, and I needed a weapon.

"Tell me," I said. "Russell James is not your real name, is it?"

He looked up from his vodka-pouring business, startled.

"I thought everyone knew that," he said. "I was born in Germany. Of course it is not my real name."

I was sorry I'd come, even sorry that I'd taken the "German" jab. The last year had taught me the often unmanly art of self-defense. There was no need to use it on an old man, no matter what his intentions were.

"I took my name," he said, "from two men I admired: Bertrand Russell and Henry James. I read them in German and then in English. They were the best that writing and thought could be. Besides, I thought it a good joke on people like Lothar Kleinholz."

I was on guard again. He knew Kleinholz, of course. And who knew what web bound him to the studio and, even indirectly, to me?

"I would guess your secret was safe. Kleinholz never read Russell or James. Not even in synopsis."

Paul said, "But didn't he produce *Portrait of a Lady*?"

James ignored Paul and stood before me, accusingly. "Do you know how many pictures I did for Kleinholz?"

"I didn't know you ever worked for King Studio."

"Five," he said. "Five pictures. They cost about eighteen million. And they brought in over a hundred million. And do you know what it was like?"

The question was rhetorical. Without waiting for an answer he beckoned us outside, to the far side of his house. There, sloping steeply on the mountainside was a garden of rocks and assorted cacti. James touched a switch and the garden went white with floodlights. There were giant, thorny shapes stippled with needles in rocky soil.

"It was like that," James laughed. In the desert night it was a crazy sound, less controlled than his previous laughter. Old people were all a little insane, I thought, remembering Sordino in his seventieth year, superbly sane but mysterious with age.

"Like bringing growth out of the desert," he said. "Everything was against creation: the money men in New York, Kleinholz and his tirades, his tape recorder and his fears: half-Hitler, half little boy. But I was tough—I was a cactus and they couldn't touch me without getting hurt."

"It's different now," I said. I wanted to have it over with. I had some curiosity as to what James really wanted to say, but it was overpowered by weariness. It was too late in my day for cactus metaphors. "You must know it's different now."

"Is it?" James said. "*Is it?* Is that why you made your statement? Confidence, you cried out. Where is the confidence you need to have anything—a movie industry, artistic work, a true government—anything. Well, I'll tell you, Mr. Marks, *we* had confidence. No, don't turn your head away like that. I see what you think. . . . The old-timer is going to rant and rave. . . ." He lowered his voice and began to pace his words as if to prove that he was not simply a loony old man brooding out his retirement in the desert, chewing on old memories.

"My wife died of cancer while I was making *Black Skies,* my best film. And I was capable of loving her, caring for her, *and* mourning her while I kept faith with my work. Because I had the confidence you spoke of."

"It was just an interview in *Variety,*" I said. "They'll interview anybody who buys ads."

"Can your marketing people generate such confidence? Your research people? You tell Kleinholz . . ."

James groped in his pockets for a handkerchief; breath came to him with difficulty. I saw Paul's face half in moonlight: he was terrified something would happen to the old man. I was, for the moment, beyond such terrors.

But I was not beyond offering a word to smooth things, to move the evening along toward a tranquil conclusion. "Yes," I said. "You want me to tell Kleinholz something for you, Mr. James?" He'd found his handkerchief and covered his face with it for a second. Then he patted it gently, as if to quiet himself and whisked it off.

"Tell him," he said, "that I have not yet voted my proxies. If he would like to call me . . ."

There was no use telling him that I might never speak to Kleinholz again, that his telegram was still unopened on the bureau in my hotel room, that all this was behind me—or would be as soon as I could manage that delicate trick.

"Look," Paul said.

There was a rabbit nestled in a scrubby patch of grass—if you called those brownish, burned-off bristles, grass. It stood facing us in a catatonic trance, only its nose twitching slightly, a cartoon rabbit in a cartoon cactus garden. The cause for its paralysis spread itself quickly in the chambers of the air: a sound like dry bones shaking in a gourd. I saw the snake half uncoiled in a skinny S-form, not moving, the two figures, rabbit and snake, a perfectly still frieze of menace and terror. And I thought of Mitch Stone, serene with Christ-like blond beard, reaching down and lifting the hypnotic and hypnotized snake, the two of them weaving slightly, impossible to separate snake from man. It was a double remembrance, under the cold rattling sound: one, the scene I'd watched in the film perhaps twenty times, that scene whose inclusion in *Festival* had been the central battle in a murderous war . . . and the re-enactment just past dawn at Ventura, when photographers' bulbs flashed in the sunlight and the snake stirred and the terrifying sound began.

It stopped and the moonlit S-form slithered between two large rocks and was at least invisible and silent if not gone entirely. The rabbit remained frozen, nose twitching as before, even though it was, for the moment, safe from death.

"He thinks if he doesn't move the snake can't see him," James said. The encounter had taken the edge off our conversation. Everyone had the urge to go indoors, but no one stated it directly. Then the old man put an arm around Paul's shoulders.

"It's cold. You're not dressed for the desert," he said.

"It's all right," Paul said.

"Paul gave me his sweater," I said. "It's getting late anyway."

Without wanting to I noticed that he still had his hand on Paul's shoulder, that James's shirt was actually a sort of blouse, with the stripes running horizontally. I noticed, too, a soft, feminine upturn to Paul's lips. But I was impatient with my observations. Pseudo-observations, fake collages made from bits and pieces of Sordino and his young discovery, the beautiful, the late Karol: loose ends which could be pasted on other people, other experiences, even here in New Mexico if you were tired enough: the paranoia of fatigue. Men embraced boys in innocence all over Europe.

We strolled back in tacit agreement that the visit was over. Paul asked about *Festival*, the rock documentary, he asked about *The Lion's Farewell*, he asked about the suspects in the murder, he asked about the proxy fight for control of the studio, he asked and asked and I turned him away each time. My concluding business was with James.

We drifted through the living room and out the front door where James busied himself with an assortment of switches that spilled light halfway down the mountain. He had brought with him the Hollywood passion for floodlights. Each tree had its own special spot and there was a super-spot for the long, serpentine driveway.

James said: "You had to know what it was like to be part of the industry in those days."

"I've heard . . ."

"It's all tied together. You asked for confidence." He tagged the word with a grin. "Along with it came a certain loyalty. We were the Holy Roman Empire. Think of it! Eighty-five million people went to the movies every week. They were ours!"

He went on. Marketing, it would seem, was the absurd and desperate hope of technocrats, people who knew nothing about making movies and had to rely only on selling them. Why else, the implication went, turn to people like Marks and Robinson, communications stars of a long-gone Kennedy Washington? A good film sold itself!

"Of course, I hope you new people can save it all: research, the changing market, youth—I am not stupid, I know it's a different world today. . . ."

I gave up. I congratulated him on his house, his cactus garden, and on his young disciple.

"Paul is a good boy," he said. "I hope there will be a place for him."

"Oh, he'll probably go into the university."

"My folks would love me to teach. But I don't know," Paul said. "There's always the pull of that damned camera."

"It's a dying industry." I waved for Juan, who began to back the car up toward us.

"It has died five times in my lifetime," James said. He shook my hand firmly and thanked me for coming to visit. Neither of us mentioned Kleinholz or proxies. The moon vanished behind thick clouds. We said good-by, squinting at each other in the floodlights' glare. Juan had some difficulty

with the ignition, and James took advantage of the noisy
wait to lean on the car and say, "I have it."

I thought I'd misheard him and said, "I'm sorry . . .?"

"I have what you want. Confidence. The past is full of
people who have confidence. We've earned it."

The spark caught and the car inched down the driveway
and onto the highway back to Santa Fe. Almost a year ago, I
had apparently alerted the entire world to my concern for
its confidence in itself. But for tonight, the area of confidence seemed to have narrowed to a small plot of land with
a cactus garden on top of a mountain outside of Santa Fe.

I dropped Paul off at his home and explained that I
could not help him in the film world: that I was out of it
now. He said he understood, but I knew he didn't.

The hotel was quiet, except that in the room next to
mine a man and a woman were quarreling. I heard a bottle
hit the wall—or at least it sounded like a bottle. When the
phone rang, it was a welcome relief.

"Mr. Marks, will you be checking out in the morning?"

"I don't know."

The telegram waited, patiently, on the bureau top.
There was no sense in opening it, I thought for the hun-
dredth time. The telegram was from Kleinholz. It read:
VITAL YOU ATTEND MEETING HILTON HOTEL MAY 27TH TEN
A.M. YOUR REPORT EXPECTED. FESTIVAL SCREENING GREAT SUC-
CESS. PREDICT WORLD GROSS OF SIXTY MILLION.

Not a word about a man being held for murder; not a
word about *The Lion's Farewell*, the picture halted by the
boy's death. The predicted gross was probably Kleinholz's
usual whistling in the dark; for himself, for the studio, for
the press, and for all the proxies still to be voted.

I should never have opened that yellow envelope. I'd
read somewhere that Western Union was trying not to deliver telegrams, to discourage the whole process because it

was unprofitable. But this one *had* been delivered, and I had opened it.

My brief convalescence was over, and I was opening the window, trying not to listen to the angry sounds from the next room. I had had enough angry sounds to last me for a long time.

Rushing at me through the open window came a swarm of small insects, blinding me as I beat against them helplessly and tried to close the window again at the same time. And all the while remembering that it was the altitude, that I was in Santa Fe, New Mexico, six thousand feet above sea level. I felt my heart beating, beating.

It seemed to me it had been beating that way since I had stood—half prisoner—in Drakmalnik's warehouse on Ninth Avenue in New York almost a week before. I remembered the strangeness of standing in the debris of decades of movie props anchored in dust, surrounded by long-unused packing crates and mottled coils of rope. The accumulated dreck of a whole world. And what had happened there: real and imaginary. Fragments of conversation, musical notes played around themes of death, of responsibility. Max saying:

"And then I remembered all of a sudden what you said to me in Paris and it made me feel better. . . ."

"What?"

"On the bridge, late at night. . . ."

"What did I say to you, Max?"

"Hey, Ezra, come on. . . ."

"I'm asking you, what did I tell you?"

"You don't remember?"

"It was late. I was beat and full of brandy."

"You said: 'We've got till the weekend. Get rid of him, or he'll get rid of us.' Something like that."

And moments—hours?—later, "Oh God, what am I going to do, what am I ever going to do?"

The window was closed, the insects gone, the beating of my heart more or less under control. The Hilton Hotel, May 27, 10 a.m. I was to deliver my report tomorrow morning.

All right: sleep and wake. Pack the suitcase, call the cab, take the plane, give the report. Let it end; let something else begin. I'd done that a few times in my life.

At 5 a.m. on November 23, 1963, sitting on a chilly curbstone near the Jefferson Memorial, mourning a murdered President in his own way, a very drunken Robinson had said to me: "Our beginnings never know our ends. . . ." My grandmother used to say that, but nobody thought it was wisdom till a poet wrote it down."

Sleep and wake, pack the suitcase, call the cab, take the plane, give the report.

"Our beginnings never know our ends. . . ."

book one

rough cut

1

The chauffeur's name was Marty and he had driven Bogart and Bacall for ten years. He told Ezra more than he wanted to know at that moment, as they whirred past tall palm trees bleeding sunshine through their scruffy leaves. This canyon led to that star's home; of course, she no longer lived there, and besides the star system was dead now. And this road led to the studio's chief competitor, but of course the trades said they were in the process of selling the plant and just releasing pictures instead of producing. And Mr. Marks was not to mind the kids smoking pot and lounging in front of record stores and head shops along the Sunset Strip. A year in the Army was what they needed, though they were the new movie market and God knew this was 1970 and we'd all be out of a job if it wasn't for them.

There was a blue, triangular scar on his right cheek that Ezra could make out when Marty turned his head to make one or another point. Too late to avert his eyes from the spot.

Ezra was treated to the history of Marty as a stunt man with John Wayne, the big accident, the subsequent surgery. They arrived at the operating room and—mercifully—at the studio, simultaneously.

The guard at the front gate had his name and he was Mister-Marksed all the way up to Kleinholz's office. Kleinholz's motherly secretary, Martha, was all gray hair, combs, and glasses; very un-Hollywood. But Mr. Kleinholz was tied up and Mr. Marks would have to wait.

Ezra asked: Could Mr. Marks see Mr. Robinson in the meantime? The result of this ordinary question was: "Ah, Mister Robinson . . . I'm sorry. . . ." This mysterious response was accompanied by a blank look, a half smile, silence, and finally a retreat to the ladies' room and return, patting sculptured waves of gray hair into place as if no question had been asked. Ezra mustered a little tired charm and leaning over the desk, said, "He's very tall, Mr. Robinson. At least six foot four. You couldn't miss him."

Martha knew a joke when she heard one; but thirty years of corporate evasion froze the smile at the corners of her mouth.

"Yes," she said. "I know Mr. Robinson."

So much for charm and irony.

"Is he going to be in his office today?"

"You'll have to ask Mr. Kleinholz about that."

For the next ten minutes Ezra sat next to a table piled with copies of the Hollywood *Reporter* and *Daily Variety*. He blinked into a beam of sunlight that streamed through the window opposite him. A sense of unreality touched the scene. The people who drifted in and out seeking appointments with Kleinholz, leaving papers, retrieving scripts, all seemed like characters on film, with Ezra as audience. And, like an audience at a bad movie, he grew edgy and bored. To distract himself, he thought of the people who might have sat in this chair in this way, waiting for Kleinholz. Scott Fitzgerald, that was on record; Garbo, perhaps; Lewis Milestone had been a contract director there in the 1930s. He had quit in rage at Kleinholz. In order to finish had he perhaps sat where Ezra now sat, waiting to begin?

Ezra had waited in the outer offices of Cabinet officers many times. He had been kept waiting by the President of the United States: seven times, to be exact. The first of each of those experiences had felt much the same as now . . . the same anticipation mixed with boredom and uncertainty as to how it would go. Plus a narrow sense of irony: Ezra's own special way of trying to master experiences that threatened to master him.

A biting buzzer sounded every few minutes. Martha answered cryptically. At last, in response to one buzz she said, "Yes, he's still waiting." Kleinholz in the flesh was about to become accessible. She pressed a button, hung up the phone and pressed another button. A voice sounded: "Marks, I've got you on the squawk-box. I'm hung up here for a while with two bastards who're trying to murder me (muted laughter in the background). I want you to see some film—Sordino footage and *Festival*. Then we'll talk. If these characters leave anything to talk to (more laughter in background). Nick Bohm'll meet you at the back gate of the lot. He'll take you from there."

A click ended Ezra's first "meeting." Martha guided him downstairs to meet Nick Bohm, past rows and rows of still photographs of King Studio productions old and new. "Nick Bohm—you'll be working for him technically—but not really," Robinson had told him. "Don't ask me to explain that right now. . . . I'll define Nick for you, though. Just remember the definition of God in the Koran: A being whose circumference is nowhere and whose center is everywhere."

"I seem to recall," Ezra had said, "that it's the other way around."

"It works for Nick either way."

Ezra stopped and pointed to a photograph that looked familiar, "Who's that?" he asked the secretary.

"Sordino, the Italian director," she said; a little like saying Eisenhower, the general. And while Ezra studied the shaggy head of the old Italian, she added a word.

"Pray."

2

Out of the door and into a burst of relentless sunlight: that vision-shock sunny Los Angeles inflicts every time one leaves the indoors for the street. At the same moment a massive convertible pulled up to the curb. Gold paint and silver upholstery caught every spare flicker of sunlight in the air. In it, sat—unmistakably—Nick Bohm: lean in outline but running to paunch, silver-gray hair swinging out on top of his forehead and wild and loose in back, almost down to his collar. A suede jacket, worn but elegant, and the surprise of sneakers without socks completed the ensemble.

He flung himself out of the car (Ezra was to find that Bohm flung himself everywhere, into a meeting that was to last for hours, or a transatlantic plane flight, as if he was hurled in for a few moments and would be—must be—on his way in moments).

"I'm sorry," Nick Bohm said. He was breathless. "I should have been upstairs to meet you. But we had a crisis." He flung himself back behind the wheel. "All these freaks," he murmured over screeching gears. "Our biggest picture is a music festival—you know, rock."

"I've heard of *Festival*," Ezra said. He took the pleasure of a second's amusement. Did people who wore socks and ties need to have rock festivals explained to them?

This time the entrance was made via the auto gate leading to the back lot. An enormous square sign told the sky that this was King Studio with a great curlicued capital K. Another sign told the visitor to slow down to twelve miles an hour and to stop and wait for permission to proceed. Nick did not stop. He waved at the uniformed guard, who waved back, and they slipped along the broad studio street at thirty miles an hour. They passed signs shouting QUIET and heard the whining of buzz saws from hidden carpenter shops.

"There's a guy from *Variety* who wants to interview you." He turned a bright, vague smile to Ezra. "The trades always interview the new man who comes in to save the studio."

"Is that why I'm here?"

"That's the word. Speaking of which—you might want

to okay this." A flick of his eyes indicated a pile of mimeographed sheets lying between them. Ezra picked one up and read:

OFFICIAL BIO, EZRA MARKS
FOR IMMEDIATE RELEASE
MARKS JOINS KING STUDIO AS V.P. MARKETING
Ezra Marks has been named Marketing Veepee at King Studio, a newly created post. Marks' background is in research and educational film. He comes to the studio from activities split between consultancies to the Federal Communications Commission and teaching at Columbia University.
      After a brief stint as an executive with the Peace Corps he served as Deputy Commissioner at the FCC in the Kennedy and Johnson administrations, resigning in 1965.
      Mr. Marks, whose father once penned a Pulitzer Prize scientific anthropological tome and whose mother was a versifier, has also produced documentary films for the Department of the Interior. He is a specialist in youth projects—considered important to Hollywood pundits because of King Studio's heavy investment in the upcoming youth pic: FESTIVAL.
      Marks will report to Nick Bohm, V.P. Advertising and Publicity, Worldwide.

"That goes out to the papers today," Nick Bohm said. "Okay with you?"

"Well, I was only an *Assistant* Deputy Commissioner at the FCC, my father's book was on zoology not anthropology, my mother would destroy anyone who called her a versifier . . . and I assumed I would be reporting to Robinson. Other than that, it's fine."

"Maybe your folks won't read the papers tomorrow."

"They're both dead," Ezra said. "But Robinson isn't."

Nick Bohm stared at the road ahead. He waited about ten beats and then turned a bland, steady-eyed gaze at Ezra.

"We'll need a head shot to go out with the bio," he said.

They turned up into an oval where a fountain flourished, surrounded by a mass of red flowers with borders of tiny yellow shrubs. Someone was spending a great deal of money on landscape gardening while the newspapers were full of scare stories about the potential bankruptcy of major film studios. A pudgy little man came running out of a nearby building. He wore a belt with a great gold buckle, and on his moon-face was a look of absolute anxiety. He trampled red and yellow flowers alike underfoot in his eagerness to deliver his message. Which was: Kleinholz had said it was urgent that Mr. Marks see the promotion film for the Sordino picture and give an opinion.

"Max," Nick said patiently, "we know. That's why we're here. Ezra, this is Max Miranda. Max is our publicity manager." Max the yea-sayer; the eager bringer of the superfluous.

"Glad to meet you, chief," Max said. He was all plump desperation to please; a ball of fearful amiability, with anxiety just under the surface of every remark, every gesture.

3

Screening Room Number Six was where the film was racked. Ezra and Max sat in the back row and next to them Nick Bohm, stationed between the phone and a short microphone. He hunched over, pressed a button on the microphone, and said, "Hey, do you have the Sordino film up?"

A voice blared from a loudspeaker somewhere in the room.

"Yes, sir."

"How much?"

"Two reels."

"Go."

The lights dimmed and vanished and on the screen appeared a naked woman with her legs spread apart. Immediately a naked hairy stub of a man entered the frame.

Bohm's head ducked to the microphone.

"What the hell is this?"

The loudspeaker called out, "Sorry, Becker was showing special film to a friend. I'll put the other film up."

"My God," Nick Bohm murmured. "We used to have fifty pictures a year. Now we've got two lousy pictures going to save our ass—and he can't get the right can of film racked up."

In the silence Max Miranda muttered, "Becker and his friends . . ."

Machinery clicked, there was some yellow flickering and the light image on the screen widened to allow for a broad, magnificent shot of a grassy field. From the loudspeakers there issued the heavy pulse of hard rock. The screen was swallowed by a great close-up of a bearded face speaking to the camera. There was no lip-synch, so it was impossible to know what he was saying. But he seemed happy, even excited. Helicopters swam into view and dropped packages to scurrying figures on the ground.

Nick Bohm dove at the microphone again. "Now what?" he said. "That's *Festival!*"

"Sorry. We had it up for Mr. Kleinholz but he canceled. Shall I kill it?"

Bohm sighed a great weariness.

"Take it down. I want to run the Sordino film first." The wait seemed endless, the room electric with undischarged energy.

As the lights in the screening room went up and then dimmed again, Bohm hunched down and brought his knees up almost all the way to his chin. With sneakered feet and knuckles pressed against his teeth, he had a childlike style. It was appealing: from corporate irascibility to innocent expectation.

Ezra had seen promotion films for everything: new products of a camera company, real estate developments

in Florida, political candidates, movie trailers. From the
first shot, Ezra could see this would be different. It was
a simple one of Sordino putting down a volume of D. H.
Lawrence stories while the camera panned through the
window and down a Roman street along which a young
boy ran. Over it Sordino's heavily accented voice quoted:
"Some boys seem destined never to be men: just as some
men will remain boys forever. It is impossible to say which
is sadder. . . ."

Then, against a background of Italy, Germany, Hun-
gary, France, and Spain, Sordino sketched what appeared to
be the conventional search for the "right actor" to play the
central role: an adolescent boy of such physical beauty that
he could dominate the story of an older man of uncertain
sexuality and a young boy who controls and destroys him
without wishing to. There were the usual audition scenes,
good-looking young boys being rejected, angry mothers.
Suddenly, there was a quick cut, just a flash, of a boy's
profile during an airplane ride. And, in a Roman café, Sordino and the British star Michael Maurice were having coffee and discussing the role of the older man—the camera
focused on Maurice's craggy face. Suddenly, superim-
posed over Maurice's face, there appeared a shot of the
same boy, full-front this time. It fought with the older man's
features, seemed to disappear, then absorbed the face and
the entire screen, growing to a full screen shot of the face of
the most beautiful being Ezra had ever seen. The word
"being" presents itself before the word boy or man—because
the exquisiteness of the features made the initial effect
androgynous. The eyes were enormous, framing violet irises,
and the mouth was as curved as a woman's, undulating
like an archer's bow with a delicate dip in the middle of the
upper lip which curved up at the corners. There was an
elaborate fullness to the cheeks; the eyelashes were long,

the lids heavy. It was touching in its extravagance of beautiful detail.

After holding a long, long moment, the camera pulled back very slowly—Sordino's camera always moved with great deliberation—to reveal the essential setting of the film-to-come: a luxury hotel in Rome, circa 1900.

"What a fucking *punim*," Max said. "Hungarian kid. Name's Karol."

"Look, look . . ." Nick Bohm whispered excitedly. "—Look how Sordino skipped the usual crap . . . you know . . . *that's* the boy . . . *that's* the star I've been searching for. He does it all with the camera. Look. . . ."

Ezra looked. The scene he saw was only a fragment, designed to whet the audience's appetite for the finished film. A young Italian working-class boy had struck up a friendship with an English gentleman: a relationship in which the sexual overtones were ambiguous, expressed in tenderness and confusion. The center of the sample scene was a moment in which the boy is trying to tell the older man how much he likes him. At the same time he needs, urgently, to borrow some money. It was a bitter, comic echo surrounding the romantic statement. At the precise instant in which the old English actor realized what the boy wanted, his aristocratic face became a ruined landscape. Against that facial terrain the boy's beauty bloomed, unforgivable.

It was a scene in the grand romantic style but with its own ironic edge. The Sordino style.

The lights returned them to Screening Room Six. Miranda turned his head and squinted. He started to say something and then thought better of it. Nick Bohm fumbled for a cigarette, and finally borrowed one from Max. Both were reluctant to speak until Ezra did. (Classic Hollywood caution?) But he sat looking at the blank white square at the front of the room, his mind a tumble of thoughts and images. That amazing face stuck in his mind as if the mind were a piece of film.

"It's going to be some picture," Ezra said at last. "Some picture. He's caught that funny thing Lawrence always has between men. Like Aaron and Rawdon Lilly in *Aaron's Rod* ... or Gerald and Birkin in *Women in Love.*"

Nick Bohm looked down at his sneakered feet. Then up at Ezra, and down again.

Finally Max said, "It's a little picture. It won't cut it. These *Festival* momsers with their tits and music—*that* could do it."

"If they give Sordino a chance," Nick Bohm said, a mysterious glaze over his hazel eyes. "Just wait. . . ."

"A hundred and eighty-five million out in loans," Max muttered as the light dimmed again.

Nick hunched down again and said something Ezra could not make out.

"Excuse me?" he said. His formal politeness seemed almost archaic considering the prevailing style of discourse.

"Pray," Nick Bohm said. "Just pray."

There was apparently, in movie studios, a heavy theological commitment in times of stress.

Then came the *Festival* scenes. Strangely, the screen seemed to stretch; actually it did not change size. But the chamber-music intimacy of Sordino's camera was exchanged for the symphonic documentary style. Twenty cameras operating almost at random; certainly at the emotional whim of the young people who slept on the ground for two nights, struggled in the rain, in mud up to their thighs. What their cameras had recorded was an event in Maine when a half million young people descended on a small town and its surrounding area, petrifying the natives and filling the air with rock music, the sweet smoke of pot (and more exotic substances), and fear for the health and safety of 500,000

people in a space that could not possibly hold 100,000. It was
a familiar legend by now, had been a *Time* magazine cover
story—and immortalized on the eleven o'clock news three
days running during the summer of its happening, including
the first network seminudity. It had also been something of
a quasi-religious ceremony with the Indian rituals beloved
by the young Indians of the middle class who had gathered
at the shrine of Rock, and The Tribe. The first minutes of
film were dazzlingly different: the screen cut into so many
segments, as if to dramatize the tribal nature of the experience, no one sensibility ruling all, the music blasting a counterpoint to the visual rhythm of the cutting. It was a dramatic jump from Sordino's subtle individual probing of
character to this sense of the entire landscape as a character, the crowd as another, the music, in fact, as the main
character.

This was only a rough cut of assorted footage, and after
a few moments the director of the film made an appearance
as guide and guru.

"Mitch Stone," Max Miranda murmured. "The momser
himself."

The momser had a thin intense face, beard and all, wore
rope sandals and an Indian headband with a symbolic pattern. He was somewhere between thirty and thirty-five; his
blond hair touched his shoulders. He was slender, and his
loose and easy manner was youthful. Lines of exhaustion
appeared, vanished, and reappeared from moment to moment as he commented on the death of the ego in films, on
rock as religion. But what he said was less fascinating to
Ezra than the use he made of the screen, even in this tentative cut, using corner frames, quick cuts where dissolves
would be expected and simultaneous juxtaposition of three
and four scenes so that the eye never quite knew where to
settle—yet was able to make emotional sense of the eccen-
tric film grammar.

"Twelve million," Nick Bohm said.

The lights went up again. The two men looked utterly unfamiliar to Ezra.

"Fifty million," Max Miranda said. "If they don't burn the negative."

4

Sun-stoned, they walked toward the administration building. Nick Bohm spoke of Kleinholz, anecdotes of the man in his youth, hints of what he expected from Bohm, what he might expect from Ezra, a fraction of the story of Kleinholz's famous accident along the mountain roads of Cannes. Bohm's conversation was like spliced and unspliced tapes: skipping to the 1950s when Kleinholz sent him on the road with a kangaroo to publicize an Australian film, then jumping to the past year when his assignment was to wangle a Legion of Honor from the government of France for Sordino; moving, then, to the immediate future and the problems of the D. H. Lawrence property.

"It's too damned short," Nick Bohm said.

"For what?" Ezra said, knowing he sounded naïve.

"To sell as a novel."

"It's not a novel. It's a short story."

"R——r–r–ight," Nick Bohm said. Ezra registered something new. A stammer. Was it because Ezra seemed to be opposing him?

"We'll have to have it n–n–n—"

Ezra waited.

"—n–novelized."

"*Novelize* a D. H. Lawrence story?"

"The only way we can s—s—sell it. We need a best seller to push the picture up front."

"Nick," Ezra said. "When is somebody going to give me a straight answer about what's happened to Robinson?"

The first full smile Ezra had seen from Nick Bohm was now flashed; with it came a faint rush of garlic odor—a memory of last night's business dinner in some expensive Beverly Hills restaurant? That smile gave Ezra a hint—just the slightest suggestion—that Nick Bohm might be the most complex factor in this new situation in which he found himself. More than the studio, the pressures, the unaccustomed lingo, the open sexuality (Beckers' "friends"), the intrigues; some unanswered question, unaskable, really, about Nick Bohm's vision of how people ticked and what the world was and meant. Straight answers might play no part at all in that view. (*A being whose circumference is everywhere and whose center is nowhere.*)

But before Ezra could evaluate any of this, before he could even decide if Nick Bohm's smile was touched with simple malice as well as spice, the motherly Martha, who tended the sanctum sanctorum, was moving him toward the office where Kleinholz waited, at last. Kleinholz in his wheelchair, Kleinholz with his tape recorders going every hour of the day and night.

Nick Bohm had vanished, a tactful ghost. Ezra checked his jacket buttons and tie automatically, and was racked by a sudden sneeze. He groped for a handkerchief. Before he fully realized that he didn't have one, Max Miranda appeared from somewhere, from nowhere, pressed a clean, white square into his hand and was gone. Ezra blew and pommeled his nose, noting the ornate M. M. on the handkerchief. He'd just managed to get it tucked away when the door opened and he was walking down an immense foyer toward an even larger office. Kleinholz was waiting for him, extending his handshake over the metallic arm of the wheelchair in which he spent most of his life. Around his neck was a microphone on a blue cord. The cord was, in turn, attached to a large tape recorder on a massive table in the corner of the office. If Bohm had not warned him, Ezra might have apologized for interrupting a taping session. But taping was a twenty-four-hour-a-day business with Kleinholz. The table was piled high with tapes, tapes in boxes, tapes with loose ends trailing to the floor, enough tapes, it seemed to Ezra, to contain the history of Western civilization.

The handshake was firm and dry. In fact, outside of the wheelchair, there was no suggestion of the infirm about Kleinholz. Only his eyes, teary, red, and rheumy, looked old. He wiped them with his handkerchief.

"The worst day of smog I can remember," he said. "I'm a built-in smog-detector. Faulty tear ducts," he said proudly. "All the garbage in the air gets in my eyes and stays there till the doctor comes and washes it out. Worst place in the world for me, California."

He waved at the picture window that covered most of one wall, beyond which glittered what seemed to be a perfectly clear blue sky.

"Don't let it fool you," he said. "It's that yellow scum near the horizon. Sit down."

Ezra sat, trying to keep his eyes from the regularly revolving tape on the table. "I've never spent much time here," he said. "Ten days once doing a film for the Department of the Interior on the Chicanos."

"I saw it," Kleinholz said. "I've seen everything your name is attached to, one way or another."

"Oh?"

"We've been looking for a man for a year."

The office was a mini-palace, baroque woodwork curled in the corners under heavy wood beams. A nine-foot Steinway waited near one window. A weathered oak mermaid, with her flowing hair trailing toward Kleinholz's tape-covered desk, crouched in the opposite corner: it might once have been the figurehead of a ship. The vaulted ceiling loomed, cathedral-like, above it all: cabinets, piano, figurehead, tape recorder, desks, and a bar. There were no paintings on the wall, only photographs. Ezra's eyes took them in as a blur during the few seconds it took for Kleinholz to wheel himself, with short, strong strokes of muscular arms, to the long desk. They were mostly stars: as far back as Ronald Colman, with his eloquent little mustache and as recent as James Taylor, guitar and all. There were several Presidents; one had Kleinholz standing next to F.D.R. The President smiled; Kleinholz frowned.

"Ten years ago, a publicity man got all the free space he could grab and made ads. Today, it's different. Producers and directors are running the show. Or trying to. I need a man who knows what they're talking about. And right now what they're talking about is young people. This industry has become a young person's business. That's where you come in."

"I'm not so young."

"Never shit a shitter, Marks. You know what I mean."

"I'm not sure the analogy holds—from politics to movies."

"It holds!" Kleinholz said, as if analogies could be held by acts of will. "People are people. Every time I release a movie I'm holding an election. People vote with their dollars. There are other candidates, not only other pictures but a million other choices—watching TV, fucking, reading a book. Some of those things are even free. Our job is to un-

38

derstand the voting public, to give them a candidate they'll want that night, and to make them enter the booth with their dollars!"

There was no way for Ezra to know what the source of his sense of unreality was: the whirling tapes, the presentation of metaphors as if they were literal realities, or just the sun—drying every corner of the enormous room with yellow light. He said nothing: he knew the difference between a monologue and a dialogue.

"And do you know what they're voting for right now? Young—they're buying young. America's on a young binge. Let me tell you a truth, Marks. The movies are always five or ten years later than the rest of the world. That used to be okay when the world moved slow. But it moves like hell now. You went to Washington riding a wave, a young wave: a young President, the Peace Corps."

From under a fringe of hair so black it might have been dyed, Kleinholz looked at Ezra in a spasm of self-satisfaction.

"I do my homework," Kleinholz said. He grinned happily, with the perfect capped teeth of an aged movie star.

"I was only with Shriver for six months," Ezra said. "I shifted to the FCC. . . ." Before he could add, "with Robinson," the old man's smile was gone.

"I don't need a college degree in sociology to tell me that the three biggest grossers last year were kid films. Motorcycles, drug trips . . . We're maybe five years behind your youth revolution."

Kleinholz executed an elaborate series of balletic movements with his wheelchair, ending up with his back to the picture window so that his face was a white blur; he raised his hands high, becoming in that strange position a kind of sun-baked icon.

"This studio," he intoned, "will rise or fall in the next few months on a bunch of crazy hippie kids—with a chief

who's an Indian mystic—camped out on my back lot right
now . . . and on a bunch of very talented fags in Italy.
I've got others in various shapes—but those are the real two.
Don't ask me how I got in this spot, after making forty
pictures a year for forty years."

The phone rang. Kleinholz wheeled himself toward it
and pressed an intercom buzzer.

"Who is it?" he said, "and hold all calls." More buttons
and: "Hello, Larry. We're going to have to pass on this one.
At a million five, it was possible; at three million it's out of
the question. Even if you were to defer your share."

The conversation ended abruptly.

"There's a man who can take 'fuck you' for an answer,"
Kleinholz said, smiling sunnily.

"I've also got a proxy fight in the works. A nice, ugly
proxy fight for control of the studio—and a bunch of pot-
heads are holding a picture that can make or break me."

"How does *Festival* look?" Ezra asked.

"How do I know?"

"You haven't seen it?"

"When Mitch Stone sees fit to let the head of the studio
see it, I'll see it."

"I heard someone say it might gross anywhere from fifteen million to fifty."

Kleinholz nodded. "I don't want to go to war with those
kids. They may have the biggest picture in ten years. If it
makes fifteen million, I'm in good shape—but with a struggle. If it grosses fifty, I've won, and they can shove their
proxies up their ass."

Who "they" were remained undefined.

"But if this all turns into a war—from what they tell me
you should be a good man to have around. Look . . ." He
stared into Ezra's eyes: ". . . I need a heavy. There's a lot
of pressure on me. I go to meetings where they tell me to
come into the twentieth century. That's the kind of talk I

got to take these days. Well, that's going to be you, the
twentieth-century heavy. I don't know what the Washington
scene was like when you were there. I don't fuck around
with politics . . . give to both parties . . . play it safe. I vote
Democrat, though it's nobody's goddam business. But you're
some kind of scientific-marketing youth expert, they tell
me." (This time "they" was clearly the absent Robinson.)
"The old stuff isn't enough any more. Publicity, promotion,
advertising. Now it's market research, demographics, psy-
chographics. . . ." He looked slyly at Ezra over the bobbing
end of an unlit cigar. "Hah," he said. "You didn't expect
such fancy stuff from the old king, I'll bet. . . ."

A tape-end unspooled, flapping, flapping until Kleinholz
pressed a buzzer three times. From a door at the opposite
end of the office, a door Ezra hadn't noticed because it had
not been used, a man Kleinholz called Ape, wearing a gray,
zippered jumpsuit, like a garage mechanic's, entered and
quickly replaced the used tape with a new one.

During the process, which took about three minutes,
Kleinholz said nothing. He glanced over some papers,
grunted and shifted in his wheelchair; the bent back of his
neck told Ezra he was expected to maintain silence until the
new tape was racked and spinning. In that semisilence Ezra
heard the sound of carpenters hammering in the afternoon
air, the distant ringing of telephones, and the beating of
blood in his own ears.

At last, when the circle of tape began to devour itself
again, Kleinholz raised his head and looked at Ezra for a
long moment.

"What did you think of the Sordino footage?" he said.

"That's an amazingly beautiful boy."

"You're going to make him famous."

"I thought Sordino would do that."

"No. He'll make him a star. That's not the same thing.
These days, that may not last through the first release of the

picture. *You* have to make his face and his name famous. Nick's good at that. Work with him. The two of you should go over to Rome in a few days. I don't want that situation to get away from us."

Ezra noted the ambiguity: he was to work *for* Nick, work *with* him, work. . . .

"You should know," Kleinholz said, "there are two schools of thought. One says: the picture and only the picture will do it. That the future of the industry is not in our hands any more—it's in the hands of the directors; you're supposed to call them . . . *film-makers.*" He closed his eyes and dreamt for an instant. "As if that's not what I've been all my life." The brown eyes under wrinkled lids reappeared. "Just let them make their pictures, and stay out of their way. Don't let the studio decide what kind of picture is in the air. Let the film-makers decide. You just give them the office space and the money. Well, I say that's shit and that's death!"

Ezra expected pounding of the wheelchair and shouting. Instead it was a declining volume, down, down to a whisper: "We are going to make the kind of picture I smell is in the air. I smell *Festival* and the one after and the one after —until the wind shifts and I smell something else. Then you're going to take all that and turn it into advertising and publicity and keep it nice and scientific, right?"

The impossibility of replying to that olfactory mixture of business, intuition, and science led Ezra to fix his gaze on the revolving tape. Kleinholz misunderstood.

"You think this is crazy, this tape business, don't you?" he said.

"Well . . ."

"Crazy old king in a wheelchair taking down all this crap. Let's just see."

Kleinholz wheels to the table; a demonstration begins. Buttons snap, springs are coiled and released. New tape off, old tape on. Kleinholz's fingers control fast-forward and reverse in virtuoso performance.

CLICK. Voices are heard. Call them text.

TEXT—*Ringing of telephone.* KLEINHOLZ'S VOICE: Hello, Larry. We're going to have to pass on this one. At a million five, it was possible; at three million it's out of the question. Even if you were to defer your share.

CLICK.

COMMENTARY: When Muller calls back or comes here to talk, he'll say I gave him the impression that the project was workable at, say two million two. And there will be absolutely *no* recollection of any mention of deferring his share. This way, we'll start bargaining from a real base. My base.

Buzzhissssssthump.

TEXT—KLEINHOLZ (fragments, stopping and starting):
. . . they tell me to come into the twentieth century. . . .
Well, that's going to be you, the twentieth-century heavy
. . . you're some kind of scientific-marketing youth expert
. . . until the wind shifts and I smell something else . . .
going to take all that and turn it into advertising and publicity and keep it all nice and scientific, right?

COMMENTARY: File this one under employee efficiency. I employ about two thousand people. I pay them millions of dollars a year. Your department has about a hundred and fifty with about sixteen million to spend, so you might listen. When I come in contact with anybody who works for me, it's a good thing to know exactly what's expected of him and of me. What I just learned from this rerun is: I gave you an idea of why I hired you. I told you something of the spot we're in. And I spelled out some of the direction I expect us—and you—to go in. That way I can measure performance against briefing. And you can't say—"But I didn't know. . . ." Memories fade. Tape is eternal.

Bzzzzzzzthump!

TEXT:—EZRA: That's an amazingly beautiful boy.

Ezra laughed at the unfamiliar sound of his recorded voice. "What could that tell you?"

COMMENTARY: "Tells me you're not a fag and you're not afraid anybody'll think you are. You just admired the kid as a beautiful object."

Clickoffffff. Tape replaced.

Kleinholz patted the machine affectionately.

"You see?" he said. "Psychology, personnel relations, deals, negotiating, sexual judgments . . . everything's there —and more—if you know how to listen."

He looked straight at Ezra, and Ezra saw him, as if with the distance usually gained by time: a strong, vulgar mouth, high, clear forehead fringed with black hair, dark brown eyes used to unblinking assessment. A man who controls his environment for the clear pleasure of control.

"I've got decades on tape. Someday I'll play you some of the wild ones." A brown eye winked: lewd window on old copulations.

"I've done most of the talking," Kleinholz said. "It's a habit. What do *you* think?"

"I think I didn't know a lot," Ezra said. "I didn't know there was a proxy fight shaping up. I didn't know you were essentially down to two pictures to get through a bad time. And I didn't know you were supposed to be the nineteenth century and I was supposed to be the twentieth. Aside from that, I think it's going to be fine."

A beam from old Kleinholz. "Good. I like the positive; hate the negative."

Then Kleinholz did something startling. He stood up from the wheelchair. He grasped a cane from the side of the piano and limped swiftly across the great expanse of office. Ezra was amazed to see that the man was tall: almost six foot. The cane lent him a certain wounded dignity, tall as he was under the vaulted ceiling, bent with years and a traumatized spine.

Ezra followed him not asking where they were going, not even thinking to ask. In the room behind them the tape revolved, gathering the distant, random sounds of the Hollywood afternoon (what the wooden mermaid might say to the piano in Kleinholz's absence), waiting patiently for its next recording, revelation of error, weakness, betrayal, strength, success; whatever chance or ambition might deliver for the old king's merciless analysis.

At the door Ezra did what he'd promised himself to do since entering Kleinholz's office. "By the way," he said, "I'd like to look in on Robinson. Where would I . . ."

He was not allowed to finish. "Never," Kleinholz said. "Never use that son-of-a-bitch's name to me again as long as you're here. I brought him in, I gave him everything; but no gratitude . . . no learning from my experience. . . . I smell one thing; he smells another. Worst of all, he wants to give *my* studio away. To his beloved film-makers. His directors, his Sordinos . . . a damned Italian who never grossed more than two or three million world-wide in his whole Italian life. Don't talk to me about Robinson!"

"I wouldn't be here if it weren't for Robinson."

The old man said: "Max'll show you around the lot. Then we can see Mitch Stone." And he led Ezra out into the tumult of people waiting to offer, to importune, to negotiate.

They greeted Kleinholz with pleasure, simulated or real, Ezra with an assessment marked by distance, caution, and care.

Max Miranda was listening to a trim, middle-aged man, tense as a violin string; a long, black cigarette holder punctuated the air as he talked. Lawrence Becker, executive vice-president; Becker of the dirty movies on the wrong reel. Becker of the interesting "friends." Robbie had described him as a man to whom everything was done. "The ultimate passive: dangerous when he finally acts." Becker had been barbered, shirted, suited, shod, and shaved to a pink fare-thee-well, and he faced his expensive world each morning in the tremulous hope, as Robinson put it, "that they'd let him keep it all for just one more day."

Like Kleinholz, Becker had come to films through the seasonal hysterias of Seventh Avenue, many years before. His superelegant dress showed it, as did his concern with every one else's costume. Each shirt worn by a colleague or a competitor (one and the same) that could not be instantly identified as to store, price, and newness was a loss of points in the game that often only Becker knew was being played. Each suit that turned out to be a stroke of style which could not be countered by some fashion coup of Becker's was a disaster. Everything physical entered into the game, not just clothing. And the results of a Becker loss could be savage. A flicker of the nose and mouth would signal trouble. Robbie swore that by the end of a meeting Becker was perfectly capable of rejecting a pick-up deal on a film because the producer had teeth that were more handsomely capped than Becker's own, or wore shoes from a firm in London, newer and more elegant than Lobbs, which shipped Becker's shoes twice a year. "I'll give you the one key to the man," Robbie had said. "At any single moment of the day he has one obsessive, all-devouring fear: that, at that very moment, in a meeting, at a restaurant, in bed, at a screening, he will be humiliated."

But now Ezra, being introduced, saw simply a tense, thin man dancing his little dance of anxiety in the sun, saying, "Glad to meet you, kid. We're going to work good, and we're going to work close. I'm hung up today with some *yugurs* from the Midwest—a big chain. But tomorrow we'll talk, maybe lunch. Don't take any shit, now. Spend two weeks in the East and two weeks here every month, like me. And keep a cunt in Chicago for between planes." A nudge and a wink were added to the repertoire, along with the shifting, shuffling dance. His eyes had heavy lids, like wrinkled hoods.

"What's that? Saks?" A nervous hand glided over the lapel of Ezra's jacket. "Nice."

"Listen, kid," Becker lowered his voice and narrowed his eyes, a cartoon of conspiracy. "I hear the guy from *Variety* is waiting around to get an interview. Take my advice: don't come on like a wise-ass. You know? Take it slow-and-humble-like. Right?" With a sidelong glance at the assembling Kleinholz caravan, he said, "Gotta go catch the *yugurs*." He dabbed at his forehead with a white square; an oddly delicate gesture highlighted by all his random grossness. That goddam Santa Ana. Don't let it get you."

And he was off, leaving Ezra and Max to their hot and airless ride across the back lot to the Castle.

7

For the second time that day Ezra was driven by a chauffeur. Only the limousine was now a golf cart; and Max was a low-comedy version of Marty, the driver. It was obviously an old routine: Max's mini-tour of the Studio.

"This is the New York Street," Max said. It was a vaguely 1920s to 1930s row of brownstones and storefronts. Generations of gangsters had run down its streets chased by generations of police. "Used to be backed up with production schedules. Now we get a little TV work for it, not much."

The Western Street was much the same story. It's long,

empty gutter framed by signs (SALOON) and sagging hitch-
ing posts drew Ezra's eye like a slow tracking shot all the
way to the horizon. It had that fake bleakness ambitious
Westerns thrived on. Max pointed out that the bleakness was
no longer fake. No one thrived on this street, now.

Signs of activity increased as they approached the castle
at the far end of the back lot. Music filtered through the
afternoon air. Cars chugged by, four young people lugged a
great trunk out of a building. Then the castle itself appeared.
Max's gloss told Ezra that it had been built for Kleinholz's
production of Tennyson's *Idylls of the King*, one of the great
King Studio successes of the 1950s. Since then, fragments
had been used for various historical scenes requiring grandeur and size. But the new directors wanted reality; they
took their crews to the château country of France or to the
old abbeys in the south of England, leaving the King castle
to its fate as a kind of industry joke; a place for festivities
that required ample space for the inevitable photographers
and reporters.

For the past six months it had been the headquarters of
Mitch Stone and his merry band who had shot *Festival* and
were in the seventh month of cutting it into some releasable
form. The world they had created at the castle was more
romantic than Tennyson ever dreamed. The bright statement
of Day-Glo colors was everywhere. Young people, most of
them wearing Indian headbands, moved in and out of the
makeshift offices and editing rooms carrying cans of film.
Sometimes, they simply wore the film looped around their
neck and shoulders: celluloid snakes. A beautiful young girl
sat at a typewriter tapping out some slow legend with two
fingers: she was bare from the waist up, except for strands
of straight brown hair some of which almost reached the
pink nipples. Blankets were everywhere; hanging from the
plastic turrets of the castle, spread on the floors of corridors
and offices. Young men with hair tied in long pigtails, se-

cured by beautiful colored ribbons, passed around tightly rolled tubes from which came a soft scent that drifted through the castle and into the stagnant air. Music blasted from loudspeakers—groups that had played at the Festival and were now slowly being assembled on film. Surprise: Kleinholz has appeared. From where? By limousine, golf cart, wheelchair? Irrelevant. He limped through gorgeous colors, the rocking sounds and ripe smoke, waving to people as if he were a politician running for office. The members of Mitch Stone's troupe were only mildly curious. Those that weren't chemically stoned were, perhaps, like Ezra, stoned by the hot, dry wind that ruffled the purple velvet draperies. Along the castle walls was scrawled less-than-royal graffiti, the largest and most conspicuous statement being: BETTER THINGS FOR BETTER LIVING THROUGH CHEMISTRY.

In Stone's workroom, between walls covered with gigantic posters of the Festival, Stone moved in on Ezra, fencing first with him, then Kleinholz then back to Ezra again. Clearly, he saw himself the embattled holdout against big money, against power. But there he was camped in the castle of the mighty, promising them film that would make everything possible if—if— His cheek twitched, first just a jump or two and then so visible—or perhaps so painful— that he jammed his fist against it.

"Sorry," Stone said. "I haven't slept more than four hours a night in six months."

He looked to Ezra like some sort of wraith out of an Indian legend.

"When do you think . . . ?" Kleinholz began.

"How the hell do I know, Lothar!"

"This is a business, Mitch. We have to make *some* plans. View a rough cut. We have a lot going on this. Ezra is new. He has to plan his publicity campaign . . . start on his ads. . . . We're going to spend a lot of money. . . ."

"How much?" The hand came away from the cheek and the thin mouth above the yellow beard stretched in a smile. The question was thrown not at Kleinholz but at Ezra.

"Today's my first day. Let's talk about it tomorrow," Ezra said.

"There's no way to predict the budget now," Kleinholz said. Ezra saw Kleinholz fiddling with something in his jacket pocket; probably a miniature tape recorder.

"Then there's no way to predict when we'll have the print," Stone said.

Kleinholz focused his intense gaze and a pointed finger at Mitch Stone. "I am playing absolutely fair and straight with you," he said. "You'd better plan on doing the same with me. And don't pull any of your Indian trances on me. It's too late in the game for all that."

Stone's eyes were actually closed and his breath was coming in short, shallow spurts. But the eyes opened in a second and he said, "Good-by, Lothar."

To Ezra's surprise, Kleinholz turned and walked from the room with a solemn step. You could almost hear the muffled drums. Ezra turned to follow him. Mitch Stone gripped his arm, hard.

"Listen," Stone said. "I've got to talk to you. But not here."

The hand released Ezra and scribbled something on a piece of paper. Ezra saw the cheek begin to jump again. It was like watching an insect jumping beneath tanned skin.

Max was waiting. "Nick called. He'll meet you at his office with the *Variety* guy."

Safely aboard the golf cart, Max driving and talking: "How did the momser do with the chief?"

"There seems to be a question about getting the print of the picture in time."

"Or at all."

"Really?"

"They'll burn it. You saw those eyes."

"What does he want?"

"What does everybody want? Money!"

"No, not just money."

"You're smart, boss. He wants money, but even more he wants the picture to be *his* . . . every frame, every beat of music. Our turn'll come, too. Every ad will have to be his, every publicity story. Wait, wait. . . . He knows how desperately we need him. He'll burn the print and we'll go down the drain. . . . Wait, wait. . . ."

Ezra could not wait another minute. He stripped off his jacket and tie, tore open his collar and closed his eyes to the wall of heat against which they seemed to be pounded with every turn of the golf cart

It was passively pleasant, swerving around corners, watching cables being unloaded from trucks, hearing Max describe the tailor shop as they pass it (everyone else called it "wardrobe") and telling of Rupert, the tailor, his eccentricities, and what he could do for Ezra, through the agency of Max, if he would just buy cloth in Madrid and bring it to the lot.

At the rear entrance to the administration building they found Nick Bohm. And there followed an inspection of the enormous office being built for Ezra, directly underneath Kleinholz's office.

"You're right under Lothar, so when he stamps good and hard you'll hear him."

Nick smiled and again the ambiguity of friendliness or malice crossed Ezra's mind. Or perhaps neither: a life lived poised on the knife-edge of neutral judgment, ready to move one way or another, as survival might dictate. Ezra met the key members of the department. One significant impression: they were all older people. Most over forty. Many in their fifties and a few with that grizzled sunburned look that could have been six decades in the making.

Like Claiborne, the man from *Variety*, an old-timer, jowled, sunburned wattles, the only white in his face the pressure point where his horn-rims touch the bumpy bone in his nose. Skeptical, seen-it-all but sentimental about "the industry," his bread and butter as well as land of dreams. Ezra was forced to reach down to find the energy to charm the man; the resourcefulness to convince him that Ezra Marks had, if not the answers, at least the right questions.

Nick Bohm watched, poured Scotch, waited.

Q: *How do you feel about coming from Government to movies? Isn't it a strange move?* (Cool question; have to warm him up.)

A: Actually, I left Washington, officially, in 1965. But I've made some small films—government documentaries on minorities, right here in California.

Q: *You've been associated with youth marketing, youth research. Have you been brought in mainly to promote* Festival?

A: No. Films are being made in all kinds of new, experimental ways. But they're being marketed in the same ways the studios have been using for forty years. (A calculated risk at offending Nick Bohm.)

Q: *Do you believe in research?* (The tone was still cool. If the interview was not to be a disaster Ezra would have to break down the distance between Q and A.)

"Of course I do," he said. "Nobody wants to play blind-man's buff with millions of dollars. Would you, in my place?"

"No. . . ." Claiborne said, the Q forced to become the A.

"And it's a new world. Television, cable TV, and cassettes around the corner, the new, segmented market: we have to make and sell pictures for each of those markets."

"True," Claiborne murmured.

"And you'll agree movies are not only a business but also an art form," Ezra asked.

"Perhaps the greatest of them all," Claiborne said. He was scribbling steadily; but by now they were collaborating on the interview. In a few moments they were also agreeing that nobody ever gave Michelangelo three million five to paint a picture. There must be accountability.

The time had come, Ezra felt, to grasp the interview and make it his own. He dramatized it by standing up, suddenly, and pacing. There was a nice drama to the moment, to the movement.

"I'll tell you where the Washington background and the movies *do* come together," he said. "I joined the Kennedy Administration—and I was small potatoes in a very big Irish stew—at a moment when something absolutely irrational but essential was needed in national life. Confidence!" He paused to let Claiborne's flying pencil catch up. "The remnants of a recession, a sluggish Eisenhower world that inspired young people only to go out and get fat jobs as quickly as possible. Oh, there's been miles of copy written about all this. But the one thing that you could sense in the air in those days was—a will to confidence. The silent sound stages . . . the runaway productions in Europe . . . sixty-percent unemployment in the craft unions. . . . Please get me straight, I'm new and not sounding off as an expert. But it doesn't take so much smarts to see that young people are the big movie audience—and young people are not famous these days for having a hell of a lot of confidence in their elders. The movie business didn't get us into Vietnam and it's not going to get us out. But 1970 seems to me a little like 1960, when I went to Washington: *we need confidence.* And there is one thing to be said for us. Whether it was Jack Kennedy . . . or the rest of us workers in the vineyard . . . we managed to rally young people together with a confidence that hadn't been heard of for a long time—and isn't much around these days."

It was part of his knack, always had been: the ability to
sell an idea. It might have been one reason Robinson pulled
him out to the studio. And even if Robbie wasn't there to
hear it, it gave Ezra a charge to see if he could bring it off.
If it worked, Robbie could read it in the papers the next
morning.

Claiborne lifted his pallid face, the pencil poised. He
looked older since Ezra had begun to speak: chalk-in-the-
face. "But how about these economies, firings, threats of
studios closing, mergers; how do you generate confidence in
that kind of atmosphere?"

"I said it was irrational, Mr. Claiborne. I don't have the
answers. I'm trying to define the questions for myself."

"And the proxy fight rumors. Aren't you joining the studio at a tough time? Especially since . . ." He glanced at Nick
Bohm. Nothing! Smiling, smooth, nothing. He continued,
". . . since Robbie Robinson is no longer with the studio."

"I'm going to pull something I haven't pulled since I
dealt with the Washington press corps." Smile, a beat, and:
"No comment."

Alone with Nick Bohm, he relaxed, wiping his face with
Max Miranda's handkerchief.

"It went well," Nick said. And busied himself with the
afternoon batch of telexes while Ezra was busy in Nick's
bathroom, which was only the size of, say, a Little League
baseball field.

"I've got us on a plane for Rome day after tomorrow.
Give you a chance to get settled. Anything you'd like for
entertainment tonight?" Nick asked.

Entertainment: God knew what that word meant. A
movie, a girl. No, Ezra was bushed.

He pulled Mitch Stone's paper from his pocket; his secret appointment was at 10 p.m. on the Santa Monica Pier,
in the Speedo Club. The air conditioning and the apparently

successful interview had calmed him, ameliorated some of the Santa Ana effect, and he contemplated the meeting with curiosity.

8

The Beverly Hills Hotel is the last unchanged meeting place in Hollywood. It sits, surrounded by masses of greenery, tall oleander trees, and crowded pink-and-yellow banks of flowers, set back from—and above—Sunset Boulevard.

The hotel was unchanged, but its cast of characters had been gradually changing over the years. The days when the film industry dominated all its poolside intrigues, its Polo Lounge, cocktail and breakfast deal-making, were gone. Men who had founded tool companies in Terre Haute six years earlier and had done well would be found here discussing California diversification. During certain months of the year, plump Italian art directors from New York advertising agencies filming the new cars for TV commercials share the pool with call girls no longer even making the effort to pass themselves off as starlets. (These were harsher times; economics brings forward a certain rough honesty.) The familiar red or black covers of scripts with their gold, embossed title type still decorated the lounge chairs, though they might be scripts for television or for an industrial sales show as well as for one of the scarcer Paramount, Warner Bros., or King Studio productions.

The bathing suits and cabana jackets worn in the lobby gave a sheen of pleasure to the place, but the basic thrust was: Business. The hotel smelled of money: its presence in abundance, its pursuit, its loss, followed by despair and the rising hope of gaining it again. With the exception of the guests at the frequent weddings and bar mitzvahs, they were all getting on in years: from middle age to old.

One of these carefully dressed gentlemen, all cream trousers and tan jackets from Beverly Hills men's shops, was prowling restlessly around Ezra's bungalow. He was immensely tall, a palm tree of a man, with a high brow and serious black eyebrows. As the bellboy fumbled at the door, the man leaped at Ezra and said, "I thought you'd never show up."

It was Robinson. He looked insane, brown eyes bulging from surrounding tanned and wrinkled flesh; jumpy hands smoothing gray hair already perfectly smooth.

"Am I glad to see you!" Ezra said.

"Somebody should be."

"Every time I asked about you, I got some fishy smile." A closer look, with concern. "Are you all right?"

"No bones broken."

"Come on in," Ezra said.

"No! I don't want anybody to know we're talking."

In one series of movements Robbie grabbed the bellhop's arm, shoved a bill into his hand, hurled Ezra's one suitcase inside the bungalow and slammed the door. Then the two old friends prowled the dusk, vines tripping their feet, giant palmetto leaves overhead casting shadows like some jungle-movie set; and all the while an ineffably sweet odor trailed them.

"They think I'm out," Robinson muttered. "I suppose you know."

"Are you—out?"

"For the moment."

"What happened?"

"I don't quite know, yet. But I tried, Ezra. You know me."

"I know you," Ezra said. "I also remember the first class

I took with you at Emerson Hall, when you stuck a phrase into a lecture on the political future of cable television: 'Who strives to the utmost, him can we save.' "

Robinson laughed: a straight laugh without irony. It seemed to ease his spirit for a moment. "Goethe in Emerson Hall. Dazzle the graduate students with fancy footwork." The laugh slowed and went away. "It didn't work here. As soon as I got some authority, some clout, I started lining up directors, started to plan deals for pictures. We were already into the banks for big money. Only real film-makers could save us. Any studio that could have a string of projects by Arthur Penn, Robert Altman, Larry Peerce, Frank Perry, Sordino (for class if not cash), and some of the younger ones you wouldn't recognize but who are maybe one picture away from a big one . . . that would be a studio worth saving. 'Who strives to the utmost,' right?

"They had my name off my parking space on the lot two hours later. I think they painted over it. You could hardly see where the letters had been." He made some funny gestures in front of his own eyes.

"Do you know I have these floating spots in my vision, did I tell you? The doctor says it's normal—but you can't tell me it's normal to have all that crap moving in front of you when you move your eyes."

He paced around Ezra, fears of brain tumors chasing convictions of betrayal and plans for comeback and vengeance through his mind; a glimpse of a Robinson Ezra didn't quite know. A man who slept poorly, the aggressive optimism of the studio day drowned by the night in which he tossed, fantasies of blindness and poverty crawling out from beneath the pillow.

Robbie grew calmer. "Okay," he said. "I'll tell you, so you'll know for your own protection."

They walked past a bungalow blazing with lights and

music. Two armed guards leaned against porch steps and ignored their passage.

"The desk clerk said Governor Reagan is visiting the Burtons or somebody, tonight," Robinson said. "Get used to the feeling of unreality. They measure Easterners out here by how long it takes to go away. Mine never has."

"I've heard what Kleinholz thinks about giving his studio away to film-makers."

"All he wants is to ride the crest of *Easy Rider*—beards and drugs and heavy rock. Well, who the hell knows how long that's going to last. And that's where Kleinholz and I split. What did you think of the old guy?"

Ezra touched Robbie's arm. They were both more settled now and the touch confirmed that. It pushed Robinson on without waiting for a reply. In his rush to tell he was like the survivor of some great disaster.

"If you saw him for more than five minutes, then you know what's on his mind. *Festival* is going to save the studio. And after that, more festivals. But he can't handle those youngsters. He can't even handle Sordino any more. He's lost the knack. Or times have changed—and there's more handling needed and less weight."

Looming over Ezra in a dark center of the uncharted park in which they wandered, Robinson placed both hands, paw-like on Ezra's shoulders.

"Ah, don't count me out, Ezra. I've got plans." Robbie had always had plans; it would be his epitaph: Here lies Robert Robinson. . . . He Had Plans.

But the immediate plans were for dinner. Under the stress of the day Robbie had skipped breakfast and lunch. The plan-within-the-plan was to see if Robbie could still get his old table at Chasen's. By the time it was clear that the table would be theirs, the heaviness had gone out of the experiment. They muffled private laughter as they ordered martinis from the sanctity of the privileged area just to the right of the entrance.

Robbie indicated a booth guarding the entrance to the large inside room. "That's been Kleinholz's table," he said, "for over forty years."

"Not Lothar Kleinholz, author of *The Electronic History of the World?*"

"Himself!"

"Where is the essential wall socket?"

"Haven't you heard of batteries?"

"Ah . . ."

They were giddy: the one free of the depression of banishment, the other made comfortable by the temporary presence of a friend. They ordered the mandatory Chasen's Caesar Salad, then steaks, wine, and more martinis.

Alcohol eased Ezra but returned anxiety to Robinson. He replayed a partial tape of his defeat.

"They used the budget of the Sordino picture to get rid of me. Sordino wanted an extra million and a half and I backed him up. But it was just an excuse."

"Who's 'they'?" Ezra was developing a curiosity about "they."

"Kleinholz. Maybe Becker, too. Maybe Bohm."

"A lot of maybes."

"That's what those two are like. Becker and Nick Bohm will never jump till they're sure it's safe."

"My new employer mentioned a proxy fight."

There was color in Robbie's face again. He poured each of them a fresh glass of wine.

"There are a few things you'll have to be told—sooner or later."

"Sooner?"

"Later. Anyway, I behaved well. That's a small comfort. Every time a studio head has made a disaster by the Great

Ape Trick there has been a line of executives ready to say: 'Yes, boss.' I said, 'No, boss.' It felt good."

"What's the Great Ape Trick?"

"You know: one picture makes millions so you ape the subject, ape the style, the director, whatever. When *The Sound of Music* made eighty million dollars and saved Fox it almost destroyed the industry. They spent two hundred million in imitations. All flops."

In the car driving back to the Beverly Hills Hotel a very quiet, drunken Robinson murmured, "That's the plot summary, Ezra: The Great Ape Trick with absolute studio control . . . versus the moviemakers taking over the movies." And intoned, "Two worlds, the one half dead, the other struggling to be born . . . or however that goes. I've bet my life on the newborn baby."

The moon trailed the car lazily. A white penumbra promised some occult West Coast weather phenomenon for tomorrow. Knowing he would have to do without Robbie, at least for the moment, Ezra's thoughts could not chase tomorrow: they went backward instead. It was odd how little he recalled the public, the progessional hurts of the Pied Piper days; days when he'd followed Robbie, giving up a vaguely defined academic career to grope his way into a glamorous but shadowy life in government. No details of the day the Senate refused to appoint Adam Yarmolinsky to head up the Peace Corps. ("McNamara's got him at Defense and I'm on my own," Robbie had moaned.) Or the day Ezra's plan to reorganize the Census on a more scientific basis was shelved for "re-evaluation." ("Do you know they're still counting noses—the way they did it when Woodrow Wilson was President?" Ezra complained bitterly.)

But it didn't matter; it didn't slow them down. Perhaps it was because of the general sense of possibility in the air. If one project didn't work another would. Until one, two, three murders, too many assassinations, one or two too many public funerals fouled that air, until American troops began to fill up Asia, until it became clear at last that public television was mostly for children; until one, two, three friends began to drift back to teach at Cambridge, to a network job in New York, to practice law in Denver. . . .

"I'll tell you something I'll bet you don't know," Ezra said. He turned the car onto the Freeway exit, past the ugliest motel in the world, hanging over it like a curse, and onto the curve of Sunset Boulevard.

"Tell me, old buddy," Robbie said softly. His eyes were closed.

"I know the moment you decided to get out of Washington."

"The very moment?"

"Give or take a few hours. Also the time, the place, and the unlikely cause."

"Ah, the cause," Robbie said.

"Remember the girl I was living with in the fall of Sixty-five?"

"Penny?"

"Nina."

Robinson opened his eyes. "I remember her well. Good long legs, blue contact lenses over brown eyes, small breasts."

"You've gone Hollywood. You only remember parts."

The memory had grown suddenly full of portent: like certain dreams which seem to promise the answer to everything once deciphered. The scene grew fat with detail in Ezra's mind. They had been playing tennis: mixed doubles at the Colony Club: adjoining courts occupied by Southern Senators, junior executives from Defense. The club was a favorite with McNamara's people. Nina was a sweet and tender young statistician at Defense with a strong forehand

and, as Robbie recalled, good, long legs. She was Ezra's
partner. Robbie was teamed with a friend of Nina's.

It had all happened very quickly. Robbie lunged for a
ball, yelled with pain, said it felt as if he'd been shot in the
leg.

In the taxi to the emergency room of Walter Reed Hospital Nina told Robbie that he had torn the plantaris muscle. She had played a great deal of tennis, and she had said
it with a quiet confidence that did not help Robbie's pained
state. "You'll need something to raise your heel—to take the
pressure off the calf."

At the hospital they slipped him into a wheelchair and
took X-rays. They waited for the results in a small room
with an emergency operating table, an intravenous stand,
and two folding chairs.

"Do you realize what we must have looked like in that
charnel house, in our tennis whites and sneakers, dangling
our rackets?" Ezra said.

To distract Robbie from the pain, Ezra had struck up a
conversation about the politics of public television, Robbie's
daily professional preoccupation. Washington is a shop-talk
town. It was a natural thing to do. The surprise came from
gentle Nina. After a few moments of complaints: "Can't get
things moving, opposition from private business. . . ."

"I've heard this from you for months," she said. "And
you don't really believe what you're saying."

"How'd you discover that?" Robbie said, an arrested
grimace on his face. It came as a surprise to Ezra. Nina had
always spoken with a kind of exaggerated respect to Robinson. He was older, had been a professor, was a wheel in the
FCC.

"It's part of my thirty-per-cent theory," she continued.
"I mean, part of you has to know that public television is a
political toy. But you came to Washington, anyway, right?
The idea is that the airwaves belong to the people. But like

every idea in Washington, it's about thirty-per-cent true. What's seventy-per-cent true is: the sponsors, the large advertisers, the product lobbies. They see to it that the airwaves don't get delivered to the people—no matter who they're supposed to belong to. But I've heard you and Ezra talking, week after week, about this problem and that problem as if there was—like—thirty-per-cent opposition and seventy-per-cent possibility of truth, justice, and hope. Instead of the opposite."

If she'd intended it as some sort of shock technique to distract Robbie from his pain, it had worked. His hand had left his leg and was waving at Nina. The grimace of pain was gone from his face.

"You've got it down pretty neat, haven't you?"

"No," she said. "It only comes out like that because I'm a statistician."

Nina was unfazed. "Actually, I was playing with other numbers. Ten–ninety was just too cynical. Fifty–fifty is what the liberals want you to believe. And. And ninety–ten is the way it sounded to a lot of people for about two months after Jack Kennedy was elected. But all in all, I think thirty–seventy is about right. Enough to give you a little hope. But not enough to really change anything."

And she hadn't let up. For the fifteen minutes or so that it took the X-rays to come back she poured it on. A kind of para-Marxist 30-per-cent–70-per-cent theory of how much— how little—power and hope the people of a country could gain from the rulers: the givers and getters. All presented from under a sweeping, fine, sweaty brow, elegant brown hair over a perfection of frilly tennis whites and a perfectly fitting blue and white sweater—in the gothic setting of a hospital emergency room—with nurses' blood-flecked uniforms and dirty white shoes roaming back and forth.

It was no wonder Robinson found such an epiphany irresistible. By the time she'd finished he was admitting how much he'd been fooling himself, how little was happening, how much he needed a change.

The doctor who brought the X-rays was a small Filipino woman.

"You have torn the plantaris muscle in your right leg," she said. "You'll have to wear a raised heel."

"I know," Robinson said. And everyone except the bewildered doctor laughed. By the time he could walk without limping—about five weeks later—Robbie had left Washington for a job with CBS.

Back in the perfumed gardens of the Beverly Hills Hotel Ezra said, "So you're leaving me behind again."

"I'm going to Rome tonight. To line up support. Sordino can help. Maybe Becker will come in when I get stronger. What time is it? I'm on the ten o'clock flight over the Pole."

"It's nine. At ten, I have a secret meeting with Mitch Stone. I'm due in Rome myself in a couple of days. With Nick Bohm. I'll see you there."

"Don't be fooled by Stone's love beads; he's a powerhouse. And don't be fooled by Bohm's helpfulness and 'good' advice. He's a quiet killer. Take care of yourself."

"Now that you're not here to protect me. . . ."

"Listen, I got you seventy thousand a year by bulling my way in and opening the door for you."

"Why *did* you? Outside of needing a friend in the jungle?"

"Because, if I win, I can't count on Nick Bohm. I'll need you."

"And how would you add up your chances of winning?" Robinson smiled. "Thirty–seventy."

"As usual."

"But if number seventy comes up, don't sell it short. You'll be Nick Bohm. One hundred thousand a year and up."

"And you?"

"Walk me out. I don't want to be late."

Robinson turned toward Ezra. Even in the half-light he could see Robbie's eyes were traced with red jagged lines.

"When I was a kid," Robbie said, "every other house had pigeon coops on the roof—and some guy with a long stick who used to open the cages and then kind of guide the pigeons in some flight pattern around the roofs and the sky. I remember those swoops and coming back and swoops again. What were those guys doing?" Robinson blinked tired eyes. "Were they exercising the birds? And how come you never see that any more, that swooping of all those graceful birds? When did pigeons get to be just a drag, dropping crap everywhere?"

It was Ezra's turn to advise his friend: "Don't let memories do you in," he said, looking straight up at the taller man. "I told the *Variety* man, today, we need confidence! You're Robbie Robinson. You have plans. 'Who strives to the utmost. . . .' "

Robinson straightened up. Standing in the auto corridor outside the hotel he was again a tall, swaying, graceful, and graying figure.

"Remember, Ezra, everybody knows what they're doing here. It's a source of strength. I hope you know why you're here." A hand raised. "See you in Rome, old buddy. Farewell . . . and welcome."

Gone was the planner of plans and the mourner of youth's pigeons. Dispossessed, the Roman proconsul on his way to Rome to recover his commission and his glory.

9

The games were Swoop-the-Loop, motorcycles whirling down a neon highway, electric lights flashing on and off as the player lost or gained the track or SMACK collision or BLINK and the game was over. The games were Red Baron, Spads, and Fokkers splitting the skies while the noise split eardrums. The games were Highway Patrol, your electronic car swerving and hopping to avoid the law's electronic beeps. The games were also Hot Dogs and Speedo and Guitars and Banjos for sale and fresh-caught sea food, fish pulled from the Santa Monica Pier or just beyond, where Mitch Stone waited for Ezra. Jimi Hendrix bombarded the air with electronic statments from an invisible source. The black-and-yellow night rocked with it, and the sea rocked around it; everyone seemed to have come out for the evening, even though at the pier itself the air hung hot, heavy again. Mitch Stone described the Santa Ana effect. It was something Californians did: explained local weather phenomena, mostly unpleasant ones, as if they were very special. Ezra didn't get it quite straight, not listening too closely, but it had something to do with reversal. The Valley would be cool tonight while it was hot at the shore, the opposite of the expected.

There were other surprises. Nick Bohm was there with a small, pretty girl; she had intense, watchful eyes and a shag of startling red hair. With them was the Hungarian boy, Karol. Nick was showing him how to operate the Highway Patrol pinball game. In the flesh Karol appeared larger than life. Film had not represented him in scale. He was very tall, a plant-stalk of a youth, slender except for a fullness in the face. Stripped of the Sordino/Lawrence mood he had a brilliant, forthright smile. It could be a boyish or a girlish smile. Some androgynous hesitation hovered over him as he laughed in the honkey-tonk tumult of the pier.

Mitch Stone, too, had someone with him. A tall, tough-looking man, older than Mitch, with his hair tied in a long pigtail behind his neck. It seemed Mitch had a partner, Jim Leggatt: a cooler customer, eyes clear, unfatigued, but with his own air of desperation. Not the exhausted hysteria that Mitch radiated. Rather, aggression held in check under politeness, under irony.

Sailors drifted by, looking for girls. Cars oozed past the wooden shacks on their way to and from the water's edge. Nick and the boy joined the group. A photographer appeared from behind Karol and began clicking and winding. Nick deftly directed the boy: "Play that game, turn away from the camera, don't smile so much, don't look so glum, you'll be in sunny Italy in a week working your ass off for Sordino."

"A poor choice of metaphor, all ends considered," Leggatt said. And added, to Ezra, "We should get together and talk. How long will you be in town?"

"I don't know. Long enough to talk."

But Mitch grabbed Ezra by the arm and guided him off toward the end of the pier, away from Leggatt and Nick Bohm.

Tonight Stone seemed more reasonable. He told Ezra about the Festival, how Kleinholz had given him the money to take ten cameras and his band of followers and photograph four days and nights, uninterrupted. He spoke of the spirit that pervaded the Festival, the sense of love and concern: half a million people taking care of each other in six fields of grass, listening to music, taking drugs under each other's beneficent guidance, helicopters dropping food, water, medicine.

"There's a saying, which at least four or five Indian tribes have in their mythology—in different ways, usually in the form of a question and answer," Mitch said. "It goes: 'Did God make us?' And the answer is: 'We make each other.' "

Mitch managed to appear both shy and fierce at the same time. The hollow eyes told of his exhaustion while he went on about those four days which, thanks to the film he was now editing, would never vanish. In fact, this outing was to be brief, and he would be on his way back to his movie lab in a little while.

"If you wanted this to be a meeting just between us, why did you ask Nick Bohm along?"

"Oh, Nick's all right. We were talking, and he was telling me about the boy, Karol, and I suggested the pier as a good background for a photo layout."

His tone was softer, less intense. "I have a good feel for publicity. Besides, general secrecy isn't the issue. It's Kleinholz; his ears are everywhere."

"And his tapes."

Mitch smiled his special smile. It never fully stretched to the corners of his thin mouth. If smiles had colors, like hair, it would be a blond smile, washed out and not entirely sincere. Only his scowls, which were more frequent, and darkened his face, seemed to carry the full authority of his existence. Ezra watched that gradually disappearing smile, wondered why the man had asked to see him and why it took everyone in this new life so long to say what they wanted. Could it be because the enterprise they were involved in, the tangle of advantage and disadvantage, motive and countermotive in the making of films, was so complex that they were never quite sure what they wanted, or should want? At the same time Ezra observed this detached young man with his washed-out blue denims ragged at the bottoms, his sandals, his red and brown headband (apparently never removed) his fringed Indian-style shirt, and realized with a perverse enjoyment that the life or death of a major film studio might depend on him.

Mitch went on: he just wanted to get to know Ezra. To tell him something of the feel of the picture by giving him a sense of the event. He went on to describe the climax. On the third day some Hopi Indians who were friends of his had initiated him into the Brotherhood of the Snake. In full view of half a million people Mitch had entwined himself with two snakes, rattlers, had whispered a sacred chant, and had come out of it unharmed; proof that the spirit of the Festival had communicated itself so deeply to him that even dumb, cold-blooded reptiles could sense it. It was captured on film and would be the high point of the picture.

"But nobody sees any film, moving or still, of that ceremony until I know where I stand with Kleinholz and Becker. They're going to kill that scene." He paused as if to connect Ezra with the two betrayers of his film.

"Are you sure?"

"Becker mumbled something about people being afraid of snakes . . . that it might be a turn-off. That man has the soul of a donkey."

"I don't know. . . . We could do some research."

"Not on my fucking picture, you don't. This picture will have everything on the screen that I want or there won't be any picture at all."

The cheek twitched again.

"There's a sickness in this business, in this whole place, and I'm not going to let it infect my work. You're new in this. I haven't got you figured out, exactly. But you have to understand the kind of man I'm dealing with."

The kind of man was Kleinholz. The type was a mystery to Mitch. Why should the classic movie mogul, that magnificent cliché archetype, manipulate power in the unique, ultimate degree? There were men in General Motors who controlled great sums of money, men in U.S. Steel who had economic control over the lives of thousands and thousands of people. Yet the mythologies of ruthlessness and desperation could not be compared. Kleinholz was one of the last of the founders. He was bred on absolute power. But—and here was the marvelous mystery—absolute power over artists and over an art form that confused and baffled better and worse men than he. How do you apply such inbred power in a time when the money fountain is drying up and people like himself, Mitch Stone, make a movie out of thin air, a chance music festival and a half million kids who love music and people and—incidentally—movies?

There was a story that Becker had told Mitch. ("And I admire that son-of-a-bitch. He's the pure article: a killer to his bones. When you sit down with him you know that only one of you is supposed to get up alive.") It seemed Kleinholz had once, in the long ago days of Cary Grant and Irene Dunne movies, assigned just such a project to a famous dramatist: Sidney Howard or Elmer Rice—somebody like that—a man who'd won the Pulitzer Prize some years before. Kleinholz had a cold and, being confined to his bed, had called the writer to come to his home with the script. On arrival the writer was shown to a tightly closed door from behind which Kleinholz's hoarse voice called out instructions to slide the manuscript under the door and . . . wait. The Pulitzer Prize winner waited. Standing by the door, sitting, dawdling in the plush living room drinking a whisky—there is no way of imagining the scene that can spread salve over the humiliation. Finally, after an hour and a half, the manuscript was pushed back under the door. It had been torn, neatly, into sixteen pieces. It was Mitch Stone's personal opinion that no corporate analogy for such behavior existed. Its boundaries of psychology were so extreme as to border on the pathological. But could a whole industry embody an illness? It meant the establishment of new norms.

"Here's our difference," Mitch said. "If he called me I wouldn't go. If I went, I wouldn't have waited. And if he tore up something I'd done, I'd go somewhere else and get it made. Like the last three Presidents of the United States in the jungles of Asia, Lothar is helpless. They bomb, and he bombs—for the same reason."

Mitch waved his arms, became a bomber plane, "What do you mean I can't control these slant-eyed gooks any more —*Boom. Ppppccchhhaaaa*! What do you mean Mitch Stone wants final cut of his movie. *Crasshhh*!"

He laid a finger alongside of his nose and closed both eyes briefly. "Indians know how to handle white men like him. Patience and cunning, that's what you need."

His subsequent pause threatened to turn into a kind of trance; or so it seemed against the background of the teeming pier. The moment had come for Ezra to move.

"What is it you wanted to say to me, exactly, Mitch? I mean all this has been about Kleinholz. Do you want me to take some message back to him? Is that the idea?"

Mitch just smiled that blond nonsmile again. He strolled back toward the brightly lit games area, Ezra at his side. It was as if the question had never been asked. Leggatt joined them, laughing; it made him sway like a rocking ship's mast.

"Your young man seems to have joined a party of sailors. Nick left him alone for five minutes to take the photographer to his car and—presto—*finito il bambino*!"

"Where's Nick?"

"In full chase. He may as well practice now."

"Practice for what?"

Leggatt's brows arched to meet each other: a black bridge of irony.

"You're taking him to Europe and dropping him in Sordino's lap, with Michael Maurice waiting in the wings. . . ."

Ezra frowned; he was on the defensive again. "I think the boy's straight," he said, feeling dumb. He'd made the company man's public-relations reply.

Leggatt gazed at Ezra from over a pinched joint.

"I don't think he knows what he is yet. It's what *they'll* make of him that can cause the trouble," he said. "If the sailors don't do it first."

Then with brisk authority he suggested that Mitch's return to the editing room was long overdue. Having arranged to be alone with Ezra, Leggatt quickly told him the reason for the meeting. They were counting on him to do an authentic, youth-directed campaign. They were counting on him not to let Kleinholz dictate some old-fashioned approach to the advertising and publicity. That would plant the kiss of death on the film. They were counting on him for everything.

"Believe me," Leggatt said, "these young people *are* different. I've lived with them, slept on the ground with them for four nights during the Festival. These are not the buttoned-down, Ivy League Peace Corps kids you did your demographic studies on. These are kids who are constructing a counterworld to yours—a sacred one to them. If they think you're into a rip-off of their thing, we're all finished." He was chanting now. "Believe me, Ezra, there is something new going on, and nobody in Washington or Scarsdale or Shaker Heights knows about it. And for sure nobody at the studio knows it. I'm counting on you to know it. You have to be with them, be part of their lives, know how to speak to them. Otherwise, we're finished, the picture's finished—and you're finished."

He paused and swept a gesturing hand from his pigtailed hair to the beads around his neck, to his rope-tied trousers and, finally, his bare feet.

"*Why*—" he said slowly, "—*do you think I dress like this?*"

And having, for once, communicated a direct demand, Leggatt was gone. From the flashing neon all around, there appeared long red hair, nervous bitten lips, long skirt seductively parting as if by its own will: a tense package of girl, pretty enough to be—what?—model, actress, starlet.

"Listen," she said.

"Yes?"

"I'm Honey Williams."

It was stated as an answer. But what was the question? A quick look told him that Honey Williams was about to cry.

"Listen," she said again.

If things were to progress at all he would have to take some action. "Are you Nick's girl?"

"I have to speak to you. . . ."

"Sure."

"He'd kill me if he knew."

"People don't kill people so easily," Ezra said. "Don't be dramatic." He observed her brown eyes and red hair. "You're Irish?"

"Spanish on my mother's side; my father's Irish. You don't know how marvelous Nick is," she said. "The main thing is: you have to trust him. Give him a chance to do what he can really do."

Everyone, it seemed, had a special request to make of the new man in town.

"Honey," he said, "you've got it wrong. I work for Nick."

Honey cocked her head sideways in a quick motion; it threw her hair in a cloud around her face and expressed impatience.

"You know what I mean," she said. "But if you let him show you—he knows everybody in town. The directors and the actors all trust him. He's the only *one* they want to deal with. Ask Sordino." Her mournful manner was gone, swallowed up in the enthusiasm of her plea. She took a deep breath. Ezra became aware of how difficult such an act was in the heavy air. He decided he'd had enough, for the moment, of demands, direct or indirect, rational or fantasied. It was hot; it had been a long day.

"Okay," he told Honey Williams. "I'll be working closely with Nick. I'll give him every chance there is."

She smiled and swirled her hair again. She stepped close to Ezra and kissed him on the mouth. He had a double twinge. A sensual stir and then the remembered words: "Anything you'd like for entertainment tonight?" He shook the connection off as absurd. What he could not shake off was the sense that he had received a small token payment for something he did not know how to deliver.

10

Heavy, rich night-blooming jasmine is all around the bungalow, the villa the studio has provided for my comfort. But my comfort was to have been Robinson. And all he has left me with are the words, "I hope you know why you're here." Such grand existential hopes for such a simple presence. Or not so simple . . .

When I was fifteen I remember setting myself a magnificent task. I chose four of the smartest boys in my class and arranged to write their term papers for them. It was no simple case of adolescent cheating. Everyone knew those four students could pass any test. The task I set myself was to write essays that would sound like each of them and maintain a high level of excellence. It worked: everyone got a good grade, not one teacher guessed the truth. But some unknown informer finked on me, not to the school, but to my father. Arnold Marks was, as far as I could judge at the age of fifteen, all of a piece and always had been. A passionate zoologist, he worked on and carried with him, the manuscript of a book that won him a Pulitzer Prize. Its thesis was that man's aggression was learned, not innate. And it used his observations of wild fowl as data. This was long before Lorenz and the other ethologists proposed the contrary. I doubt if his book could win the Pulitzer Prize today. The act I'd committed baffled him. It was not aggression. No one had been hurt. The intent was not even, strictly speaking, dishonest; the outcome would have been no different had the boys taken their own tests.

He didn't bring it up until that summer. We were spending the summer at Brandeis, where he was a Visiting Fellow; my mother was on tour giving readings that July. He waited until we'd played a game of paddle tennis and I was sweaty and silly with heat and fatigue. We drank Cokes, sat on towels, and he asked:

"Why did you do that?"

"I don't know," I said. The classic answer of childhood miscreants.

We sparred back and forth in the manner of parent and child, until I thought I caught a glimmer of what bothered him most.

"It didn't mean anything," I said.

"That's just it," my father said. "Then why did you do it?"

Meaning would have explained—if not excused—all. Four years later, a year before he and my mother were killed in a meaningless car accident on the Pennsylvania Turnpike, he joked with me about it.

"It's the family ailment," he said. "Logophilia. We're hooked on the idea that everything has to have meaning." And I told him, then, that there had been three questions behind my experiment: Could it be done? What would I get out of it? What would it feel like?

He never accepted or understood that. We let it drop.

*But after he died, I think that encounter—that logophilia—
took me over, by inheritance. It took me to a job in government. But now I am thirty-five-years old. When do you stop
being a prodigy, a Washington whiz-kid? Why had I accepted Robbie's wild and undefined offer, in the first place?
It's 1970. The public world that began—or seemed to begin
ten years earlier is gone. (Robbie realized this first, with
an assist from Nina.) For five years I've kept a foot in both
private and public camps.*

*But what do you do when Nina's 30–70 equation sums
up your daily life? When the public life dies on you—is
literally assassinated? What you do is, you go private! You
go public because you've been teethed on principles, hooked
on logos. Then pursuit of truth, the pursuit of facts. But
always, too, the pursuit of what they mean.*

*That's why people like Robbie and me go public: teach at
universities, join the federal-this or the state-that, or the
foundation for this-or-that. But when you go private all
you're left with is winning or losing. (Nobody ever argues
about what winning or losing means!)*

What am I doing here at King Studio?

To find out: Can it be done?

> *What will I get out of it?*
>
> *What will it feel like?*

11

KLEINHOLZ TAPE #8362

KLEINHOLZ: Nick wants to use that Sordino promotion
film on network TV. Be diplomatic, but get it.

EZRA: It's apparently complicated. Michael Maurice and
Sordino are both uptight about the boy. Somebody wants the
promotion film killed.

KLEINHOLZ: I've been handling fellows like this for years. Movies breed sexual competition. It's a law of life. You saw the footage?

EZRA: It's a beauty.

KLEINHOLZ: Get Sordino's permission to use it. In writing.

EZRA: We don't need it legally.

KLEINHOLZ: But legal is the last resort around here. Most of all, until a picture is in the can—and in the theaters generating revenue, what you need from these creative sons-of-bitches is what I call Operating Good Will.*

EZRA: *(a laugh)*: As opposed to *real* good will?

KLEINHOLZ: Real good will I got from my father. A wonderful man, dead at fifty-three from a life of poverty and murderous work at a cloak presser's iron, with lots of real good will. Don't bring me that. Get me written permission, and make Sordino happy to give it.

12

TWA Flight 862. NY–Rome. A Boeing 707.

The TWA passenger agent saw them swiftly through the gate and onto the plane before anyone else boarded. Nick spread out his gear comfortably through the cabin.

"Don't you know why Becker has got to hate you?" Nick hunched down in the seat staring intently at one of the hostesses, a skinny little red-headed girl who kept repairing something—the freshness of lipstick, the tautness of stockings—every few minutes. It made for an interesting show.

"It's because of the whole making of a movie: look, a guy

---

* Ezra's note: Definition of Operating Good Will. The successful acquiescence of others to your will, without their precise understanding of what has happened.

brings a script to the studio. They like it. They don't know
why they like it. Everyone says: 'A wonderful script.' But
nobody knows what they mean. It's not an exact science.
What they forget is: It's not even an exact art. If you look at
a painting, there are some standards, even if you don't give a
shit about them. Line, composition. Mostly this gang—and
any of the gangs that decide things at studios—like a script
if it reminds them of another script that did well."

He turned away from the redhead's eternal correction of
herself, toward Ezra.

"But there's one little thing they don't know. That
there's an element of mystery in the creative thing. Christ,
you should hear Sordino on all this."

"You should hear Robinson," Ezra said. "He calls it the
Great Ape Trick."

"I've heard," Nick said, wearily. Apparently safe in mid-
air it was all right to speak of Robinson. "He lost that battle.
Listen, have you got a cigarette?"

"I don't smoke," Ezra said quietly and beckoned to the
redhead, who then hovered over him for the entire ceremony, through the smoke and nonstop talk.

"Ape Trick or not, you never hear them say things about
a script like tension, or definition of character, or too many
climaxes spoiling the big one. Simple things like that. Do
you know in 1949 I quit Sam Goldwyn to go live in New
York for a year and study creative writing at The New
School for Social Research? That's on Twelfth Street."

Ezra nodded that he knew the location.

"I was back in eight months. Never wrote a line. And I
never found out why. But I'm losing the thread," he said.
"What? Oh, yeah. The basic reason why publicity and advertising are so powerful is that everybody else is so weak
and confused about the whole process, the whole product
you call a movie. So they pick a script and people to turn it
into a movie, and they give them the dough and the go-

ahead. After some months, in comes a piece of film. A work of art or two hours of entertainment: *something*! They still don't know. And you can't be too hard on them. The critics don't agree. What the fuck would they do sitting in that dark screening room if it was *their* dough and they had to decide before the fact. I knew a writer once who used to say to the producers and the studio brass, after the sneaks in Glendale or Pasadena, when everybody had an opinion about what to do, he'd say: 'Fellas, where were you when the paper was white?' He died like a dog a few years ago. His liver was like a piece of used carbon paper. Writers drink a lot."

The redhead brought Nick a whisky sour.

"Okay, so they're in the screening room—*you're* there with them, by the way—and they look at, say, eight million dollars up on the screen. Eight million *spent* dollars. All gone! And they have to decide, sometimes pretty damned quick if the banks are breathing down their neck for repayment of some loans at twelve per cent, whatever the hell the prime rate is at the time. Decide if it's any good. So—enter Ezra Marks: the new marketing genius. Sitting in the dark and perilous room, when the lights go on, *you* are the focus of all eyes. 'What do you think?' 'How do we sell it?' '*Can* we sell it?'

"And," he added, "in the middle of all this high-stakes uncertainty, come the fears. You're living in the middle of a great example. *Snakes will kill a picture*. You could do research until Gallup pops a gut and not convince Kleinholz that the snake scene is great, will help the picture—or even, sadder-but-true—won't make any difference either way. He's afraid of it. It's too bold, the way Stone did it, and most of all too-fucking-plain-unfamiliar. So it's war; like most wars totally unnecessary, and the wrong people get hurt."

He finished his whisky sour with a last despairing toss of his head.

"A guy like Sordino falls in love with a story by D. H. Lawrence, dreams of doing *The Lion's Farewell* for maybe ten years and finally gets somebody at the studio to take a chance—I had a lot to do with convincing Kleinholz to do it and don't think it doesn't scare me when I think about what's going to happen if . . . Anyway, it's not just Sordino, it's any artist. Willie Wyler, John Ford, George Stevens . . . they work like bastards for years to get it down right. And six guys turn to a seventh guy—usually somebody with no talent of his own—and it all comes down to him."

"Kleinholz told me these two theories," Ezra said. "The other one says the picture does it, no matter what we do."

"Yeah? Then let him live that way. Our marketing budget is twenty million bucks and we spend millions more in media every year—the second largest chunk at the studio—after the production budget. Why do you think Becker hated you before you ever got here? He books the picture in some sort of pattern: big cities first, or some chains he owes a favor to, or vice-versa; or, more usually today, he takes a nice theater in New York, maybe in the East Sixties, opens the picture and waits for people like us to get the word out to the trade and the rest of the money-paying world. He doesn't know how to make the picture a success. He hopes you do. But in the meantime he's helpless. So we're back to that 'word,' right Ezra? But that 'word' has gotten pretty complex today. We still do the whole bag of tricks. Personal appearance tours, for one. But who do you tour when stars don't sell tickets any more? Stunts, clowns jumping off bridges, working a territory before the premiere for a week with promotions on radio and TV, with seminars and talk shows and sky-writing and a girl diving naked into swimming pools with the name of the picture tattooed on her ass—all that does is guarantee that a lot of people will know the name of the picture. What it doesn't guarantee is

that anybody's going to want to see it. That's why they turn
to you with fear, in that screening room, and that fear
turns to hate like a shot. *Because they don't know how to do
it any more.* You made your big manifesto to the trades; you
asked for confidence! Well, they don't have it any more. So
now they ask you: Which star should we feature? Do stars
matter any more? Do they matter only in certain kinds of
stories and not in others? Should we emphasize the love
element? Love pictures are big this year—but our picture
doesn't hit the theaters till next year. Should we talk about
the murder in the picture? Does murder still sell? Two murder pictures flopped this year.

But this year, don't you see, as Alice said to the White
Rabbit, is really next year, so what should we do about that?
Maybe we do some copy testing for the ads. But Becker and
Kleinholz don't believe in that. 'Don't give me that shit,'
Kleinholz says, 'I can smell a dog from a money picture a
mile away.' All those artists turning, at the end of the trail,
to Kleinholz's nose. But most of all to . . ." He paused. Some
vestigial sense of tact or politics poked through the whisky.
". . . to us, to make or break the work of art they've killed
themselves to put on film."

He sank his head in his two fanned-out palms and murmured, "Ezra, you and I are up to our necks in such a pile of
shit." His eyes closed for a second, shutting out reproach
and self-reproach.

"Okay," Ezra said. "How would you handle things if you
had your way, Nick? You've been in the business a long
time."

"All my life," came the even softer sound.

"Then what would you do when the film hits that screening room—who would you have sit there, and what should
be the operating system? You must have some notions after
all you've been through."

Ezra waited as the chest in the next seat began to rise

higher and lower more deeply until the breath turned absolutely regular and exhaled with the gentle hint of a snore.
It seemed Nick Bohm was only posing problems, today. So-
lutions would have to wait.

13

The first Roman day and evening: a kaleidoscope of
blurred impressions. Arrival, encounters, introductions,
screenings, evaluations, plans. All organized by Nick Bohm;
yet all with a random air.

Perhaps this was because everything was filtered
through Ezra's groggy head and queasy stomach. (This last
began during the walk from the arrival gate to passport
control and never let up.) On that first day in and out of the
Hotel Excelsior suite there moved a succession of people who
worked for the studio, for Ezra's department, or, often in
some undefined relationship *with* the studio . . . some head-
quartered right here in Rome—but some from London or
Paris, a few from New York, all appearing because Ezra and
Nick had appeared, as if conjured by someone's spectacular
will. The names blurred along with the faces: Giannini . . .
Archer . . . Rossi . . . Becker (again). There was even an
unpronounceable little man from Bombay, in Rome to see
screenings of what he kept calling "product," and who was
toothily eager to discuss expanding billboard coverage in
India.

On the plane, Nick had briefed Ezra about everyone he
was to meet. The most interesting of all was Umberto Rossi:
at once an original and a type. He was Assyrian—of whom
there were only a few thousand left in the world. In the
distant days before movies, his family had sold camels,
women, boys, and various other commodities. The precise

origins of Rossi's personal fortune were cloudy and imprecise. Real estate was sometimes mentioned when the subject came up; a small loan to Lothar Kleinholz at a crucial moment thirty years ago was another piece of revolving mythology. More importantly Rossi was the head of the company through which King Studio released their "product" in Europe. He also headed his own company which co-produced and co-released with King Studio.

A small man, elegantly compressed into a tight white suit, Rossi chain-smoked cigarettes that smelled like perfume.

"Welcome," he said. "I've heard about and read about you. I tried to see you in Los Angeles but I got tied up and then you had left."

The assembly and reassembly of studio personnel so swiftly in any country in the world was an amazement to Ezra.

Some strain of guilty common sense made him mention this to Rossi months later, in the course of a trip to Paris.

Over a drink at Fouquet's, Rossi said, with his white-on-tan smile, "It is a special thing. Do you know what single element keeps investors away from movie studios? T&E."

"T&E?"

"Travel and entertainment. A balance-sheet statement—like the bottom line everyone is so fond of talking about. Well, this is the only business in the world where travel and entertainment can amount to ten million dollars a year. Do you know how that sort of thing looks in the *Wall Street Journal*?"

But Ezra did not think, then, of the *Wall Street Journal*. He thought of magic. The magic of all those swift flights through the dark: to land and appear, exhausted but quickly groomed, at the bar of the Plaza-Athénée in Paris or the Pink Elephant in London, or Harry's Bar in Venice (the names change but the principle is eternal), sleepily talking

of below-the-line costs, of pick-up deals, of photographic
layouts for stars no one was certain could guarantee a penny
at the box office. And all the while some conservative inner
voice was wondering if any results would come from these
expensive conversations, followed by long, moonlit walks
back to the Danieli in Venice or rainy strolls back to The
Dorchester in London; wondering all the while if any concrete results would justify the loose and lavish spending of
money as if its limits did not exist; as if only accommoda-
tions and speed and effectiveness in reaching destinations
and decisions mattered.

Nick Bohm, the Master of the Revels, gave the kaleidoscope a shake and they climbed into one of the ubiquitous
black limousines. They were driven to a compound of low
brick buildings in which they moved from one screening
room to another, seeing films. A few whispered "hellos," and
the lights dimmed. But not before Ezra saw that on his left
was a prim and pretty dark young woman. In the darkness
she whispered that her name was Lisa, that she was his
translator, that she worked for King Studio in Rome and
Paris, that she spoke *presque seulement le français* and that
the film they were to see was produced in France by a man
named Leroux, whom she did not trust and who had no
taste; it was in French, but *malheureusement* the dubbing
had not as yet been done—and that she would do her best.
Her best was, at best, confusing.

The discussion afterward was brief. Becker led off. "This
guy Leroux wouldn't know how to say shit if he had a
mouthful." In such terms, apparently, major business decisions were settled. Umberto Rossi nodded and turned toward Ezra, who said, "It's mostly talk and no action. And so
much talk in a foreign language— I'm sorry." With a shrug
he disqualified himself.

Nick Bohm joined them. "Leroux is one of the best directors working in France." Becker raised a smartly cuffed hand and turned the thumb down. They were, after all, in Rome. Rossi smiled and Leroux's film was finished.

Becker and Rossi proceeded to engage in a symbolic, competitive ballet: the choosing of a restaurant for lunch.

"Hostaria dell 'Orso." Umberto Rossi said. "Let Mr. Marks see the Rome film colony in full bloom."

"Hell, right after lunch he gets to see Michael Maurice, the kid, and Sordino," Becker said. "That's enough film colony for one day. There's a new place in Trastévere Dick Zanuck told me about. Let's try it."

Ezra observed Nick's barometric pressure. It registered in those gray eyes. A shift inward, as he saw Becker putting the weight of his entire self against the choice of a restaurant for lunch. A fox refusing to be caught in the hunt.

"I've got to pick up this artist," Nick said quickly. "We'll meet you at lunch."

Becker seized his opportunity. "Gigo's," he called after Nick. "The driver knows where."

Rossi took defeat gracefully. He rounded up cars and drivers for the rest of them. Becker shot his cuffs and tightened his already tight belt a notch. He could always refuse a pick-up deal, like the Leroux film. But the smaller victories were tougher. Ezra had the feeling the man wished lunch was over; he'd won the initial victory. From now on, until the next screening, he could only lose.

In the limousine Ezra was matched with Becker. "You started off wrong, kid," Becker said. He worked a cigarette into a holder. "You didn't take my advice."

Ezra could remember no advice.

"With the *Variety* guy. You came on like a whiz-kid. Confidence . . . Jesus! In the middle of a proxy fight you talk about confidence!" He grinned over the holder and the perfectly set collar of his shirt, an impish parody of F.D.R.

"Everybody probably figures you were standing in for your buddy Robinson. What the hell, hah?" He spoke in a hoarse whisper.

"How could I stand in?"

"He's sucking around Rossi and Sordino. Rossi has King stock up his ass, been buying it for years, taking it instead of dough."

"I didn't know that. It takes a month before you find the men's room in a new job."

"Not in this business." Ezra wondered why he spoke in whispers.

The restaurant was small but had a sidewalk terrace swimming in sunlight. Only a few yards away, trucks were being unloaded and then loaded again with great sides of beef. A young woman sat with Nick Bohm. She was small; ash-blond hair curved easily up from a high, pale forehead, over blue eyes. She wore a blue skirt and a pale blue blouse; a touch old-fashioned. When she spoke, he understood. She said, "Hi, I'm Kim Cross." The first word came out: Hah. She was from the South. That explained the time lag of style.

Nick made a precise and formal introduction, carefully giving Ezra's full title. Kim had no title. She was simply going to do a painting of Karol to be used as the basis of the publicity and advertising campaign.

"Kim is not a commercial . . . I mean . . ." Nick said. His customary poise fluttering away.

"I see," Ezra said, politely.

"No," Kim said. "You couldn't possibly. But I'll do a good painting of the boy."

She gazed at Ezra, blue eyes wide open as if the statement were unfinished—and dared him to challenge it.

From the other end of the long table Becker and Umberto Rossi collaborated on the menu. With their palace

guard of King Studio, European staff, and Lisa, the perfumed simultaneous translator of the morning's film, they
made one party. Ezra, Nick, and Kim made up another.
"I'll never get used to seeing movies in the morning as a
way of life." Ezra said.

"I like it," Kim said. "But it's not a way of life for me."

"Do you do much movie work?"

"Some posters, illustrations, ads—sometimes a real
painting. Exactly as much as I need to live and paint in
Rome and not one bit more. I exhibit in New York and keep
a studio there and in L.A.—it costs money to travel. Shows
don't always sell." She leaned forward as the waiter distributed the small plates of fettuccine. "The trick is, to get in
and out before they get you."

Nick Bohm stepped in. "You're talking to the wrong people about that," he said.

"Am I?" Kim said still addressing herself directly to
Ezra across the narrow table.

"I'm new," Ezra said.

"I know. Rome's a small town. Movie-Rome is even
smaller. Are you married?"

"No."

"Living with anyone?"

"No."

"How old are you?"

"Thirty-five."

Nick Bohm drank his cold Frascati, watching them,
smiling, as if thinking of something else.

"I'd like to see your work," Ezra said.

"I've already auditioned." The wide blue eyes could narrow as quickly as a cat's.

"That's not what I meant."

The second course was veal. A small commotion at the
other end of the table indicated that Becker had ordered a
particular wine and was not satisfied in the captain's han-

dling of it. Much of the conversation was in Italian. With
quiet malice, Nick translated for Ezra. The captain had
placed the wine on the adjacent radiator. The heat would,
naturally, spoil the wine. There was only one thing wrong
with Becker's fastidious concern. It was a warm day. The
radiator was producing no heat. Nevertheless, for the sake
of Becker's endlessly vulnerable *amour-propre*, the wine was
returned and a new bottle summoned.

The shared delight in Ezra's corner smoothed over the
rough edges of his encounter with Kim. Now it was Nick's
turn.

"Nick, Nick," Kim intoned, leaning back in the cane
chair, "How can you work with people like that?"

"It's easy."

"Is it because somewhere down beneath the Gucci loafers
and the Mister Guy sport shirts, you're really like that, too?"
She's slept with him, Ezra decided. It was the only way to
gain license for such remarks. The expression on Nick
Bohm's face forced Ezra between them.

"Isn't there an old saying, Kim: You mustn't bite the
hand that feeds you?"

"That's just it, Mr. Marks...." (Southern formality used
as a form of contempt.) "That is precisely what separates
man from the dog. A dog will lick your hand as long as you
feed it. Any hand! Fido makes no moral judgments. On the
other hand, man does and should, on occasion, bite the hand
of the feeder. It's a special form of communication. It tells
the feeder that a bowl of food—" she indicated the deli-
cately seasoned veal she had barely touched "—does not buy
the whole person."

She stood up and said, "Excuse me. I'm sharper than
usual today because I made an arrangement for tonight that
I'm sorry about. I want to see if I can unmake it." She
walked toward the back of the restaurant to a wall telephone.

Ezra watched the backs of her legs and the upper thighs

under the skirt. Was she wearing pantyhose? It was hard to tell from a distance. Mustn't go Hollywood, Ezra thought, recalling his joke to Robinson: seeing women as parts. Still, she had good legs; long for her small torso.

"That's Kim," Nick Bohm said, cryptically. Then added, "She takes whomever she wants, doesn't take anybody else."

"Except tonight." Ezra was impressed by the lingering affection in Nick's tone. He was not an easy man to insult.

While waiting for Kim to return, Nick spoke of plans for the "novelization" of *The Lion's Farewell.* He had a friend who could do a fine job (Nick always had a friend). And, Ezra being noncommittal, he went on to suggest a scheme for the buying of copies of the book, once it was out. They had a staff of field men all over the country: each man would buy books, amounting, all in all, to nine or ten thousand books, enough, if geographically well planned, to land *The Lion's Farewell* on the best seller list. After that, it is no longer merely a book, it is a "best seller." People ask for it, recommend it, talk about it. And when the movie arrives there is a built-in audience waiting to buy tickets.

"You mean we can manufacture a best seller."

"You can try."

"No!" Ezra said. He was about to lose his detachment and fought to hold it. But the no came out sharp and hard.

"What do you mean, Ezra?"

"Don't count on me for that kind of stuff."

"But we've always done it. I mean, especially when you have the lead time. With production just beginning, with a good writer doing the job, we have a chance to make it a big book."

Nausea wandered in Ezra's stomach and finally, dangerously higher. He had been expecting rotten choices to be forced upon him: Robbie's warnings, the universally inherited culture of Hollywood lore that promised deep dark dealings.

Nick Bohm was enumerating the books that had flowered into the beautiful green of large money under these tender ministrations.

"I don't care if you did it with the Bible," Ezra said.

"We *did* do it once, with the Bible, John Huston . . ." Nick Bohm began; and Ezra's anger slid into laughter.

Kim came back looking pale. Nick made a light remark about the unmaking of the evening. But something in the quick way she drank a glass of wine as soon as she sat down told them that the moment for jokes had passed.

14

After lunch, Ezra's agenda included meetings with art directors, free-lance photographers, makers of documentary films (all of whom wished to help Ezra promote King films. They were, like most of the world, friends of Nick Bohm). There followed, too, meetings with Nick and Ezra's Italian staff, Rafaello Giannini and his crew. All of them had been with King Studio for over twenty years. What was the basis of this superb staying power in a world of flux?—Giannini: unctuous and servile; Ezra knew at once there would be no help from him, only treachery . . . a look at—and approval of—sketches for ads introducing several new films Ezra knew nothing about . . . and, presto, he was blinking in the dimness of a screening room while tall, sweatered Archer, the King man in London—an American turned British Continental years ago in the service of Kleinholz—introduced him to Michael Maurice. In the back row Kim sat quietly, waiting for the screening to begin.

Maurice was as he had always been in the British films in which Ezra had followed him since childhood: dry, muted elegant. What the films had not prepared Ezra for was the bitterness, the style of malicious wit, as well as a face full of wrinkles, like an aerial map of a canyon. As Ezra shook hands with him a photographer materialized behind them and began clicking off shot after shot. Nick Bohm stood next to the photographer, murmuring at him, and suddenly the boy, Karol, was thrust between them. He squinted nervously and said hello under the barrage of little light-explosions. Even in the confusion of the moment his physical presence was startling, the effect of his personal beauty such that one would imagine no one immune to it.

"How do you do?" Michael Maurice said. "I understand you're the man who's going to make our boy the biggest thing since Rin-Tin-Tin. Please don't. He's difficult enough now."

Nick Bohm said. "Ezra's been dealing with Mitch Stone. *That's* difficult."

"Youth . . . youth . . ." Archer said. "There's no holding them down."

"Come, ducks," Maurice said, tugging at Karol's hand. "Let's all look at the movie about how we found you."

Karol pulled his hand away violently. His features were ice-cold.

Ezra thought: it's gone that far. He thought: It's going to be ugly.

Becker arrived, accompanied by Lisa, the morning's translator. Becker's hand rested on her rump; she wore it lightly, as a trained horse wears a harness: an acceptable condition of servitude. A few moments after the film began, the door opened and a stout, older man was framed, for an instant, in the sunlit doorway, long hair swept back from a high starting point, pronounced cheekbones, almost Oriental: Sordino. He wore a dark silk scarf in folds around his neck. He squinted, closed the door quickly, and groped his way to a seat, alone, in the last row.

For some reason this particular print had an Italian

track and Lisa repeated her morning's function, whispering
heavily French-accented English phrases in Ezra's ear. This
time, however, it was much easier to follow, since Ezra had
seen the footage at the studio. When Karol appeared, it
happened. The clichéd effect that almost never occurs but is
assumed, always, to exist, waiting for the right combination
of elements. Something magnetic was present, in addition to
the physical grace of the face and the slender form: a sullen,
sleepwalking quality that seemed to provoke and deny at
the same time. And in that obscure communion that audiences in dark rooms share, Ezra could tell that everyone else
felt it as well. His work with Karol would not be too difficult. The boy would make himself a star. The little film, itself, was an excellent piece of work: with the exception of
the usual *March of Time* narration such documentaries always have. It was fast-moving, well cut, and intelligent.

Ezra whispered to Nick Bohm, "Change the track. Get a
natural-sounding voice, instead of the pre-fab announcer.
Even in Italian I can tell we'd be better off using an actor."

"Good idea," Nick said. He scribbled in the dark.

The lights bloomed. Michael Maurice yawned and murmured, "What a bore. I can't see that it could be of the
slightest interest to anyone in the world—except of course,
those of us who burn with love and admiration for Karol."
And he turned to Archer for confirmation. Above the buzz
of conversation, it may have been only Ezra who heard the
young boy mutter, "I'd like to burn you. All of you. . . ."

It was then that Sordino stood up and leaned over the
back of Maurice's chair. He hissed a series of Italian sibi-
lants at the actor. There was no misjudging the tone: it was
angry, punitive. Maurice's pitted face flushed. He said nothing. Sordino then touched the boy's arm gently and smiled.
He bowed stiffly to the others in the room and vanished in a
blast of sunlight.

"What the hell was that?" Becker said.

"Sordino," Nick Bohm said. The boy giggled. Now it was Maurice's turn to stare at him blankly.

Outside, light-blinded, Ezra found himself face to face with Kim.

"That's going to be an interesting circus," she said.

Still sorting out the complex intrigues of the screening, Ezra was in no mood to play; in spite of her very long legs, in spite of the way her hair curved over the corner of her eyes. He nodded and turned away.

"Listen," Kim said. "If you'd like to see some of my stuff..." He turned back. "Yes...?"

"I'll be at the French Institute. That's the old Villa Medici above the Spanish Steps. They have some Rouaults I want to see. I'll be there at five. My studio's a few minutes away."

The remainder of the day was taken up by a trip, guided by Nick Bohm, to the set of *The Lion's Farewell*. It was at the Villa of the Quintilli, next to the Via Appia Nuova. The approach was littered with shards of pots and semiburied small and ancient buildings. It was here that Sordino had built a replica of the Albergo Appia, the great hotel of the 1890s in Rome. All modernizations had been removed and everything was articulated in terms of the period, down to the authentic daily newspapers in the lobby. A television crew from France accompanied them, and even those cool Gallic characters were impressed at the extraordinary care with which Sordino had "dressed" his set, had re-created another time with the greatest tact and delicacy.

The ambiance he had created was extraordinary. The rococo hotel, its velvet draperies, its perfect marbles, its inlaid columns. Here one could easily imagine the character of the older man playing out his drama of frustration.

Five p.m. The Villa Medici. Walking up and down with

Kim, looking at Rouault's clowns and kings. In Rome one looks at buildings and paintings, not movies.

"In 1952," Ezra said, "when I was a kid of seventeen, everybody talked about Rouault as a master. Then his reputation sort of vanished. Is he back?"

"I don't know and I don't care. I'm looking for a certain dark glaze he gets with a light source underneath. It's technical."

"For Karol's picture?"

"For my own stuff."

"You paint portraits?"

"The figure."

"Only the figure?"

"That's what interests me. But it's never *only*. The composition . . . never mind. You'll see—if you've got eyes."

"I've got eyes."

"I know! I could feel them watching me when I got up to make a phone call at lunch."

"Your back was turned. Maybe they were Nick's."

"Nick has no eyes. Just a gray haze that sees what's necessary to see at the moment. It's a studio knack."

Playing her game Ezra said: "Is Nick your lover?"

"No. We slept together once. But he was never my lover. He's been supposed to marry Honey Williams for years now."

Out of the gallery and up the long steep narrow walk to the beginning of the Pincio Gardens. They arrived in the half-light of six o'clock.

"There's no light like it anywhere," Kim said.

They leaned on the stone wall. Rome tumbled down the hill beneath them. "I keep a studio in L.A. For commercial work. But this is where my eyes are. I don't think I'll show you any work here. I've changed my mind. I've got the assignment anyway, right?" She laughed a little. Ezra pointed in the distance where the Hilton stood, spoiling the classic outlines: rigid lines, a dead square in the lambent light.

"Too bad about that," he said. He was taking up no more of her challenges that day.

"It's convenient. They have a good hairdresser."

No sentimental traps for Kim. He laughed, unexpectedly. She did not ask why he was laughing. Instead, she said, "Have you seen Robinson, yet?"

"No. Have you?"

"He's a very busy little boy. I think this time he wants to go all the way."

"Do you know him well?"

"Just in and out of L.A. Friends of friends. And don't ask me if . . ."

"Okay. I didn't ask."

"How far in it are you? And why?"

"That's the last thing Robbie asked me. It made me think a little."

"And. . . . ?"

"I'll save the big description when we have more time. But it's partly like what you were doing at the Rouault exhibit."

"How?"

"You gather technical skills. Then you want to use them. If you can use them where everybody says how wonderful you are—and you like yourself for using them, excellent. But when that stops . . . either you go somewhere and teach them to kids or you use them where they can be used."

The blue eyes were wide again. The mouth half open in thought. "So you think it's all about skills. . . . Then you've told yourself about half. You probably don't know the other half yet. I was married to a man who . . ."

Her silence was so long, so insistent that the subject was closed. Ezra had a quick feeling of delight at having met her; just a sense of pleasure at her presence, however peripheral, in this menagerie in which he was the newest animal.

She chose that moment to say what he might have said: "I like you," she said. "It's nice that we met."

The dark-yellow light, the quick feeling, her words, then, all impelled him to the natural action. He brushed the wave of ash-blond hair from the side of her face so that he could see and hold it, and kissed her.

"No." Kim said against his lips.

"Oh?"

"No reason," she said. "Just no."

15

There was a message at the concierge's desk: would Mr. Marks please come to Mr. Becker's suite. But it was Robinson who opened the door.

"Surprise," he said. He filled the doorway but behind him Ezra saw a paper-strewn couch and Becker in a purple and yellow robe pacing up and down. No smile accompanied Robinson's greeting. He seemed somber. There was a nervous charge to the air between the two men in the suite.

"Be with you in a second," the distracted Robbie said to Ezra and occupied himself with rolling up a large piece of paper half resting on the couch, half on the floor. Becker was in an excited state.

"Hello, kid," he said. "Come on in and live. Eat dinner yet?"

"I'm not hungry," Ezra said. "I'm still on New York time, or L.A. I don't know which. My stomach's not too hot."

"An occupational hazard. But we'll get you something hot, don't worry," A wink. "What'd you think of that meshugaas, today?"

"Maurice and the boy?"

"He's humping the kid, I'll lay you odds."

"I don't think it's that simple. Not yet, anyway."

"I'm staying away from that *faigele* Maurice. I deal strictly with Sordino. And we talk money, dollars, cash—no art shit. I'll get him down to the numbers I want.

"Have a drink. I got everything. Scotch, bourbon, these fuckers even put champagne in the refridge. What the hell, it's not even the studio that's paying. It's Uncle Sam, right?"

In his robe he wove whirls of cigar smoke around Ezra's head, and strutted across the room, a peacock of uncertain pride. Near the end of the long living room, in front of a closed door, he paused. Voices sifted in, muffled. Then there was a loud crack of laughter. Becker's head turned toward Ezra. He, too, pushed out a fragment of a laugh. It did not come out easily; the man did not know how to laugh, Ezra decided. It simply was not one of the things he did naturally. Becker had probably taught himself to do it, painstakingly, in front of a mirror. He gave the impression of a man who had pasted himself together from various parts he assumed were desirable.

Becker pressed an ear against the door. Then he hunched his shoulders beneath the robe, drew on his cigar, threw a puff at Ezra. In the next moment he had vanished into the bedroom, leaving the two friends alone.

"Did I walk into a heavy scene?" Ezra asked.

"Moderately, old friend, moderately heavy." With Becker out of the room, Robinson breathed easier.

"Tell me about it," Ezra said. He sipped the vodka and tonic Becker had forced into his hand. "But tell me slowly and clearly. It's been a long, hard, Roman day."

Robbie crouched in front of the tiny refrigerator in the corner of the living room, searching for something. "Becker has plans for relaxing you. Becker is big on relaxation." He straightened up with a bottle of Coca-Cola in his hand.

"Have to keep my wits about me. I have just been wandering all over London. I stopped off, on my way here, to see John Schlesinger. I want to get him coming off *Midnight Cowboy* if I can. I saw John Huston. One new John, one old." He settled himself next to Ezra and drew on his Coke as if it were a martini he desperately needed. "Don't discount sentiment for the Old John. Sentiment is a large item among movie people . . . if not among stockholders."

They sat next to each other on the couch. There was only the hum of the air conditioning and Robbie's description of his Odyssey. They could have been anywhere: after the specific newness of Ezra's recent experiences, the anonymity of the hotel room was pleasant. He let Robbie drone over his consciousness. The energy of Robbie's plans had always been a comfort; something you could relax and count on.

". . . the word is that Arthur Penn wants to do the Balzac *Lost Illusions* and has a great script on it. . . . Penn is bankable since *Bonnie and Clyde*. I'm seeing him tomorrow . . . nobody's doing costume pictures . . . but that's just my point. . . ."

In his fatigue Ezra groped his way toward a central point.

"Don't you need some center, some point of leverage, from which to deal with all these people?"

"The young man learns quickly," Robbie said. The answer is yes. I need a power base, and I'm on the point of settling it."

"Would you care to describe it to an old friend?"

"Not just yet."

"That's the second turndown of the day."

"Who else?"

"A painter. Kim Cross."

"Ah, the Iron Belle. Her noes and her yeses . . ."

Robinson jumped from the couch, a suitcase was torn

open, a rubber band removed from a scroll, the scroll un-
furled on the floor. It was an immense graph. Robinson
placed chairs on the edges to hold it fast.

"Here it is," he said. "The graph that's going to devour
the studio. Do you have any idea how hard it is to mount a
proxy fight. There's a zillion shares of stock out. Compared
to what I'm trying to do, here, the U-A proxy fight back in
the Forties was kid stuff. Shares—big blocks—owned by
distributors, by other studios, small blocks by widows and
orphans. Look at those lines, zigzagging there. It's like poetry." He was dancing crazily on the stretched-out scroll.
"United Theatres—Brodkin—and International Circuits—
that's the Berry brothers—they're coming in with me. If I
can get Umberto Rossi to come in— " He bent down and
swept the graph with scoops of his hand. "Here and here.
The Berry brothers have been quietly buying it up for years.
Like Rossi. And now they're scared."

"Why?"

Robbie pointed. "After-tax losses last year: thirty-six
million dollars. This year will be about seventy-seven million.
Over sixty per cent of the stockholders' equity lost in one
year. Kleinholz's mistakes. And they're afraid of more of
those mistakes. Listen, when I get enough film-makers and
projects behind me, and enough stock pledged to me, we are
going to mount the biggest pressures these old guys have
even seen. We'll put in new management . . . a new ball
game . . ."

The spark was catching. Ezra had not thought Robbie's
plans to be so sweeping. The fatigue of the day was gone.
He was once again planning with Robbie. No one could,
after all, follow a man twice to two such emblematic cities
as Washington and Hollywood unless some metal in his
character was tugged by some magnet in the other man's
make-up.

The magnet was perhaps something as simple as the

grandeur of Robbie's plans. They had always been immense. Immediately following graduation, Robbie had followed a golden-haired and golden-moneyed girl he loved to Europe. There, the epic ideas that had terrified his parents and made his high-school friends laugh, became almost real. He'd bragged for so long about his devotion to Homer—the golden girl was a classics major as was Robbie—he found himself, one day, telling a representative of the Greek government that he could guarantee Marlon Brando to star in a production of *The Iliad.* All the Greek government had to do was provide the Army and funds for the battle scenes; Robinson, and the genius of Homer, would do the rest. While many of his friends were occupied with ideas of social reform, with Marxism, it never occurred to him that the answer to the riddle of history—as well as daily life—was not contained in individual heroism. *The Iliad* was his *Das Kapital.*

The Greek functionary must have sensed the authority in Robinson's vision of himself—but not his anxiety at being embarrassed before the girl he loved. He got the money, the men, and the boats. The battles were heroic. Of course, they were a little hard to see on the processed film as Robinson did not know too much about lighting exteriors—or interiors, for that matter—but they were full of vitality. When the money ran out, there was still much wonderful material to be shot. But Marlon Brando was inaccessible, and Robinson had to leave Greece very suddenly and the golden girl never forgave him for lying. It was simply proof to him that she was not the golden girl he'd thought. He married her anyway. But he never forgave her for the lack of vision. And eventually he drifted toward women who'd kept their twenty-one-year-old belief in great and grand projects. Some of them were, in fact, twenty-one. Marriage did not stay among Robbie's plans.

Having done his proxy dance, Robbie appeared relieved

of his earlier heavy mood. He beamed a smile at Ezra as he rolled up the giant graph.

"It's not all that different," he said. "Remember, for about six months when I was legislative contact man for the FCC; convincing a junior congressman from Michigan and a heavy-weight Senator from California to back a budget program . . . there are certain sibling semblances."

"You lost that one."

"I'll win this one. But I can't discount support from *anyone*. Would you believe that Becker, that nervous wreck you just saw in here, has one of the best reputations in the industry for squeezing the most money possible out of the release of pictures everybody knows are dogs?"

"Is he with you?"

"He won't jump until he's sure the ship he's on is sinking —and the new one is safe and sound. Rossi can help there."

Class was over for the day, Robinson had appointments stacked up for the rest of the evening. The bedroom door was flung open and Becker reappeared.

"Hey, kid," he said. "I want you to meet a couple of friends."

The magic door closed again.

Saying good-by, Robinson said, "I'm staying at the Grand. Give me a ring before you go back. Maybe we can have a less hurried time—dinner." Then he laughed. "No, why kid ourselves. It's going to be on the run like this until we straighten out." He paused, towering over Ezra, eyes no longer bloodshot and bleary. "Don't get the idea," he said, "that"—he jerked a hand toward the bedroom—"all that has anything to do with me and my quest for the Holy Grail. Becker and Rossi go back a long way. People who do business together have many and complicated ways of keeping each other happy. Some businessmen go fishing. Some get theater tickets—some arrange poker games. Enjoy."

And from the hotel corridor, a last *envoi*: "Don't talk in

the limos. The drivers are all spies. They tell Giannini, who tells Becker, who tells Bohm and Kleinholz. Be paranoid. It's only normal."

Ezra was sorry he'd accepted the drink. His unsettled stomach roiled at the acid strike of the liquor.

Becker opened the bedroom door. On the large double bed Lisa, the translator of the afternoon, was sprawled; next to her was Umberto Rossi. A girl with long yellow hair was kneeling on the bed, kissing and pressing Lisa's flesh from her knee to her crotch. Lisa was moving under the other girl's touch as if she were greatly moved and aroused. Ezra could not tell if it was authentic or fake. Umberto Rossi might have been wondering the same thing as he propped himself up on an elbow to watch the scene more closely. His free hand caressed Lisa's breast, an almost flat setting for a rose nipple, in her prone position. The sheets were in rumpled disarray, and the kneeling girl's butt loomed large in the composition so startlingly unveiled.

"Gentlemen," Umberto Rossi called out. "Come and join us." His manner was most gracious: clearly a generous man.

"Here comes Mrs. Becker's little boy," Becker said, advancing a few steps into the room. He did not remove his robe. Behind them, in the living room, the phone was buzzing: that hard, sharp buzz European hotel phones have. Becker took a few steps forward. Breathing and the distant harshness of the phone were the only sounds. Becker was opening his robe and Ezra fled to answer the phone.

It was Archer and the news was bad. "There's been a fire. The whole set is a wreck. It's under control now, but it looks fishy." Archer's anglicized accent had vanished under the moment's stress.

"Some King Studio executive ought to get down here," he said. "A little cat like me can't handle big stuff like this— and I can't find Nick." Ezra's flash of memory had the feel of truth, Karol muttering under the nastiness of the screening-room atmosphere that day: "I'd like to burn you. All of you. . . ."

In the bedroom Becker was wrestling in some obscene contest with both girls. Lisa was kissing his mouth while the yellow-haired girl was on her knees, her head almost vanished between his legs. Umberto Rossi was behind Baby, reaching down to her in preparation for more interesting combinations. In the anarchic twisting, the random movements of all four, Becker's eyes crossed Ezra's. There was something panicked in that look; when Umberto Rossi pulled Baby aside for an instant the reason was clear. In the midst of this feast of sensuality, surrounded by this schoolboy's pornographic dream, Becker was not aroused. Some wire had failed to strike a spark with some other wire. Impotence was his spirit's answer to the occasion and its elaborate opportunities.

Having seen the look and registered its cause, Ezra was now implicated. He decided to interpret the look as a plea to be saved—never to be admitted or referred to again, but to be acted upon. Out of a number of motivations: simple humanity, pulling a man out of a mass of dung in which he's buried himself; the chance to put Becker, subtly, or not so subtly, in his debt; Ezra couldn't quite tell himself. But it didn't matter any more.

He said, "Sorry to break up the party. But there's been a big fire. The whole hotel set is gone. Sordino is in an uproar —and the police and the newspapers are asking questions." Pause. The Laocoön tableau began to ooze apart. *"You'd* better get down there. Right away!"

"Yeah," Becker said, quickly. He tugged nervously at his robe, then slapped Lisa lightly on the behind. *The Salvation of Becker:* School of Modern Italian Painting.

16

"Je ne suis pas confortable parlant anglais. Peut-être on peut parler français?"

"Mon français, ça n'existe pas. S'il vous plaît..."

"If you insist," Sordino said. "I will try." His tone expressed displeasure. Ezra had won his first small skirmish. He could tell from the sound of Sordino's initial sentence that the director spoke English well enough. It was a matter of pride. The two men stood on a small arc of a bridge: the high ground from which the director-as-general could control matters in progress. Sordino was beyond rage. He expressed fatigue and a dignity that would not allow him to squabble over which language to speak.

Dingy gray flakes covered the charred magnificence of the hotel set beneath them. Two police vans were parked on either end of the long street with a searchlight from each truck moving over the scene. A mélange of carabinieri, members of Sordino's company, and firemen poked through the ruins. A few feet behind them, Archer led Becker on his own little guided tour.

Sordino said, "Perhaps I should have had the cameras going."

"Cinéma vérité...?"

"Your friend Mitch Stone, that is what he would have done. He stands for the new, does he not? The unplanned, the better over art for life." He corrected himself quickly. "I mean life to be more important than art."

"I know what you mean. There was no script for *Festival*."

"I am old-fashioned," he said. "I did not set the fire. Therefore I did not film it." He laughed, a heavy sound.

"Will it take you long to build again?"

"I don't know," he said. "Some things are not entirely destroyed. Maybe a week, two, three. It will not destroy the budget. I think about something more important." He coughed several times; a brief spasm; smoke or nervousness. "Look, let's not play a fencing match you and I," he said with sudden force. His gaze floated over the scene below: a sightseer observing the site of a famous fire. He said, "We know who did it. So we may put that behind us now."

"Oh . . . ?"

"I think perhaps everyone knows. Where do you think Nick is?"

"I don't know."

"He is with the boy: now is, naturally, tears and remorse."

Below them the lights suddenly clicked off. The two police vans started their motors and began executing a series of maneuvers: a little ballet of big cars trying to exit from a tiny street. Only some smears of light from the half-moon lit the destroyed set and beyond it, the Tiber's dark waters. Becker, Archer, the Sordino people, the police, all appeared to have left.

"Good," Sordino said. "They leave. Now we walk."

"The police . . . ?"

"It will be all right."

"I don't know how such things go in Italy."

"They have questioned me. Nick will talk to them tonight. He knows someone in the department."

"Have they spoken to Michael Maurice?"

Sordino laughed. "He's hiding somewhere. Poor Michael. He knows how much it is his fault."

Was it the moment to move, to pressure? To bargain silence in exchange for permission to use the "discovery" film? Ezra decided against it, and they moved down the small hillock that led to the burned street. Alone in that unreal street, Ezra and Sordino moved like ghosts over a battlefield. In the lobby the fires had mysteriously skipped certain

objects: a swath of purple drapery at the entrance, with a
coat of arms and a Latin motto Ezra could not understand
... a magnificent settee with lion's-paw legs carved with delicate curvature. Two brown birds splashed in a puddle of
water left by firemen's hoses. Over them loomed a gigantic
table meant to stand in an entrance hall so enormous as to
seem intended for entrances and exits of great importance.
Sordino moved about touching things, brushing ashes from
a mantelpiece, stooping to move a soaked newspaper from
his path.

"Let me tell you, now, why it is so important that I make
this picture," he said. "We are not on the same side, we
cannot be, at the end. Even if we find a large *rapport*, when
the picture is finished Kleinholz will say, tell him to cut
twenty minutes out . . . tell him to shoot that scene in a
different manner because we have to promote those wom-
en's clothes with the picture . . . not those men's clothes—or
some such. And you will be forced to tell me—and it will be
the usual war. But for this one moment I will tell you.

He lifted himself onto the table. His legs dangled, childlike, he smoked a cigarette, and told Ezra, "My cinema is
done by a visual naming of things. The most beautiful thing
in the world is just to name something: but not with words.
I let the camera name an object by framing it, staying, lingering on it, let the eye name it . . . perhaps an echo of the
real name exists in the mind of the audience. Woman, chair,
boy, glass, vase, mountain. There are so many beautiful
things in the world to reveal. That's why they say my films
are slow, but that is not true; they are not slow, only careful
to name things to the eye in the right way so that they begin
by being visible to the audience and end by becoming invisible in them—a permanent gift, named once and for all.
That is the first thing Adam did in the Garden of Eden, you
know. He named all the creatures. That is what I do with

my camera." The old director led Ezra on a tour with commentary.

The period he had chosen, the period of Lawrence's story, was perhaps the last moment in modern history when the world still believed in itself. "Is not an original idea," he said. "All the professors have written about this for forty years. The people staying at the Albergo Appia in 1912 were the chosen of life. They knew that they were at the center of a charmed and perfect world, with a beginning, middle, and end. Cause, effect, good, bad: these were not mysteries, they were the natural processes and material of life.

"Then where's the drama?" Ezra asked.

"Ah," Sordino said. "The one mystery was—is always—the mystery of the self, of sex."

The dream tour continued as Ezra listened to the aging homosexual speak of his vision of sex: a process with something ambiguous always, at its heart. Once, in his twenties, he had consulted a psychiatrist in Milan: a man of some wit. Sex, he had said, does not work. Do not be fooled. It works for a time, for some people, not all. But, basically it does not work. It is not a function, it is a metaphor; a theater in which a fantasy-play takes place (without intermission) that is as unlimited as any art. The means are simple, the result is complex. Something mysterious happens between the intention, the means, and the result—something that makes it the most powerful and the least reliable of human operations. And that is what this film will be about. A man of the earlier, more confident time, a celebrated artist, a man who has gained the world, and finds, through an encounter with a beautiful young boy, that he does not any more have power over himself.

"No symbols," he said, and added a grave and wicked smile. "That's for Antonioni, symbols. And no *goticismo*— that's for Fellini. And absolutely no operatics, we leave that to Visconti. The look of the boy and Michael's acting will make it all." Sordino sighed. "I am so—*fatigué*—and the film has not begun yet."

The Rolls was white, the driver skinny and silent. They drove at what seemed to be, from what Ezra could gather from a fast look over the driver's shoulder at the speedometer, a hundred and fifty kilometers an hour. Trying not to look at the buildings and trees as they blurred by, Ezra wondered if the speed demon in the front seat was a spy too. "Motion Picture Chauffeurs, Inc., Industrial Espionage at Reasonable Rates." Sordino was not the only one who was *fatigué*. Ezra's own small plot had now to be executed and then he could go to sleep. He was not sure if the weapon still existed ("We know who did it," Sordino had said) but it must be used.

"Michael Maurice seemed quite difficult with Karol, today . . . at the screening." Tentative opening.

"Quite."

"This is why there is a problem about using the promotion film. . . ."

"You understood it is not for me, it was because of Michael. . . ."

"Yes."

"He is torn, Michael. Karol troubles him."

"Troubles . . . ?"

"You understand, Michael is one who has the bad sex. He is not in control. It is one reason he will be magnificent as the Lion. The air conditioning is *tròppo freddo*." He said something to the driver and the buzzing stopped, the windows rolled down, and the Roman night entered their conversation.

"But if he is going to drive the boy to be as unhappy as he is, you're going to have a lot of trouble."

Sordino turned a blank face to Ezra. It might have been

the old man's death mask. "That is my job," he said. "I will
handle it! And Mr. Robinson, I think, can be of assistance."

"I have my job, too," Ezra said. It was the moment for
Operating Good Will or it would never be. But the reference to Robbie threw him, and Sordino moved past him.

"About *publicité* for the film," he said. "Nick told me you
must use it—and that you want something for the grand
patron, Kleinholz." He patted his pockets, and produced a
confusion of papers. "It is here, somewhere, or I will have it
sent to your hotel." Having taken the lead, for the moment,
Sordino softened. He shifted his bulk and half-turned toward Ezra. "Your little film will tell the world how we found
Karol, you will do a fine campaign for the picture, and
everyone will come and buy tickets—and all this unpleasant-
ness, Michael's nerves, fires—it will all be forgotten. Mitch
Stone came to Rome once to tell me that old-fashioned
masterpieces are finished. No more! Now comes only the
Happening, the *vérité*. But don't believe him. We are going
to make a masterpiece."

Ezra relaxed. His poisonous plan had been unnecessary.
Between the three of them, Nick, Sordino, and—in some
mysterious way—Robbie, his small mission would succeed.
Sordino spoke, then, of people, of the studio. At the name
Robinson, again, Ezra's attention was flagged.

"It is a good thing," Sordino said, "people like yourself,
like Robinson, coming into films. In Italy, of course, we are
used to government people working with us. But we are too
much with ourselves, for years, movie people. A little king-
dom of our own, telling each other the lies and intrigues we
wish to hear, torturing our enemies and rewarding our
friends—and always assuming we do it in the name of *le
cinéma*—of art."

Ezra chose to take it straight. "Do you think we can
really change anything?"

Sordino laughed. It was an old man's laugh, a mixture of cough and laugh, rattly with phlegm.

"I hope not," he said.

17

Later, before saying good night, they strolled toward Ezra's hotel. Sordino dismissed the car near the Piazza di Spagna and they walked the five or six twisting blocks upward through mostly sleeping streets toward the Via Veneto.

Suddenly, he grabbed Ezra's arm and pulled him into a doorway.

"What ... ?"

"S-s-s-s-h-h-h. . . ."

Sordino breathed asthmatically, waiting. Ezra waited, too. Then, up the street came two figures, one of them swaying, murmuring, shuffling. The other one (it was Karol, Ezra saw at once) was trying to sustain, to calm, and to quiet his drunken companion. Michael Maurice, of course, would have none of that, and was struggling and hissing objections at the boy. This charade continued for a moment or so and then was gone. Sordino seemed to have stopped breathing. Then, when the couple had passed, he stepped out into the street again. Silence. There seemed to be nothing for anyone to say.

The old man chose to say: *"Buona notte."* And bowed from the waist—a gesture as archaic as the notion of a masterpiece—and disappeared into the darkness of one of the little streets surrounding them. The director had vanished, taking with him the mysteries and ambiguities of a sexual life that did not work.

18

The international operator had some business with Signor Marks and Signor Bohm awaited him in his suite. Signor Bohm was surrounded by colleagues and friends: Archer on the phone, Giannini, and several dark-suited Italian men brooding over sketches laid out on the floor. But Nick was enthralled by a massive chrome instrument with more dials than Ezra had ever seen on a radio. Nick, himself, looked a little blurred around the edges, like an old publicity photo of himself. He sat on an ancient couch fiddling with the dials, producing squeaks from all over Europe.

"Hey, Ezra," he said. "Listen to this: Istanbul."

"Yes," Ezra said. "How did it go?"

"Italian police are murder. Wait a minute, I think that's English. Maybe the BBC. Hey!" he yelled at the Giannini group. "Hold it down, will you!"

But the BBC had faded into some Middle Eastern music, twangs and whines. "Sordino gave it to me," Nick said. "It can get everything—short wave, regular stuff, FM, as far as Egypt." His hair was mussed, his tie open, his tired eyes wide with pleasure: Christmas morning for Nick Bohm.

"Will there be any charges?"

"I don't think so. When I was a kid, I loved all this electronic shit. I don't know a thing about it—but it kills me. Let's go inside, I can't hear a damned thing."

In the bedroom, over the sweet syrup of a French singer Ezra continued, "Do they know who did it?"

Nick shrugged. His basic repertoire of gestures expressed ignorance, innocence or insufficient information. Evasion was a way of life. "I guess so," he said.

Ezra decided guessing was not enough. "How did you do it? Did you have to pay?"

"I have a friend."

That was the standard, government-issue Nick Bohm reply. He returned to his new toy. Ezra decided to wait that one out.

"What happens the next time the kid breaks loose?" he asked.

"He only did it to scare the shit out of Michael Maurice. It worked. But he scared himself even more."

"He could have killed somebody."

"Not at that hour. It'll be okay, Ezra. Don't make such a big deal out of it."

"I thought this picture was life or death?"

"Yes and no. We're in such trouble that *every* little thing is life and death. We can't afford *any* failures."

"Sordino likes you." It sounded flat and stupid.

"That's what I'm here for. Everybody has to like me." It was an odd way to say: stay out of my relationship with Sordino, but he'd said it.

Ezra said, "Okay, I'll choose you who gets to call Kleinholz and tell him."

"Tell . . . ?"

"The fire."

"Oh, he knows."

"How?"

"Pick your man. Becker would be my guess. It'll be an excuse for him to suggest scrapping the picture."

"Why would he want that?"

Listening to the music, patting pockets for nonexistent cigarettes and cultivating that absent-minded style that committed him to nothing, Nick said, "He thinks the picture's going to be a loser."

"Is it?"

"Remember my big speech on the plane?" Nick Bohm could unleash a smile, when he chose, that was absolutely winning. "From now on *you'll* have to make that guess."

Then he declaimed:

> "You, who slowly leak
>
> From the heart of the world,
> Leaving us to seek
> A truth not quite dead,
>   but curled
> Against our hearts
> Like a torn flag
>   never unfurled. . . ."

"Can you figure—my kid Jenny wrote that last year? What makes them so depressed? Maybe I'll give her the radio for a present—if she doesn't drop out . . . if she, maybe takes her third year in Europe."

"Adolescents are depressed," Ezra said.

"But can you figure my girl writing stuff like T. S. Eliot? Now that nobody wants to read Eliot any more? The kid's a loser." He banged a hand down on the radio. In the silence that followed Archer's nasal British voice sounded from the next room: *"Look, the whole set, all the props, everything's burned or smoked."* Pause. *"Well, if he can't get it when we need it, then he's the wrong man for Frankfurt. We'd better call Drakmalnik in; he'll get it. It doesn't matter a damn what period—Drakmalnik will get it."*

A phone was hung up and Nick said, "What do you think, Ezra? You think we'll work together, okay?"

Ezra paused to take in his own astonishment. Did Robbie's and Honey's ambiguity about who was in charge of whom extend to Nick, himself? Was it this special situation? Or twenty-five years of eating fear?

Low and cool, Ezra said, "Sure."

As if eager to change the subject, Nick said, "Did Kim show you her work?"

"No. She decided against it at the last minute."

"She does that a lot. I saw sparks between you two."

"They only went one way."

Nick turned a blurry face to Ezra. A primitive despair seemed to have joined with his fatigue. Perhaps he'd caught depression from his daughter's words; perhaps he'd been subtly frightened by Ezra's cool response to his question about working together. "Perhaps" was a word never far from Nick Bohm.

"Try her again in L.A. She shuttles from here to there."

"She's a strong lady." The downward curve of Nick's delicate, almost feminine mouth seemed about to form a question; the kind of unspeakable question that exhaustion can produce. But no question came. Instead, he said, "Ezra, everybody's available to everybody. It's only a question of when and how long you can wait."

Approximately five miles from the Vatican, the Gospel According to Nick Bohm had been delivered.

19

Sometime in the night there was a knocking at the door. It was Honey Williams. Nervously gay, aware of the hour, of the odd circumstances, she pushed the dazed Ezra back toward the bed and shut the door behind her.

"As soon as I got to Rome I knew I had to see you."

"Why?"

"The Eee King said so."

To Ezra, exhausted to the point of paralysis by travel and tension, it sounded as if she'd said: The King said so.

"Who?"

She held up a paperback book. The cover read: *I Ching.*

Book of Changes. By this time he was back at his bed. He sat down abruptly, unable to stand. Then he was horizontal. Honey sat on the edge.

"I thought maybe you wouldn't have understood what I said that night—you know, at the pier in Santa Monica. About trusting Nick."

"Understand ..."

"Nick thought I was crazy to do it. He got mad. So I started throwing the pennies. I always throw the pennies to find out what I should do. And all the answers were about you."

"What were the questions?" he murmured. He saw her through a mist of eyelids and lashes, a swirl of red over a twist of red lips. Either she was now lying on the big bed or Ezra's depth perception was drowning in the residue of sleep.

"The Po Hexagram was the first to come up. See. . . . Six crossed lines joined at the top. . . ."

"Oh. . . ."

"It says: Po indicates that in the state which it symbolizes a movement from heaven to earth is indicated. (That means from head to toe)."

Hands were unbuttoning a pajama jacket he had no recollection of having put on.

"And it says: *in this condition all the waters leading to the fountainhead, the reference is to authority.* That has to mean you."

"Mmmmmmm."

One hand held the book, the other hand was busy, scurrying fingers, sliding, slipping tips. The air conditioning told his numbed senses that he must be naked.

"The seat of power will be troubled yet must be calmed. See that?"

She was back on power again. But the nuances and implications were a little different now. No, he did not see, he

would never see anything again, as he drifted on a slow ride
behind his eyes, beneath his trembling skin. Honey drifted
down toward the seat of power that was growing quite visibly troubled. Her mouth followed those floating hands, but
by-passed centrality, titillating peripheries, making slow,
tongueing circles that descended below his knees, behind
them, and the bed was turning—no, it was he who was
turning, and her mouth was mumbling obscure rituals
against parts of his body that had not been visited by stran-
gers in time out of mind. Honey's rhythms were creating
hexagrams, tetrahydrons, forms never before experienced.
There was light trickling in from somewhere; a thin beam
whose presence suggested that some look might be taken at
all this. Through that little light there crept the subtle sense
that what was happening might be sad, ludicrous, or simply
comic. But this vanished and his entire sense of himself became local. As simple and uncomplicated as pleasure.

20

In the morning there was an envelope under the door. It
contained Sordino's permission to use the promotion film.
Operating Good Will had been attained. Mouth pasty and
eyes still sticky with sleep, Ezra noticed that he had slept
the night in his pajama top, alone: visible evidence that his
own Operating Good Will had been solicited.

During breakfast in the room, Kleinholz called. Just
knowing that he had Sordino's envelope allowed Ezra to be
comfortable with any potential Kleinholz storm. None came.
The old man was relaxed and joked about the fact that it
was midnight in California. The fire was already old stuff;
he had other matters he wanted Ezra to think about on the
way back: publicity problems about *Festival* and a number

of films Ezra had never heard of. Stockholders were getting restless; product had to be removed from cans, to which it had been consigned as worthless, and made to produce money in theaters.

Only just before the end of the conversation did the real reason for the phone call, and the summons home, surface. The conflict over who was to control the cut of *Festival*, snake scene and all, was in full bloom. A board meeting was scheduled, legal was fully mobilized. Even the studio guard system was being overhauled. The negative was still in Stone's hands.

"I haven't seen a foot of film," Kleinholz said. "Call me as soon as you're back on the lot. Have a safe trip."

The taxi driver had to shake Ezra to wake him up when they arrived at the airport. It was named Leonardo da Vinci Airport, and a producer who sat next to Ezra on the plane pointed out that Leonardo, like today's film-makers, had also worked for money, for a patron, not unlike the major studios. Ezra did not argue with him.

Halfway over the Atlantic the movie projector broke down. Ezra slept all the way to America.

book two

director's cut

1

The sun edged a semicircle over the horizon, and the limousine turned off the Freeway and headed for Ventura. The driver was again Marty, the ex-stunt man. No longer garrulous, this early morning. More of a listener, now, Ezra wondered? (*"Be paranoid," Robinson had advised.*)

Still, Nick and Ezra spoke easily: Nick with some irony about Ezra coming back to Los Angeles to find his "confidence" speech had been reprinted in every possible trade magazine and newspaper. In a terrified industry the man who speaks of confidence inherits the confidence of others.

"Talk is talk," Ezra said. "Now we have to deliver." But the weeks since his return from Rome had been occupied with his own orientation. And, somewhere along the line, he had passed into a split state of consciousness: in part, accepting an outrageous new way of life as if he'd always been part of it; in part, keeping an eye fresh for the incongruities, experiences containing elements of the fantastic.

Ezra had eaten breakfast at 5 a.m. in his suite. Now, leaning back in the seat talking to Nick, he felt as if he'd been doing things like this all his life: rising before dawn at the command of the studio head, to witness strange Indian rites involving rattlesnakes, drugs, and music.

Still sleepy, he let Nick Bohm move the conversation: From studio politics to the awful fog that periodically cursed Los Angeles mornings—to his concerns about the Sordino project.

"Michael Maurice is a fag," Nick said. "Sordino is a man who has homosexual relationships."

"Not too much of a fine distinction?"

"MM is a tormented son-of-a-bitch who develops passions for busboys which could overthrow the British Empire. An amazing actor, too, an artist. Hey, Ezra." Bohm laughed, unmaliciously it seemed to Ezra. You grew quickly sensitive to that particular nuance at the studio.

"You know what happened last year when MM came up for the Queen's Honours List, again? It seems the old girl said, 'How about Michael Maurice this year?' (I got this from Sordino.) And the chief equerry, or whoever the hell decides these things said: 'But your Highness, we already have our homosexual peer from the cinema.' And she is supposed to have said—what a sweet lady, I met her at the royal opening for Duke Wayne's last picture—she said: 'But can't we have two ... as in Noah's Ark?' "

Even Marty felt free to laugh. Ezra looked out at the streets from which the sun was gradually driving the rolling wisps of fog. Little house after little house running past the car with only an occasional child out, too early, sitting on the grass to observe their elegant passage.

Nick patted every possible pocket to see if he could find a forgotten cigarette before cadging one, as he inevitably did. He told of the stormy history between the British star and the Italian director; a love affair long since finished, two pictures made together, one a disaster, the other a great success. The problem was: the success had come first and the disaster hung over their heads, a darker cloud than the memory of their affair, ten years earlier. Sordino had been married, was still—in the Italian manner—married. More importantly, for the heterosexual credentials Nick was obviously trying to establish for the director, he'd had several big love affairs: a famous singer, an American actress. Now, of course, there was the question mark of the boy.

Nick succumbed and took a cigarette from the driver.

"I have a teen-age daughter," he told Ezra. "At least you don't have to worry about *girls*. Just get them the pill or a coil and hope for the best. Honey says—" Ezra's stomach jumped, his cheeks and jawbone tensed. "—that girls are less susceptible than boys at Karol's age."

Another Nick Bohm "perhaps." Perhaps he knew about Honey? Perhaps he had sent her? Perhaps he had no idea?

"Be there in about five minutes," Marty said.

"No photographers," Ezra said.

"That's what the guru insisted."

"Eyes," Ezra said. "At least we can report how it looks to the eye; how it feels to see it. Do you think Mitch believes in the whole ritual?"

"Believe," Nick muttered. "Believe . . . what does that mean?"

In an enormous field rimmed by hills whose tops swam in gray fog, Stone, Leggatt, and company had pitched camp: tied-dyed tepees, bright red, blue, and yellow shimmered in vagrant sunbeams; a great circle marked by stones had been shaped in the center of the field. The young girls, of whom there were at least a dozen, were bare to the waist; their headbands bore the same red, blue, and yellow patterns that circled the tepees. Several Indians wandered around the circle, or sat before the tents. The spicy scent of pot was there, but it was difficult to separate it from the incense that burned in jars, and from the sweetness of the fresh-cut field grass. An emaciated Indian in front of a tent near the car tended a large basket, the contents of which did not bear too much thinking about. The Indian's face was painted white from the nose up and black from the nose down to the chin and neck.

They were silent for at least a moment after getting out of the car.

It remained for Marty, sage Marty, to have the last word. Breaking his respectful silence, he said; "These fuckin' kids! They all want to be niggers or Indians!"

A half-naked girl approached the car, and Marty threw the car quickly into gear and screeched down to the parking area.

"Hello, Nick," the girl said. "We're all down this way."

"Hey, Pat, how are you?"

"D'you see me in the picture?"

"Mitch won't let anybody see the picture, sorry, kid."

Ezra could not match Nick Bohm's cool. Pat had hand-somely round breasts, and Ezra's eyes stayed there in frank communion, as if her nipples were eyes.

By this time they were all concentrated in front of the largest tent, more like a circus tent than a tepee. Mitch Stone arrived from inside the tent, wearing only a pair of jeans below his tanned, muscled chest. His face, like the Indian guarding the large basket, was painted black and white. The blond beard mitigated the effect of the white paint, but it was all quite startling. Leggatt was there, too.

"Perfect symbol of the youth movement," he said, echo-ing the driver but more gracefully. "White wanting to be at least half black."

Mitch gave his partner a look of contempt and vanished into the tent again.

"Those two," Nick said, mysteriously, "Love and peace . . ."

The time was approaching for the start of the ceremony. Nick appointed himself Ezra's guide. He explained that the tent in which Stone was preparing himself with prayer was a substitute for the kiva, an underground room about eight-feet deep where the snake societies of the various tribes held their councils and their ceremonies. When Mitch appeared, Nick noted that he wore a small bunch of eagle feathers at the back of his head—the eagle, he added, was the natural enemy of the snake. Around his neck Mitch wore a Navaho silver necklace (though the present snake ceremony was basically a Hopi one). There seemed to be as many contra-dictions in Indian life as in the white man's.

As the sun grew brighter and the rites proceeded, Nick poured. He was a fountain of facts, illuminating, confusing, irrelevant, voluminous. He had obviously buried himself in

the basic material of certain Indian ceremonies in order to
get some handle on what Mitch Stone was up to.

A stillness settled on the field, and Mitch knelt in front
of a large, thick-necked bottle in which were two large rattlesnakes. Ezra felt a chill. Nick flashed a smile. He whispered, "There's a line from some poem about snakes 'And
zero at the bone.' Right? Right. . . ?"

Two Indians stood on either side. One, Nick said, was
the gatherer, who was responsible for bringing the snakes in
and washing them so they'd be clean for the ceremony.

"The original purpose of this kind of a dance," he said,
"was to bring rain."

He squinted up at the porcelain sky: the fog was thin-
ning quickly. It would be another clear, scorching day.

"We could use it. But this stuff, today, is to make Mitch
a member of the Snake Society of the Navahos. Those two
guys are delegates from the Society. Watch the one with the
little whip in his hand." The "little whip" was two eagle
feathers on a wood handle. Its function became clear as
soon as the gatherer removed a snake from the bottle and
threw it on the bed of clean white sand. The snake began to
coil almost immediately, a sickening piece of live jewelry,
mottled bronze. Easily, as in a dream, the other Indian
waved the whip over the snake's bulging head. The coil of
its body unraveled at once. Nick said, "A snake can't strike
unless it's coiled."

There was a silence over the field now, accompanied by
two sounds: Mitch Stone's chanting, and Nick Bohm's murmured commentary. From that point on the strangeness of
the scene reduces it, in Ezra's consciousness, to a series of
still photographs: the eagle-feather whip poises over the
snake. Nick: "Must be some ancient memory of eagles attack-
ing. They used to swoop down, grab them in their claws,
and drop them on the ground from high up. Then eat
them." The chanting stops. Mitch Stone holds the snake in

his mouth. Repeat that snapshot: holds the snake in his mouth. Nothing from Nick, nothing from anyone. With both hands Mitch Stone holds the snake's body that hangs down from his jaw. The two Indians begin to dance around Mitch Stone as he moves slowly around the stone-marked circle. Ezra's eye catches the face of Pat, the bare-breasted girl. There is not just astonishment, but worshipful awe on that lovely young face. Next to her, his arm on her shoulder, is Cody, a black reporter, also young, who appears to be sharing her emotion; even though Nick claims he cannot be trusted. For the moment, like almost everyone at the scene, he is beyond deceit.

Stone kneels, still holding the slow movements of the snake in his mouth. Around him the two Indians draw some symbolic form in the sand. From Nick: the six directions of Hopi mythology. The four regular ones, plus one line up to the heavens and one line down to the underworld.

The next few moments blurred into chaos. Ezra saw Nick wave, signal behind him toward where the cars had been parked. There was a clicking of cameras, a plunge of crouching photographers, a girl screamed. Stone grasped the snake with both hands and threw it on the ground. It coiled and was uncoiled by the gatherer's whip, coiled and again was unwound. By this time Mitch was running around in furious circles, yelling something which Ezra could not make out. Nick grabbed his arm and called out something equally unintelligible.

Finally Mitch found what he wanted: the sight of Nick's face.

"You son-of-a-bitch," he yelled. He was dripping paint and sweat. "You bastard— If I see one of those pictures in a paper I'll kill you."

He kept trying to push his way toward Nick, being held back by Leggatt's long frame and the general crush of people separating them. He broke through far enough to land a fist on the side of Nick's nose; still shouting, he was pulled back into the crowd. The last thing Ezra saw was the snake slithering back into the narrow-mouthed bottle.

In the car, Nick squeezed a handkerchief against his bleeding nose; a thick red blob dripped onto his shirt.

"What was all that for?" Ezra asked.

Nick Bohm looked at him with a weary smile: the look of a man who has just run the mile and broken a record, or made love happily—a look of fulfillment.

"What for?" he murmured almost drowsily through the bloody cotton. "It was my assignment from Kleinholz."

"Assignment? Getting a man killed?"

"Getting the snake business on film. Nobody got killed."

"That was just luck. And it's *already* on film. It's in the movie."

"We can't get a look at it until he's ready. God knows when that's going to be. In the meantime, the word-of-mouth spreads. By the time he *is* ready, the kids will be looking for that scene in the picture. And I have a good hunch the studio's going to want it cut out. Did you see that—*thing*—in his mouth?"

Ezra stared straight ahead at the ribbon of road, thinking, everyone's fantasies of persecution were justified. The screenwriter waiting outside Kleinholz's door, Stone expecting betrayal on the Santa Monica pier.

Later, Nick said, "You know the real good of what happened today, Ezra?" And answered himself with the rare stammer that announced emotion:

"*L-l-l-et them kn-n-ow who's in ch-charge!*"

He blew a final period of blood into the crumpled linen.

Let them know who's in charge! Nick Bohm: dreamer of impossible states of clarity and order!

2

Kleinholz opens the board meeting with little attention to form. Statement: There is to be no snake scene in the final cut of *Festival*. Ezra turns and looks at Nick Bohm, standing against the wall, swollen-eyed, brooding sleepily like Ezra, a publicity-guest of the board. Ezra has visions of laboratories held open all night, developing film so that Kleinholz can view it before the meeting. Cardboard containers of coffee with cigarette butts swimming in them in midnight screening rooms, silent witnesses to Kleinholz's disgust. The snake ritual Kleinholz reports, is a monstrosity. It will turn audiences off, will make *Festival* a kids' and kinks' picture: a two-to-three-million-dollar gross. The studio is aiming for a forty-million-dollar gross. And up. Cutting the snake scene is a declaration of war, and various studio employees report on security. A complicated discussion follows. Original negative matrices are said to be on the lot with dupes at Technicolor. It is the original negative that is the central problem. Stone can change or destroy it if open war erupts. It must not leave the lot. There is a twenty-four-hour-a-day guard at the Music Building, where Stone is editing. Once it is off the lot—stolen, in effect—Stone will dispute the delicate question of what is whose property. He doesn't believe in the idea of private property, anyway. The blackmail will begin immediately.

You cannot give final cut to wild kids like Stone or tricksters like Leggatt. Double the guard! Triple it! Anyone who works for the studio and is found helping them smuggle any piece of film off the lot will be fired and blackballed in the entire industry. The agenda then addresses itself to *The Lion's Farewell*. Already, the sound of the title evokes the tone of the enterprise and makes it a stranger in this room. What do such as these know of lions or farewells? They live in the present and feed on financial advantage or failing that, each other. The recording executive at Ezra's right murmurs that the record album cannot possibly do well; another voice, belonging to the man responsible for selling films to television after they have exhausted the possibilities of theatrical film rental, says he cannot be expected to sell it to television, unless substantial changes are made—and everyone knows Sordino does not make changes—not for the Pope, let alone a TV network.

Becker, elegant, gold cuff links glinting stylishly, rises, cigar in hand, to set the record straight on certain controversial aspects of *The Lion's Farewell.* Shaking his head sadly, he states that the dispute over the budget had never been *his* affair. Robinson the late Robinson, had wanted to do the film at two million six, giving Sordino concession after personal concession that raised it from the original budget of a million five. In the course of the ensuing dispute, Robinson had resigned. (As if there had been no session in the Hotel Exelsior. . . Becker will never jump until he's sure the ship is sinking.)

"However, gentlemen," Becker said, "even though Mr. Robinson is no longer with the company, we are stuck with the fucking higher budget. The issue is" (with a swift glance at Kleinholz) "are we running this company or are these cocksuckers with cameras running it?"

The lot is filled with signs of imminent warfare as Nick Bohm and Ezra leave. Six extra uniformed policemen are heading for the Music Building. A bus parked, sideways, at the street next to the exit at the auto gate, two guards checking everyone in and out, with special attention to parcels and packages of all kinds. At the auto gate itself, workmen are rigging up a new electronic device. The days of Kleinholz summoning Pulitzer Prize playwrights to his bedroom are clearly over. To even attempt the same control today requires full mobilization—a state of siege.

3

May 5th
(Soon after returning from Rome.)

I am going blind.

For two days I have sat in a screening room and seen four full films each day. As well as fragments of pictures so awful that a few bits from each reel are sufficient reason to explain why it was buried in the first place. We are the proprietors of a cemetery, going through the graves, one by one, disinterring, looking for a sign—any sign—of life.

Leaving the screening room with Becker, or Nick, or Max—or any combination thereof—I walk onto the sunlit lot with an old familiar childhood guilt at hiding in the movies during the day: supertruancy. I glance at Becker. Does he feel it? There is no way of telling. And I do not know how to phrase such a personal question to such a man. Did he have a childhood?

Instead, I take a sanity break to clear my head and stroll over to the Music Building, where I watch the soundmen dubbing and redubbing tracks on whirling reels. Then I walk blinking into the sun and stop by the Fire Department, where the Chief plays chess with one of his men. He tells me how glad he is the studio is getting moving again. Down the New York Street, with its 1920s façades of buildings against which have been shot hundreds of the movies I watched as a child . . . stopping off to talk to William Watkins, the studio police chief for thirty-three years. He tells me the security precautions taken with the Festival group are the tightest in the history of the studio. His front teeth are rotted and his smile is dotted with black. The studio dentist has never been called upon, even though his services would be buried in some film's budget. Perhaps Watkins refused. Can he be the only honest man on the lot? He tells me the details of taking the driving test for my California license. I am not to worry—he will go with me—and, somehow, a copy of the answers to the written test will be on or near the desk. The driving test instructor will know I'm a studio executive. Watkins winks. There will be no problem. Cured of my illusions by the Watkins wink, I walk past transportation, where cars are up on blocks being repaired, being gassed up, being polished for the executives to whom they will be delivered before noon. At the Executive Dining Room of the Commissary. Harvey, a black man who prefers to be a Negro (twenty-two years with the studio), will serve me lunch that will send me back, strengthened, to the ordeal of the dark: at least two more films before nightfall.

Such speculations distract me from the fact of Kim's arrival. She teases and my memory teases. Her tease: a postcard from Rome, addressed to me at the studio, bearing a fragment of a sketch—Karol's classic profile. Does her touch of continued interest tease more than that firm "No" against my lips, in the Pincio Gardens? The drawing power of refusal is immense. She arrives tomorrow. Distractions . . . distractions, too, from Stone's phone calls, which I have learned not to answer; from Leggatt's brief visits, heavy with unstated threats: no cuts or no picture. Fortunately, Kleinholz is traveling: New York, London. He returns in two days. If such frantic travel wiped me out, what does it do to a semicrippled man of seventy or more? Perhaps he only sends a tape-recording of himself.

May 20th

It begins—and perhaps ends—with language.

". . . brings to the leisure-time industry more than three decades of experience with the powers and personalities that have shaped the contemporary world of . . . born in Brooklyn, New York, he attended public school there and early in life formed the ambitions which later culminated in such enterprises as . . . Stuffed language, dead as a medieval

manuscript. What is known as a "bio"; your life, anyone's life, in several well-chosen clichés, proving that men are indeed born equal and entitled to the same, deadly words. . . . Language, not death, was the great leveler.

In my diligence I keep after Max Miranda to describe each man's function. I get a variety of slippery answers. But I am persistent and I discover that so many of them duplicate each other's work that Max is terrified and expects—as does everyone—a blood bath.

One man totally resists my efforts at clarification. An aging, gentle soul, he floats around the office, arriving when I am not there and leaving at some undetermined time each day. He is in International Publicity but does no demonstrable work. I speak to him and he tells various tales of publicity stories placed in foreign periodicals. But they are all about stars no longer under contract, for pictures long since sold to television.

Finally, I nail Max; Max, the compleat concierge to the studio. Max knows all. But he will not say a word. I threaten to fire the man at once unless Max speaks. Max speaks. It seems the man's job is to get medals for Lothar Kleinholz from foreign governments. The Order of Siena from Italy, an honorary CBE from England. His crowning achievement: having Kleinholz made a Chevalier of the Legion of Honor; only someone told Kleinholz that Chevalier was kid stuff and only a Commander was worth anything. The medal-gatherer is now in the doghouse. He is currently trying to climb out of it by mounting a movement to get a Congressional citation for Kleinholz. It will be timed for the following year to coincide with the release of Festival. *At this point Max has me. I am helplessly entranced; an archaeologist faced with the ruins of a culture whose ways are so unthinkable that judgment is for the moment paralyzed. Only curiosity and an aesthetic awe are possible. In the wake of this, the man's job is temporarily safe. Max gazes at*

me with relief. Somewhere in that devious, amiable face
there hide the shards of surprise.

"Max," I said, "there's a line by a great French writer
which I try to use as a guide. And since we're going to work
together, closely, you might think about it."

"Yeah?" Max is ready for new guides; always useful in
the jungle.

"Neither a victim nor an executioner be."

"Neither—" Max repeats carefully, "—a victim—nor—
executioner—" He shakes his head. "It doesn't work, Ezra."
In his bewilderment he forgets to insert his customary boss
or chief, "I can't believe it could hold up. Who said it?"

"Camus," I said. "Albert Camus."

Max shook his head again. He would think about it.
But—no victims, no executioners. It didn't sound right.

June 10th

　　Two days of my life lost in a fuzzy mist of résumés,
personnel interviews; crossing and uncrossing of legs, trying
to remember first names, what I want in my staff. I want
competence and everyone offers loyalty. I want imagination
and everyone offers studio experience.

　　SHY, WITH HORN-RIMMED GLASSES: FIFTYISH.

　　". . . helped Metro reintroduce Gable after the war . . .
you know . . . 'Gable's back and Garson's got him. . . .' "

　　SKINNY, SQUINTING, FORTYISH.

　　". . . handled launching of new talent at Universal, Fox,
and Goldwyn. Don't let them tell you . . . star system dead."

　　If they only knew that I am improvising myself and my
job every day they would not be so nervously smug in their
armor of studio experience. No, that's wrong! They would
simply assume, as perhaps they all do, that being new I
need old hands to show me the ropes. But none will realize
how thin are the ropes they are walking on, how dangerously frayed.

132

I've hired three new people, shifted a dozen others around. But with it all a sick, helpless feeling, I will have to rely on Nick Bohm, Max, Archer, even Giannini. I will not get imagination or honesty; I'll get precisely what they promise: experience and loyalty. But the experience is of another, vanished world. The loyalty is to other people; to that other world; to each other.

June 18th
Sunday morning in Hollywood.

Hazy sun, late, sleepy breakfast, smoggy feeling in the chest: heavy breathing.

Freeway dreams . . . Honey Williams takes me brunch-shopping at the Hollywood Ranch Market. It is open, she informs me with the sense of imparting eternal secrets, twenty-four hours a day. We stumble out to the car loaded down with eggs, papayas, butter, wheat germ. For every ordinary item of food there is one nut food. Honey speaks of Ying and Yang. She does not speak of Nick Bohm, who is drag-racing his custom-built Maserati at Redondo Beach.

Honey tells me her dreams—wild affairs, often painted in brilliant colors, with mad, violent denouements. Sometimes, when something happens, such as the old man with wild eyes laced with blood and a bespittled beard who begins to yell at us that love is filth and only God is clean—the daily California lunacy, she will say: "You know, I think I dreamed that last night. . . ." And she understands its meaning well. Sometimes an all-too-clear justification of sweating in my bed on a sunny Sunday afternoon, while Nick Bohm sweats over a steaming pile of metal miles away.

"Are you and Nick going to marry?"
"Yes."
"When?"
"Well, maybe yes. He wants more than he's got."

"*Ah, that....*"

"*It's okay for you to 'Ah.' Do you want an orangeade? Never drink lemonade. It's bad for your potency.*"

"*If you and Nick don't get married, what will you do?*"

"*String along. It's kicks. He's going to buy me a dog. I guess Becker was drinking lemonade in Rome, huh?*

"*Who told you about that?*"

"*It's all over the studio.*"

"*Doesn't it bother you? That a thing like that can't be kept secret?*"

"*Listen, Jews and Protestants worry about that. I come from Paterson, New Jersey. I'm a Catholic. I know what people are like.*"

"*Are you a good Catholic?*"

"*I haven't missed mass or confession since my confirmation; except when I was sick with scarlet fever, and once when I was fifteen and I was run over by a lady in a station wagon in Newark.*"

"*Will you tell your confessor about sleeping with Nick and me?*"

"*I'll tell him.*"

"*And what will he say?*"

A tiny laugh. "*He'll say: 'Stop!' *"

"*And what will you do?*"

"*Priests! My mother knew a priest when he was a young man. At parties he used to do a perfect imitation of a rooster crowing. Priests! I'll tell him: Father, this is California, L.A. You have to move with the times. Then he'll give me my penance and I'll do it and come back here and do this—and this—and ...*"

Sunday evening in Hollywood.

A cool wind blows through my nose and mouth and into my eyes. Vague feelings of detachment. The hotel suite is a mess. Honey is not the tidying up kind. Next week I'll rent a house. Max Miranda warns me that an apartment is beneath my studio status and would damage my standing. He lives in a tiny apartment. Honey tells me there is some awful tragedy in his past. I'm curious about that, but do I care about Max's vision of my proper living style?

How deeply am I getting into all this?

Sunday Freeway vagaries. The day between Saturday and Monday.

Myself, between what?

I have nothing objectively new to add about Hollywood. The place escapes me; it rests secure in its bed of prereceived clichés, truths. All I have are certain images. . . .

Images: the winding hills of Bel-Air (where, Honey tells me, they put down plastic white blankets on their lawns to simulate snow at Christmas—but even that fails to surprise).

The old women on street corners wearing coats in the killing summer heat, selling maps of the movie stars' homes, a maniacal glint in their eyes. (Honey: "I've never seen anybody buy one, or even stop. But they're there every year.")

The endless Freeway guarded by looming hills whose slopes are always being graded, readied for more and more settlements of aging couples who come to California to die and then forget what they came for.

The afternoon bars on La Brea or Genesee or other such place-names. Girls with thin, hard, too-red mouths and beautifully curved bodies, and eyes all make-up, depth and shadow, no substance; and their men in cowboy boots and nail-studded collars, and pants worn low-slung and crotchy, a cigarette stuck to every mouth; the talk all of agents and TV castings and the deaths of old people in the neighborhood and how to make extra money by a little drug dealing . . . the sex-talk surprisingly un-erotic.

But everyone knows this Hollywood: this banal, plastic

wasteland. There is no mystery left in its familiar, depressing details; only in the unyielding mysteries at the bottom of the details. It is the mystery of the studio that interests me. The studio from which the exterior Hollywood landscape drew its vitality for so long. Now, vitality gone, it continues to do what passes for living while the studio struggles for its own life; a corporate-human state within a city: Vatican to Los Angeles' Rome.

4

KLEINHOLZ TAPE #9193

EZRA: I've got a way for you to see *Festival.* All of it!

KLEINHOLZ *(contempt)*: I'll see it. I bought it! It's only a question of how soon.

EZRA: How soon would you like?

KLEINHOLZ: Now!

EZRA: How about next week?

KLEINHOLZ: What's the kicker?

EZRA: I'll set up a sneak of the picture.

KLEINHOLZ: But . . . ?

EZRA: With the snake scene.

KLEINHOLZ: Son-of-a-bitch. . . .

EZRA: But that's the point. That's our leverage—and it's Stone's leverage. And we both get to see if the people faint or love it.

KLEINHOLZ: You've worked this out with Stone and Leggatt?

EZRA: All I need is your approval.

KLEINHOLZ: Do it! *(Pause)* Does Nick know?

EZRA: Not yet. I thought I'd line you up first.

KLEINHOLZ *(admiration)*: You're learning.

5

Like a dream, like an archetypal funeral procession, the black Cadillac limousines followed each other, nose to tail, along Sunset Boulevard. In stately rhythm they slid onto the Freeway, where the pattern was slowly broken up by changing lanes, alien cars slipping between them. Gradually the one became many, absorbed into the wild flow of traffic.

Twilight hung over the Freeway, blue-black, laced through with poisonous yellow-green ribbons and bags of smog visible against the far horizon, mixed with the blinking lights of passing suburban cities. One of these, Glendale, was the destination. For four decades it had been one of the key places; the mysterious witching sites to which terrified and superstitious producers brought their films: an altar on which rites of darkness told success, failure, life or death, according to ancient patterns. In Glendale the people spoke and the Film Gods trembled. Tonight, *Festival* was being "sneaked" in the air-conditioned splendor of the Glendale Granada. Two months, also like a dream—one of those dreams that upon waking seem clearer than reality. It was as if Ezra had always been at the studio. Absolutely no *segue*. At the same time its strangeness was all-pervasive; he felt it in his teeth, in the drawing of the skin over his cheeks as he smiled at each new person met in the line of duty. . . . It was like no other experience he'd ever had; no other environment was so enveloping. . . .

Somewhere up ahead, in one of the other cars—with Nick Bohm, Becker, and Graham, the studio treasurer—sat Kim. Weeks of inconclusive encounters—quick drinks, afternoon coffees—had come to an invitation to join the studio entourage to the sneak. Both of them were aware that they were circling each other. Ezra, uncertain about her motives, knew his was simply fear of closed lips.

". . . I hope everything goes nice and smooth—the way we want it tonight. . . ." Max was saying. Max had been uncommonly silent for the first part of the trip; his moon-face empty of expression, even of his usual worry.

"What do you mean?" Ezra said. "What could go wrong?"

"With those meatballs? With freaks, freaky things happen. You gotta stay one step ahead of them all the time."

"And—are we ahead?"

"Let's see how it goes, boss." He smiled weakly. "Let's see how the snakes go over."

The traffic was slowing to a crawl. Max said he thought it was unusual for 7 o'clock in the evening. They were passing a feed-on point in the Freeway. From some dimly-lit suburban town cars were creeping onto the crowded Freeway. Miles of red lights glowed and dimmed, glowed and dimmed.

"Everybody's coming to the sneak," Ezra said, to joke Max out of his gloom.

"Don't be surprised at anything," Max said. "The kids've been waiting for this picture for a year. It's not a picture, it's a religion. Like the fucking snake ceremony . . ."

The jump from the private language to public language was a personal amusement for Ezra. He had supervised the latest publicity release on *Festival*. "Long-awaited motion picture record of a great event. Landmark of the youth-culture . . ." had initialed it, feeling as if he were approving a statement in an ancient language. What if it had said: "Not a picture, a religion. Like the fucking snake ceremony?" The line of red lights dimmed and the car began to move.

Something odd was happening. They had reached the Glendale exit after a half hour of inching along. Finally free of the Freeway, the service road, too, was blocked. At the

first traffic light Ezra could see that along the four inter-
secting streets an endless line of cars lay, like a painting of a
traffic jam. The moon shone obligingly and the scene was
tranquil. Then the first horn began to sound a honk of
rage.

"Son-of-a-bitch!" Max said. "He did it. The momser did
it."

"Did what?"

"Look!"

Max pressed the button that unrolled the window and
leaned his head out into the gasoline-night. Ezra craned his
neck. He knew at once what Max meant. Car after car was
painted bright yellow or green and red, with graffiti spilled
from front to rear. Peace flags featuring doves or the international peace symbol flew from at least a dozen aerials Ezra
could see. Some of the cars were Fords or Dodges or some
vaguely recognizable make. But many were jalopies held
together only by the imagination and will of their owners.
One convertible, or simply topless, car had about fourteen
people in the back seat. The rock music of countless radios
sharpened the night air. The gods that would pass judgment
on tonight's film were the gods of youth.

"He did it," Max murmured, "he wasn't going to take a
chance for a minute."

"Could Mitch gather—*that*—on any given night?"

Max pressed the button again and the sounds stopped
behind the closed window. "Like that," he said and snapped
his fingers. "There'll be a thousand of them in that theater
tonight. And at a certain crucial point—Wow!! Nick must
be busting a gut. And Kleinholz!"

"And how about us?" Ezra said. "How are our guts,
Max?" Max sat on the edge of the seat, round and suddenly
composed: a smile touched with unaccustomed irony sat on
his pink Kewpie mouth.

"You've got *me,* boss. Don't forget that," Max said. "You've got Max Miranda on your side." Ah, loyalty!

About two miles and twenty minutes later, Nick appeared on foot and rapped on the window.

"We'll have to start at nine instead of eight."

"This gang wouldn't care if we stay for two weeks," Max said.

Behind him, looming over Nick's shoulder, was William Watkins. Ezra met the studio cop's gaze and, unbelievably, Watkins winked. That Watkins wink could only be ominous. Ezra quickly decided that the responsibilities of office demanded something more of him.

"Hello," he called out. "I hope there won't be any trouble tonight."

"You can count on me, Mr. Marks. I'm in radio contact with the State Police; they have a helicopter on the way for surveillance."

Nick was in a wild state. Not anger but confusion and surprise, staring eyes.

"Are you sure we've got the right print?" Nick asked Max.

"What do you mean?"

"With the snake ceremony in it."

"Sure."

"If it's not there, they'll tear the place apart. They've been primed."

"And if it *is* there, they'll go ape," Max said.

"Well, are *we* all set?" Nick asked.

Max nodded. "All set and primed."

Nick smiled, loose-lipped, at Ezra, "Everybody's primed," he said. "It's all a question of who goes off first, right, Ezra?" Ezra was included in the magic circle of conspiracy.

Before he could ask Nick for details, the caravan began to move. Nick ran; Watkins winked again and was gone.

Leaning out of the window Ezra saw Nick climb into a hip-high Maserati. There was a girl in the back seat and one sitting in front. The one in front was Kim. He could tell by the loosely combed ash-blonde hair. The girl in the back seat could only be Honey. Somewhere after leaving the studio Nick had exchanged the limousine for the sports car —probably picked up at a rendezvous point by Honey. The notion was troubling.

Glendale was a shambles. Too small a town for so many human bodies and cars. Pressing forward toward the theater entrance, Ezra was fronted by a flying wedge composed of loyal, ferocious Max and two of William Watkins' men. Up ahead, almost beneath the theater marquee, was Nick, fronting for Kleinholz, who had opted, this evening, for his wheelchair; a wise choice, there was a magic circle of safety around the old man. Behind him came Ape and his equipment. Hair and bright colors were everywhere. Ezra looked for Kim but did not find her until they were all standing inside the theater lobby, where the theater manager, elegant and hysterical in his tuxedo uniform, was begging Kleinholz to call off the preview. As a contest of wills it was pitiful. Kleinholz simply ran over the man in his wheelchair. The poor manager was reduced to insisting that the fire laws be obeyed.

Mitch Stone appeared wearing a plaid blanket, his hair loose around his shoulders. Kim was chatting amiably with Leggatt, while Nick and Max busied themselves organizing seating patterns.

"This is the big night, Lothar," Mitch said.

"Didn't have to be quite so big, did it?" Kleinholz said.

"The news is out."

"You rigged it."

But the wheelchair could not flatten Stone. He possessed

a tribal certainty that made Kleinholz and all the other executives seem shaky. Each person from the studio pursued
his specific function, from Max and his seating arrangements to Watkins and his security, to Kleinholz and the
manager counting the house; those same functions that had
not changed in thirty years. Only the people in the seats had
changed.

"Sit with me," Ezra said to Kim. Deafening sounds
erupted from speakers all around them.

The legendary Festival weekend unfolded. If Max and
Nick were primed with some secret explosive, the audience
was bathed in an electronic aura of its own making. It pulsed
with the music, it laughed raucously with the laughter on-
screen, it was breathless as the snake ceremony began.

When Mitch Stone was kneeling in the dust holding the
snake in his mouth, a young man stood up and began shouting something. The electronic aura was shattered. People
twisted to see what was going on.

" . . . sadistic shit . . ." he was yelling. "How can you sit
and watch this disgusting . . ."

"What did he say?" Kim whispered.

Ezra said nothing. He tried to see where Nick Bohm
was. The manager and several ushers were running down
the aisles. Then a young girl began to scream. It was the
strangest thing Ezra had ever heard, a live human female
scream in an enclosed theater backed by a throbbing rock
score. Another girl (or the screaming one) ran up the aisle
to the back of the theater. The yelling and the ranting continued, joined by the angry calls of the faithful—and by
more rebels against the human/snake images on the screen.

"Primed," Ezra remembered, as the house lights came up
and the screen faded. The manager had apparently recov-
ered his courage after his collision with Kleinholz. He refused to allow the film to continue in all this chaos. Next to

Ezra and Kim, sat Max, wearing the same pursed-mouth expression of determination he'd had in the limousine. A form of loyalty had just been expressed. The stampede was beginning, a rush of people that made Ezra begin to think of emergency exits and trampled bodies.

"You planned this, you son-of-a-bitch. Those screamers were plants." Mitch Stone raised his fist at Kleinholz.

"You're crazy. People can't stand this snake business."

"My people can!"

"You admit they're your people. Ape, did you get that?"

Brief scuffle between Ape and Stone. It ends when the manager forces himself between them. The tape continues to turn in some hidden recess of Ape's jumpsuit.

"People could have been killed. . . . Look at them. . . ."

"It's a miracle that . . ."

"You should have thought of that before. . . ."

"*You* should have! Don't think this changes anything, Lothar."

Mitch Stone's blanket had lost its quality of repose—it was twisted askew on his shoulders; he loomed over Kleinholz's wheelchair like a murderous madman. Nick Bohm shouldered past Ezra. His eyes had lost their usual vagueness; in them, now, was a cool excitement. The floppy gray hair was wild.

"Come on, Mitch," Nick said. "You could see the guy was the real thing. Maybe he was a nut. But there are a lot of nuts in movie audiences—and you don't want this kind of thing happening every place the picture plays."

Nick lived for these moments. It was a climactic episode in the Publicity Dance, an elegant genre in which truth was subordinated to style.

"Listen," Mitch Stone was trying to control himself, measuring his breathing. "Listen—nobody's-going-to-leave-this-lobby until Leggatt gets back here with the guy and the girl who pulled this stunt."

"Don't make threats, young man," Kleinholz said. He spoke with the calm of a man who's already won his game. "You loaded this theater with a couple of hundred extra kids to stack the deck. But it didn't work—and your snake . . ."

"Backfired. . . ."

". . . selling entertainment not . . ."

". . . goddam crazy snake-religion . . ."

". . . millions tied up. . . ."

"Don't shove. . . ."

". . . three years of my life on this picture . . ."

". . . out of here already . . ."

". . . till we find those shills . . ."

It could have lasted all night. Realizing this, Ezra had a flash of a solution. He went hunting for Watkins. Max was actually the man to find, but Watkins would be next best. Ezra's guess was that the two people in question were actors hired by Max. They'd been too convincing to be amateurs. If they continued to act in front of Mitch Stone the episode could safely end.

He found Watkins standing in front of a studio first-aid truck that had appeared from somewhere. Ezra did not explain his plan to Watkins. He wanted no complicit wink. He just ordered him to produce the two in question, as if their existence on the studio payroll was mutual knowledge.

They were inside, the man munching a sandwich, the girl touching alcohol to a cut knee. It had been a strenuous evening for two unemployed actors. They were not happy when Ezra informed them that their job was not quite ended. But they accompanied him to the finale.

The battle in the lobby was in new crisis. Leggatt had found Max and was shaking him. Nick stood nearby, holding Max's glasses, while the theater manager struggled to free the sightless Max.

When Ezra delivered the two actors to the starting points of their respective performances, Leggatt released Max at once. The look of gratitude on the round face was ludicrous. As Ezra began to speak he was aware of the eyes turning toward him. He was taking part in the Publicity Dance.

6

Later, Kim and Ezra explored the house the studio leased for him. Still, semifurnished, it was like a giant hotel suite, studded with pieces of earlier lives: a phonograph record of the 1955 Academy Awards, a catalogue from the museum at Santa Barbara. And on the wall in the bedroom, pencil marks, with names scrawled next to them, along with numbers.

"Look, here's Irving," Kim said laughing. "Irving Thalberg no doubt."

"Short," Ezra observed somberly. "Like many great men."

"And Gary, only three foot two."

"Gary Cooper, the child. This room, this wall, is an archaeological collection illustrating the history of Hollywood."

"Here's Audie...."

The game died, and Kim wandered through the house, gazing through glass doors and broad windows. Alone with Ezra, she dropped the style that protected her among crowds of youngsters and studio executives. She did not seem quite so tall, so distant, now. In public, as at that first lunch in Rome, she sheltered herself with separateness. In privacy she could afford to be less private.

"You're very quiet," Ezra said.

"It's been a noisy evening. I'm trying to figure something out."

"About . . . ?"

"The evening." She shook her head. "All that about a movie."

"About several million dollars."

"I'm not sure," she said. "You had a stroke of genius with those two fakes."

"Did you see Kleinholz's face?"

"No," Kim said. "I saw Nick's face, though. You're going to have trouble there. He thinks you planned that glorious denouement for your personal glory. He's not a simple man. And poor Max."

Kim laughed a silly little sound. It was pleasant to hear a trivial noise from her; she'd been so serious all evening; he'd taken her seriousness as a judgment on the proceedings.

"You've got a friend there for life."

"I've got a friend there for about half an hour."

They were interrupted by Kim's discovery, through the picture window, of a large tortoise in the garden. They went out and knelt to examine it. Kim stroked the back of the monster and murmured to it. It was strange to be there with her, in the movie-night.

"You like turtles better than snakes?"

"I didn't mind that scene—I thought it was kind of hypnotic. Until the hired help started screaming in the aisles. Stay there," she said. She usually carried a sketchbook like a third arm. Something in the shape his position formed, sitting next to the still turtle interested her eye. The garden behind the house was floodlit; the inevitable pool rippled in yellow light; fruit trees made little clumps of mystery every few feet. Below, the sudden slopes of Bel-Air slid down to Sunset Boulevard.

Kim sketched him while she spoke. She loved the figure, stubbornly. During her student days in New York no one of any consequence was bothering with the human figure; abstraction was all. But Kim stuck and the wave had caught up with her again. Galleries blossomed with nudes; museums bought figures of all kinds. Once again the human had been rediscovered. She exhibited rarely, cherishing a certain contempt for the atmosphere of fashion in the galleries. She kept sketching, painting the figure. She kept her contempt. It was as precious to her as her talent.

The moon hid, then reappeared from behind a thin scarf of clouds. Ezra sat as still as the turtle.

"This is my first sitting," he said. "Is it all right to talk?"

"Sure. Ask me anything."

"If it doesn't please you, why do you come here?"

"It's simple. Coming here lets me make the money to live in Rome, and show in New York. It's not so simple really. I was shanghaied—by a writer I met when I was studying at the League in New York."

"You've had a husband, then."

"A husband has had me."

"That bad?"

"Very bad. He was a talented writer. That was part of the reason I married him. He had a way with words—so he had his way with me. Southern girls like words. Don't fidget."

"What went wrong?"

"Everything. He came out here a couple of years after we got married. I came too. That's the way you did it in those days. It was all so damned *dumb*," she said. "You take somebody who does something well—he writes—so you pay him well. Out here they know how to pay. Then you make him a producer and pay him even more money. Oh, damn it, I don't want to talk about all this."

After the rage in her voice there was the silent hum of tires on pavement, wind in trees; charcoal pencil hissing on paper. A few moments later she said, "Do you think I'm a strong woman?"

He had to smile. "You give that impression."

"I wasn't always. As he got weaker, I got stronger. I had to."

"What became of him?"

"He's second in command of one of the other studios. No names, please." She stretched her arm, flexed her drawing hand. "Listen, honey," she said, dipping into ironic Southern as one dips into a bowl of cream. "My daddy was a drunk. I know about weak men and strong women."

Ezra thought of Nina, long legs and smart-ass style, he thought of a girl named Lily whom he'd wanted to marry, but couldn't any longer imagine why—perhaps because he'd been about to turn thirty; he thought of the many girls and women, of the swinging pendulum between assent and refusal, first on his part then on theirs, like a film and sound track deliberately out of synchronization. What had kept them out of synch? Perhaps some unstated, unrealized sense that he wasn't yet in synch with himself; that there was a self stranded in an airplane, the New York/Washington or New York/Boston Shuttle. The sense that whoever the girl was, perhaps they'd better wait till that plane landed, till the figure disembarked, till you could hear what he would say—and whether the words would move at the same speed as the mouth articulating them.

". . . no complaint any more. He taught me how to get into the movie graphics business. I taught myself how to keep getting out—before you start telling yourself what you're doing is really terrific—before you forget where you leave off and they begin. What are you in it for, Ezra? Don't move. Just talk."

"Robbie asked me that my first day."

"And . . . ?"

"It's not too neatly defined. I spent a lot of years trying to make everything I did mean a hell of a lot. What is grandly known as the public sector, the new frontier . . . whatever. I've developed a lot of skills in the meantime.

Maybe now I'd like to see if I can use things like sociology, methodology, demographics, all kinds of techniques for the sheer pleasure of seeing them work. And for the sake of the crazy numbers they put on the checks made out in my name. Do you understand?"

"I think so, yes."

"I call it going private."

She laughted, unexpectedly. It broke her concentration, broke the spell of the sitting.

The turtle craned its neck; it seemed uncomfortable inside its speckled shell. A leaf clung to one of its back legs. Suddenly, it began to move. The speed was surprising.

Kim stopped laughing. "Damn!" she said. "Just when I was getting it."

She waited a moment. The turtle stopped. She watched it, pencil poised. Ezra watched both of them, the turtle's back gleaming, mottled, in the yellow light; Kim's eyes, dull, sealed. Her hand began to glide over the paper. The turtle began again, turned sideways so that the shape of the pose was changed. Ezra stretched. Then, with what seemed like a surreal series of actions, Kim dropped the pad and charcoal pencil, fell to her knees beside the turtle, and turned it firmly, gently, on its back. The cartoon-like waving of webby feet and jerky movements of the scaly neck went on for some seconds. Then, just as firmly, she turned the animal over again. This time it was utterly still. Calmly Kim returned to her station and picked up the pad and charcoal.

"Turn a little toward me," she said to Ezra. Ezra turned. Neither he nor the turtle moved until she finished the sketch.

Later, though, knowing better, he presses the issue. She surprises him by responding, dry wit encased in wet mouth, careful hands carelessly touching his cheeks while they kiss. They are in the bedroom facing sliding glass doors that gaze down at the slippery, twisting roads falling dizzily down to the boulevard below. It is a vertiginous embrace, unexpected, unreal.

There is almost no furniture in the room; a floor-level bed, just a dressed-up mattress, really, and one stuffed yellow chair. Knowing her conflict, feeling her half-response, he pulls her onto the chair with him, hands slipping on sweaty thighs below her skirt. Angry at his own haste, knowing he is handling it badly, but knowing there was no other way, or no way at all, he loses her. She slips away, angry at herself, too, tugs herself together while he sits, defeated.

"I wanted to," she said later. They were standing outside the front door. He flooded the driveway with light. "Then all of a sudden I couldn't . . . not even a not wanting, very definitely a 'couldn't.' "

"Oh . . . ?"

"I'm sorry. I had a vision."

"Voices, too?" he said. It was impossible not to have some bitterness.

She was turned away from him toward the blinking bracelet of lights, a slim, fugitive figure with messed-up hair, like a bird's nest, from the back. She spoke quickly; it was as if without this eruption of words, she couldn't leave.

"Don't joke about voices, or anything," she said. "A vision, I said: all the marvelous young men, with their bright good looks, with their marvelous new disciplines, with their sciences, their this-ologies, their this-graphics or that-o-graphics, I saw them—okay I saw *you*, I saw my ex-husband —all of these marvelous men—ready to be used in the service of shit. Power-shit, money-shit . . . And there's no way for any of you to do anything more than teach these skills to

each other in universities—or to work them for gold in
these shit-mines . . . somethin' wrong, Ezra . . . somethin'
wrong . . ." The eloquence was pure Southern jeremiad and
she lapsed even farther South in her dropped g's. "It was a
turnoff," she said flatly, turning back to him. "I'm real sorry.
It's funny. I puzzled about Nick Bohm. Everybody puzzles
about Nick Bohm. All smoke, all vague gesture and style.
But he does what he was *trained* to do—fancy-dance, sing
the promotion songs, blow pretty smoke rings for the people. Where's the mystery? I'll tell you. It's you, Ezra,
now. . . ."

7

"Hello . . . ?"

"How'd the sneak go?"

"What the hell time is it in Rome?"

"Twelve noon. Why?"

"Why? It's 3 a.m. in L.A."

"In the real dark night of the soul in L.A. it's always
three o'clock in the morning."

This was a jubilant Robinson. "Try and wake up because
I have news. Projects," Robbie crackled in that reedy trans-
atlantic-telephone voice. "Projects and proxies. I have almost enough to push for a seat on the board. For me or my
man."

"Board?" Ezra switched on the bedside lamp as if seeing
better would help him understand.

"Of directors. There's big movement going on. The projects are going slower. I've lined up some beauties: Huston
and Billy Friedkin came in. Mike Nichols has a powerhouse
project. But they're all waiting until they see about *Festival*

—and the Sordino picture. They want to be sure there *is* a King Studio. That's why I'm calling."

"The sneak was a disaster. It's too complicated to explain on the phone. But it's a terrific picture. All I have to do is fight Kleinholz to make it stay terrific."

A series of crackles and bleeps intervened. When Robbie's voice was clear again, *"Ars gratia artis."*

"What?" Exuberance was making Robbie incoherent.

"An old Metro saying. Listen, I need you over here. I've got my power base. Well, a mini-power base. But it's a start. You'll read about it in the funny papers tomorrow. When can you come?"

"I had a bad night, Robbie. I'll call you tomorrow."

Click of phone. Click of lamp. Sleep. In the morning, not surprisingly, he woke with a headache and an erection. The erection went away.

8

The story was featured in all of the trades. The real news came at the end.

Rome: *ROBINSON SEES MAJORS CHANGING OR DYING*
Former Executive V.P. of King Studio, Robert "Robbie" Robinson sees the future of the major Hollywood studios as dependent on their opening the gates of power and control to film-makers. "Everybody talks about the studios becoming only distribution arms for independent companies owned and run by directors and screenwriters. But the truth is: the studios exert as much control over the product as if they still had the power—which they don't." Robinson has just signed on as Executive Producer of Sordino's Italo-American production The Lion's Farewell, *ironically to be distributed by his former home base, King Studio.*

9

Outside the sun was hot, the sky blue-clear; inside steam swirled and Kleinholz huddled in a white, hooded robe. Outside was a two-hundred-yard archery range and an olympic swimming pool in which Ezra had observed several executives' wives swimming. Outside two agents played tennis on Kleinholz's grass court, while a music publisher kibitzed.

Inside were hot wet stones, in the Finnish manner, and Becker waiting sprawled sullen in his white terry-cloth costume. Inside Kleinholz held Saturday morning meetings, one by one, as long as the sweat poured. He could not swim, he could not play tennis any more—but he could steam, he could talk, he could scheme.

"I'm taking the picture into the cutting room. . . . Don't be so surprised. You read the cards. 'Disgusting. . . .' 'Violent. . . .' 'Sacrilegious. . . .' "

"I read them. But I'm still trying to figure out who wrote them. Our people . . .? Our people's friends . . .? I can't even figure out which of the rave cards were written by real people or by Mitch Stone's kids. We're playing cowboys and Indians and I can't tell who's who."

"Listen— You were terrific last night."

"Which part?"

"Your part. If you hadn't used your head and found those creeps we'd still be there."

"Lothar, those were *our* creeps."

"I'm cutting the snake scene. And some other stuff, too. The best way to handle this situation is to take charge."

"Let me do a research study. That way if it comes to lawyers you'll have extra ammunition . . . if it turns out people hate it as much as you do."

Kleinholz squinted, shifted weight. Ezra wondered where the recording equipment was.

"Okay," Kleinholz said. "Do the research."

"It would cost about..."

"Do the research! But I'd like it if everybody agreed with me."

"So would Mitch Stone."

"Are you comfortable? Drop that hood down, you'll choke to death. You have to understand me, because you're working for me. Understanding Kleinholz is easy. You know why? Listen—I once had a great English writer here, back before the war. Forster. Uh—"

"C.S.? E.M.?"

"E.M."

Ezra's glance caught Becker's form shifting. He was lying on a bench on the other side of the steam room; a stomach rose and fell regularly. He might be awake, he might be asleep.

"Sam Goldwyn had all those big writers from Europe. Maurice . . ." Pause. "The fellow who wrote *The Bluebird*. So I got Forster. It was a mess. He didn't want to write for pictures. . . . So instead I had him give a lecture to my contract writers." He laughed, a hoarse sound full of pleasant memory.

"I had him do it in the commissary. Just to remind those buzzards that they had to write good—and they had to write for me—if they wanted to keep eating. In those days, a writer was a writer. Now they have their own companies and you can't tell them from the producers without a contract in your hand. Ah, God. . . ."

His exhaled breath was a stream of smoke. "There was one thing he said I never forgot. He said in every story there have to be round characters. The hero you know. Sure, every kid knows that. But don't forget, he said, you have to have flat characters, too. People you can describe in a few sentences, with no hidden tricks that maybe even they don't know are coming up."

"It's a famous lecture."

"Well, me, I'm a flat character. Flat as the Freeway."

Kleinholz proceeded to outline the dimensions of his flatness. He had built the studio and he was going to keep control of it; he was going to make money again. The start of that would be *Festival* and the Sordino film. Simple.

Amid the hissing steam and ambience of damp toweling and sweat Ezra was reduced to leaning forward. The single line of his own nose merged in his sight with the white-swathed football that was Kleinholz's head.

"Lothar," he said, "I think I read you right, but I-will-not-do-a-fake-research-report."

Without taking a beat, as if he refused to allow a clash of wills to be initiated by someone else, Kleinholz said, "You're right! Nobody would believe it. Get Nick to help you."

From under a pile of white Kleinholz produced a ringing phone encased in cloth. From what Ezra could gather it was the Prime Minister of Ireland on the other end. After the appropriate long-distance false starts and pauses Kleinholz proceeded to tell the Prime Minister that he didn't appreciate being put off location shootings on a picture dealing with the Easter Rebellion because some damned civil servant didn't like the script. The Prime Minister would seem to be in agreement, and Kleinholz allowed his tone to be mollified and even offered to have the Prime Minister tour the studio when he came to America. All during this conversation a strange crablike being, Becker in his white toweled robe, crawled toward Ezra. Before Kleinholz hung up, the white crab rose high enough on his legs to whisper one word into Ezra's ear: "*Shit!*" and subsided to his prone position. Was Becker's critical instinct addressing itself to the question of flat and round characters? Or to Irish politics? Kleinholz hung up. There was an odd moment. It hung in the air, unresolved.

Kleinholz said, "Listen, you must have figured out by

now that the business of getting signed permission from Sordino was a kind of test. I don't give a damn about signed permissions. I just wanted to see how you do under pressure." Ezra supported a brief vision of people flying around the world signing checks and performing tasks to prove some secret worth to King Kleinholz—what would be next: golden apples, golden fleece. . . . His small victory was even smaller than he'd thought.

"Last night you came through, again."

What coming through had earned him, apparently, was being taken into Kleinholz's confidence. There were plans being made and they tumbled from Kleinholz in a bewildering flow, to the accompaniment of occult grunts from Becker now lying on the floor in imitation of a damned soul.

It would have been helpful to have a calendar in that atmosphere of smoke and heat, but Ezra had to track the plans in his head. The Cannes Festival was to be the key moment: exhibit the film—out of competition or in, if Becker could swing it. . . . Sordino would be important.

"They all kiss Sordino's ass over there."

Festival would be a great success, perhaps win the grand prize. He, Ezra, would manage the publicity so as to make the most of the moment. Then, the next day in New York, the stockholders' meeting would take place. With the impetus of Cannes behind him, Kleinholz could easily hold off the proxy threat. More grunts from Becker, prone. And Ezra remembered Becker and Robinson working over charts, graphs. Kleinholz knows that Becker may be flirting with betrayal; Becker knows that Kleinholz knows—and only the King is unaware that Ezra knows, too.

Yet, what Kleinholz said made a clear, logical picture. Until the stockholders quieted down he could do nothing. No new pictures until these two were settled, until money was coming in.

"And don't think I don't know what a certain former

executive is trying to do: get us deeper into commitments, over our heads, just so he can promise the theater owners more product—a short cut to dealing himself back in. Fuck him! I'll use him. If he can help me get the picture in on budget . . . and without everybody killing each other over the boy. . . . I'll use my worst enemies . . . I've always been proud of that."

He gargled water from a cloth-encased bottle and spat it onto hissing stones. "My father used to have an expression, *mein sunim*. It means anything bad should happen only to my enemies. But what's funny is: that nice old man didn't *have* any enemies." He paused, bemused at the distant recollection of a man without enemies.

"Wait," Becker murmured, in ominous promise. "Just wait."

Kleinholz sighed. "How many minutes?"

"Fifteen."

"Finished."

For the last five minutes Ezra had been taking his breath in small shallow portions. He bent to find a white blob, the toweled handle of the door.

"Come and watch me cut on Monday," Kleinholz said. "I'm cutting some of that sex stuff, too—not just snakes." He murmured, hissed, "Sacrilege."

Information was still flowing. It was hard to leave. Ezra said, "What am *I*, Lothar: flat or round?" It was his try at a light exit. Kleinholz stood up and shed his towel. From somewhere in the gloom he found a cane and leaned, an incongruous parody of some Caesar, naked but invulnerable. He was tanned everywhere except for a fish-belly bowl between his bulging navel and the black hair below.

"You—you're as round as *him*." He prodded Becker with his cane. Becker mumbled, a jostled sleeping animal. "I never know *what* he's thinking. *He* never knows what he's thinking. Mysterious son-of-a-bitch. And I have to depend

on him. . . ." Kleinholz turned his attention back to Ezra.
"But you're *supposed* to be round. Publicity is a touchy
thing. The way our pictures look—the way we look—to the
whole world, to the stockholders, that's your stuff."

"You mean it's like writing fiction."

"That's a good one!" The distracted humorless tone said
the session was ended.

"*Ape!*"

The door was flung open. Ape appeared with a bucket of
water and flung it at the naked Kleinholz. Wearily Becker
rose. Ezra stumbled to the showers next door.

10

There were six miniature screens on the mass of equipment against the wall. Mitch Stone moved from one to the
other, manipulating images, stopping the film on one screen
long enough to bring another one to the point he wanted—
then held both while he ran the sound track to a desired
climactic point. On the far left-hand screen there played out
a scene of a young man and woman lying in the grass. They
were naked; they made love half visibly in the tall grass.
Simultaneously, on the next screen, a young man with a
wide smile, empty of front teeth, offered a rolled-up cigarette to the audience. As he winked, on the left-hand screen
the naked young woman raised her head as if suddenly
aware that her private love-making was only as private as
the nearest camera. There was a tiny moment of suspense:
then she grinned and returned to her joyful occupation. The
sound track punctuated the movement with a witty period.

Nick smiled vaguely, and Ezra was aware that he had
just seen an elegant bit of film cutting. Stone did not laugh

easily. He was clearly pleased. He'd invited them to watch him cut because he needed allies.

"I could choose a lot of scenes to throw against them making love. This way the kids will see the joke: being offered dope as if to say—This is what your parents think, turning on means going wild, screwing in public. They'll laugh and we'll have them." He continued pumping foot pedals and pressing console buttons. Helicopters dropped supplies on one screen while next door hundreds of people bathed in a lake. It was a scene at once apocalyptic and utopian.

"With the split screen you get away from the sentimental stuff about the Festival weekend. By setting up two scenes with different emotional tones you get irony. Like love and dope. And when I want to hit the audience in the gut, straight—I just sweep all the images together into one —big—"

The pictures on all the six screens were now identical: a scene of what one of Nick's publicity releases had called "The largest single peaceful gathering in any one place in the civilized world, ever." Skillfully, Mitch dropped the music entirely. All that could be heard were the crowd noises.

Next: a surprise. As tribute to the source of his editing skill, Stone fished a book out from a pile of tapes, and dropped it on the floor. It was *The Films of Sordino*, with a blurry photograph of Sordino on the cover. Ezra was dutifully surprised at Stone's admission of influence. Sordino's kind of film-making was finished. That was what Stone had told the old man to his face. But what surprised Ezra more was the photograph: without the scarf enfolding his neck Sordino seemed much younger, less vulnerable.

"It's terrific cutting," Nick said to Stone.

Ezra watched him puffing borrowed cigarette smoke past his sleepy eyelids. It was a curious statement. Ezra knew that Kleinholz would have much to say about sex and drugs on the screen. He allowed himself to be impressed at Nick Bohm's choosing sides, dangerously. For one pleasant moment, The Studio Ethic seemed to have broken down.

11

The pendulum swung. Now Kleinholz was cutting. His console had only three screens.

Joke: "I can't afford the fancy equipment we give Mitch Stone." He sat in his wheelchair this Monday morning, swiveling from point to point as he ran up the different sequences of film. Nick Bohm stood next to him, staring blankly. Kleinholz's cutting danced a different ballet than Stone's. He turned the images by a slow pedal, got exactly what he wanted, and for the most part ignored the music. His movements showed that he had a different film in mind than Stone, even given the same raw footage. The film was the music score, the Movieola was the piano keyboard. The rest was talent, ingenuity, will—all the familiar raw stuff of art—plus some unique practical matters duplicated in no other art.

Example: Kleinholz ran up the same film of the young nude lovers. It was not such an uncanny coincidence. Nudity, sex, these were heavy components; concern was natural. Pressing a button, Kleinholz brought the picture up larger then still larger—the over-all field diminished to a close-up of the girl's face. This left the wit intact in her discovery of being observed, but eliminated the lovely pink nipples, and the activity of the boy's hands on her body.

"Great," Kleinholz cried. Then: "Damn it. When she turns to the camera you can see her face too clearly."

"Too clearly for what?" Ezra asked.

"For her lawyer or her mother."

He pumped the field down again to the medium shot, then to the long shot and was back to Mitch Stone's version.

"See—her face is too blurry now for identification. I guess I'm stuck with them screwing. Ah—hold it." Turn, whiz, flip on the adjoining screen. A shot of cops moving into a field.

"Maybe that'll take the curse off it." He swiveled his head toward Nick. "What'd you think?"

"Mitch has a guy offering some pot to the audience next to kids making love."

"Ah-h-h-h, God, doesn't that figure? Well, what *do* you think?"

Nick thought, Nick mused. Nick did a superb imitation of Nick Bohm summoning up the courage to talk straight to the boss.

Then: "If you're going for the all-kid audience then Mitch is right. If not . . ."

He left the question theoretically in mid-air. Ezra, even though unskilled in such subtleties of corporate evasion, could see that Nick had danced his way through barbed wire, retreating all the way, while applying for a decoration for bravery under fire.

12

At the end of the broad esplanade stood an obelisk. It shone, mysterious with Latin inscriptions, in the bright sun.

"They call it the Foro Italico, now," Robinson said. "But look." The letters ran vertically spelling MUSSOLINI DUX. It dominated the open area. In the middle distance there spun out a chain of sports fields and a stadium, ringed with gigantic statutes of athletes in heroic poses. "The old name was the Foro Mussolini. The fake grandeur that was Rome, for a while."

The flies of the hot afternoon trailed and buzzed, vanished when they walked through shady patches of the field, then reappeared in the yellow heat. They walked, Robinson, Becker, and Ezra, over black and white mosaic tiles marked DUCE DUCE DUCE DUCE. . . . Groups of Italian tourists wandered among the distant statues. They called out to each other and posed for pictures in marble attitudes.

Ezra had been in Rome for a week; it could have been a year. He had drawn his new environment around him like a blanket; calendars and clocks meant as little as money spent in restaurants and hotels. Time and money were taken care of by the studio. Ezra had expected to see Robinson at once. He had rushed in response to his summons. But Robbie was scouting locations as part of his new responsibilities.

Ezra stayed away from Kim in the evenings. He busied himself with catching up on the details of the European operation; a small jungle of mismanagement and venality, going by first impressions.

As he put together the bits and pieces of new responsibilities and juggled new skills, Ezra felt himself preparing for something. It was an old sensation with him. Whenever a serious move of some kind was being prepared in his head, there was—for weeks or months before—a sense of interior furniture being shifted. He did not sleep well. His stomach, legs, hands, eyes: all were tense, waiting.

Finally, Robinson had returned to Rome and had summoned Ezra to the Foro Italico (né Mussolini).

"I never got to congratulate you on your new job," Ezra said.

"I'm about to earn my money. I've redone the complete

shooting schedule so that all Karol's scenes will be finished in a week. Then he'll be gone and the trouble goes with him. Damned if I know why nobody thought of that before."

"I don't think Sordino would want to think of it."

"If he's not gone, it's all going to blow up in our faces. Maurice keeps talking about taking the boy away to Ischia for a rest. Sordino says nothing—but God help us all. The boy may crack. Yesterday, setting fires. Tomorrow. . . ?"

Becker caught up with them. "Hey, kid. That's the way to go. Upside down with your mistress next to you." To Robinson he said, "Did you ask him yet?"

"I've been waiting in the hot sun for a week." Ezra said. "To find out what was so urgent that my presence was needed at once."

They paused before a great statue of a swimmer poised to dive, and waited in the shade before moving on. In that shaded pause Robbie began to outline still another Robinson Plan. He needed an additional weapon for leverage. Something that would differentiate his group from Kleinholz.

"There's the world of economics and the world of psychoeconomics. Movies are made largely of psychoeconomics: a blend of Keynes and Freud." With men like Robinson, theories go along with plans.

Robbie called up for Ezra long evenings of theoretical conversation in Washington. The core of the remembrance was a party McNamara gave for some visiting honcho from Germany. It was just about the time when both Ezra and Robinson had been getting—for the first time—sick enough of the escalation to talk about leaving. Neither one quite knew how fed up the other was—just a general sour feeling in the air. They were introduced to the German V.I.P. and proceeded to get drunk and turn on a little in a corner of the garden. Then they played a game.

"I remember that part," Ezra said. "We had to pick the

single most dangerous title or phrase of modern times. I
don't know how I remember that. Or you. We were both
stoned out of our skulls. It wasn't just us. A bunch of us
played."

"Right. First prize was a week in Chevy Chase. Second
prize was two weeks in Chevy Chase. Washington charades."

Becker watched them sullenly, an American tourist
observing two natives babble in a foreign tongue.

"The German gave us the idea," Ezra said. "The first vote
went to *Mein Kampf*, second one to Tomorrow, the World."

"Remember what we ended up with?"

"No."

"A sweet innocuous title everybody agreed was the most
dangerous phrase in the language: *The Engineering of Consent*."

"I forgot that part. The title of a book on public relations."

"By a nice old gentleman named Edward L. Bernays.
But the implications of the idea were immense. To engineer
consent is democracy's answer to force in a dictatorship."
Robinson's wide sweep of the hand included the neighbor-
ing playing fields where the Duce had once been celebrated.
"If you can arrange for people to agree to do what you
want, whether they really want to or not—whether they
know what's happening or not—think of it . . . politics . . .
marketing . . . but most of all psychoeconomics."

Becker broke in. "Will you tell him what we want, for
Christ's sake?"

Still mystified, Ezra said, "Whose consent do you want
me to engineer?"

"You are about to use those skills for which I engineered
your hiring in the first place," Robbie said. "A giant research
proposal that will change the world of marketing motion
pictures."

Becker dabbed at his sweating forehead with a surprisingly delicate motion. "You don't have to change a fucking thing," he said. "You just have to look like you're doing it."

"What?"

"Never mind." Robinson took charge again. "That will be discussed between you and me tonight over dinner at the Hostaria dell'Orso. In full view of the entire movie colony in Rome. Reverse English. With Becker we hide in Mussolini's Forum. But everybody knows you and I are a team. We dine in public. While Signor Becker here entertains Signor Rossi with some very special motion pictures."

"Umberto expects some kind of answer," Becker said darkly. He plucked at his shirt collar; the kind of man who could not bear the thought of being seen in a wilted shirt.

They strolled back toward the exit, along the Chirico-like plain, and passed over a bridge embellished with bas-reliefs of battle scenes and sarcophagi. On the other side, Becker suddenly pointed down at a mosaic beneath their feet. "What's that say?" he asked. Robinson translated: "Many enemies Much honor."

"Yeah," Becker said softly. "Yeah."

13

Hostaria dell'Orso. The Chasen's of Rome. Five serving people to every diner. And every other diner involved in one way or another with the turning of cameras. At the bar a surprise encounter. Nick Bohm is having a drink with Archer and Cody, a black journalist who sometimes did assignments for Nick.

Cody is dressed in a parody of Hip: high boots from the East, flowered shirt from California, the red bandanna around his forehead from Harlem via Jimi Hendrix.

"Hey, man, he said to Ezra. "Thanks for the gig."

"Gig?"

"I'm doing a tape interview on Sordino for the L.A. *Free Press*. Nick told me you dug the idea."

"Sure," Ezra said. "But do me one favor, Cody. With me, talk straight English."

"Oh." Cody laughed and said, "What I meant was: I appreciate the opportunity to explore the confluence of Sordino and *Festival* with its snakes and youth gods, as a situation that will tickle the imagination of young people who read the *Free Press*."

"That's more like it," Ezra said. "Have another drink on the studio."

Over the macaroni Bolognese, Ezra entertained Robbie with his description of the steam-room meeting with Kleinholz.

"You did yourself some good as a go-between with Stone and the old man," Robbie said.

"At least Kleinholz saw the picture at last. Got hold of it so he could make dupes. Now he and Stone are both editing —and the war will continue."

"How's the reptile research coming?"

"How'd you know about that?"

"Max Miranda, who sits at the right hand of the mighty. The Messenger of the Gods."

"That was Mercury."

"That's Max Miranda."

"I have a pilot study in the works: focus-group sessions that should give a pretty good cross section as to age, sex, and moviegoing habits."

"Okay, however that turns out, here's what I need: A research plan on a broad scale, that can actually predict the success or failure of a picture, based on selected screenings. Given that first prediction, we can then plan how much to spend on advertising and publicity, determine the right—

and least expensive—release pattern. And save the millions that go down the drain chasing bad or mediocre pictures every year. Do you know where I got the idea? From you."

He dredged up Ezra's aborted plan to utilize the predictive abilities of the TV networks' election computers.

"You were going to take that data and work out a plan for the Census Bureau, so they could know ahead of time the basic professional choices of students approaching college age."

"That was to help colleges plan curricula and staff—apply for grants in the right areas of study, and so forth."

"Right."

"But it was just a glimmer. And the whole project died when I left Washington. To turn that into your engineering of consent, that's another story."

"Ah—but a glimmer is all we need. Think about it. Explore. If I can present a plan to the stockholders—to the investment bankers who control some of the large blocks, too, a plan that looks as if it has the faintest chance of turning a crap-shoot art form into a cost-controllable business. . . ." Robbie raised his wine glass. "We will have conquered fear itself."

"But three weeks . . ."

"We are dealing with shadow as much as substance, here. After we win, if you can actually make the damned thing work, even better. But all we need is a reasonable facsimile."

The last table before leaving the dining room was occupied by a large party, draped with overdressed, beautiful women in evening clothes, and dapper dark men, one of whom turned out to be Jack Valenti. As if in a Fellini movie they were introduced to Fellini, Silvana Mangano, Dino De Laurentiis, and a blur of names and faces. Valenti smiled a Washington/Hollywood smile and introduced Robinson and Ezra as the Washington wonder boys come to save the

movie business. Everyone bustled, someone raised a glass in
an unintelligible toast; it was a pleasantly foolish moment.
Ezra heard a small click in his mind. Something in him
opted to enjoy the moment; to take pleasure instead of irony
from it. It was a very small click. But he noted it, carefully.

"This is 'Auf der Bruck,' " Karol says. His fingers make
brisk, secret passes at the little Sony machine on his lap.
Schubert pours out.

"Fischer-Dieskau," he adds. "My father's idol."

"Don't move," Kim says. She rubs at a smudge of yellow
paint. Like the turtle in Bel-Air, Karol stops moving at once.

From the corner, clicking sounds remind them that Nick
Bohm is with them, telephone and all.

"I heard him sing once in New York," Ezra says. "With
Leonard Bernstein accompanying."

Karol's utterly beautiful face, already soft with its almost feminine mouth and slightly slanted eyes, softens even
more.

"In Budapest, I heard him. I didn't sleep all night. I
knew that was what I should do. Sing like that. Sing Schubert, Mozart...."

"And did you study voice?"

"Since I was five. My father is a lawyer, but he always
wanted to sing opera."

Sun filters in from the skylight. Karol moves like a
dancer, but minimally, always within the boundaries Kim
has set up. He tells of his father's love of song, sings a fragment from Schubert in a small, sweet voice in counterpoint
to the Sony. He flashes smiles, he frowns in serious remembrance, he throws out rhetorical questions to Kim ("Do you
like music? Do you have an ear as well as an eye?"). Kim
murmurs affectionate nonsense while she paints.

Giannini materializes and hands Ezra a portfolio of papers: advertising and publicity budgets for new King films

in twenty European cities. Nick Bohm is talking to Max in Hollywood.

"The Queen," Nick is saying, improbably. "The Queen of England, that's who. . . ." And goes on about the Royal showing that Becker has arranged as the world premiere of *The Lion's Farewell.*

"Becker and the Queen," Ezra murmurs. A sly look passes from Karol to him. Kim calls out, "Rest." Karol does a smooth imitation of Becker, invisible cigar in mouth, curtseying to an invisible queen. The effect is brilliant: he becomes stouter, older, ineffably vulgar, instantly Beckerian.

But it is also a disturbingly androgynous performance. Ezra thinks: If this is how he behaves to Sordino and Maurice, he must be tempting them beyond their strength. Then, in a moment of pure Viennese sunshine there in the Roman studio, he turns from his performance to sing a natural and gently turned phrase from another Schubert song. All lights and darks, his voice trails off gently, in a sad fall. Ezra asks him how old he is. "Sixteen," the boy replies.

"Are you glad to be in the film?"

A shadowed look places the answer in doubt even before it is given. "Oh, yes," he says. But it is a public answer. Doubtless, if Kim were to ask it, privately, the answer would be more complex. But his spirit is still occupied by the sounds that flow from the Sony. He speaks and sings— speaks of Christa Ludwig, Aksel Schiøtz, Elisabeth Schumann, Irmgard Seefried . . . a pantheon of European song. Ezra has read all of the interviews the publicity staff had arranged for Karol, complete with all the classically stupid questions. What movie star do you like best? What part would you have liked to play most? The true answer was now clear. Characteristically, too, gender was irrelevant. Eisabeth Schumann, Aksel Schiøtz . . . any golden throat would serve. All a far cry from the silver screen.

Kim decides that it is too much and clears the studio.

Ezra and Nick have a drink at Doney's: their first private moment in a while. Since the last one, a change in who and what they are in relation to each other and to the studio has become possible. Ezra feels the difference as they speak— and wonders at what Nick feels. But, ah, what Nick feels— that morass is not to be attempted so easily. Easier, right then, to get at what Nick knows.

Nick says, "Michael Maurice may get his 'sir' after all."

"How come?"

"The Royal premiere. If they go through with it, there's a good chance. I've seen tougher things come off."

Years of manipulation speak. Knighthoods are only extra, elegant steps in the Publicity Dance.

"The great Snake War is on," Nick continues. "Max says they're everywhere. One in the bathroom on the main floor of the administration building. One in Becker's office. I guess they didn't know Becker was over here."

"*Real* snakes?"

"Rattlers," Max says. "Without fangs or venom."

"That's nice of Mitch."

"Kleinholz is afraid to go home. He's staying at a hotel in Palm Springs and flies in to the studio by helicopter every morning."

"I'll bet he's still cutting the picture his way."

"You're getting to know the man."

"I think so."

"Listen, I thought I knew Mitch Stone. But *snakes*, Jesus! Not on film—in real life."

Ezra thinks, suddenly, what if he were to put it bluntly?

"Who will you go with if it comes to a split?"

No thunder or lightning at the speaking of the unspeakable. Just a small, weary cloud over the forehead and: "Oh God, Ezra, I've seen them come and go—the big planners, the buyers, the sellers. I was here fifteen years ago when National Theaters bought in and then sold out." As if by an effort of will, Nick's face turns in on itself, grows older in an instant, illustrating the world-weary tone. "I'll stick with the studio, however things go." And orders another Campari and soda. He seems to think he has answered Ezra's question and turns to more practical matters.

"The Royal Equerry wants some film on the kid and Sordino—just for an idea of the picture's style. So I'm getting the promo film back from the States. The only trouble is, he has to see it in two days. You don't keep the Queen waiting."

"You can get it in two days."

"It takes a week sometimes, to get film out of customs. And Italian customs!"

In the dazzle of the afternoon Roman sun, Nick tells his little scheme—such a small scheme among the larger ones casting shadows all around them. His daughter, Jenny, is bringing the can of film in her luggage disguised as home movies, should any one ask. No one searches American teenagers for contraband film; just pot and pills.

Jenny is restless (*You, who slowly leak/From the heart of the world,* her poem had begun), and Nick will be able to keep an eye on her in Rome.

Beneath the scheme and the parental concern, Ezra is listening to learn what Nick has actually told him. Will he go with Robinson, with Becker, with Kleinholz? *I'll stick with the studio, whichever way it goes.* A superb objectification of the studio—placing it above and beyond individuals.

14

No one knew, afterward, whose idea it was to go to Hadrian's Villa in the middle of the night. No one knew if you could get in or not—but it was a hot and beautiful night. On the way into the lobby they encountered Cody, who thought it was a great idea—and Max Miranda, just in from Los Angeles, vague from lack of sleep, but convinced that anything Ezra wanted to do was a good idea. The group grew, willy-nilly; someone went for more wine. Giannini was sent for, not because he was wanted but because his driver was essential to the plan.

Karol was phoned in his room and was delighted. Nick Bohm had gone to the airport to meet his daughter carrying her contraband film. Becker was available. Giannini was desperate to go back to sleep. It settled down to Ezra, Kim, Cody, Becker, Max, Karol, and the Spy Driver.

15

The cypresses, Cody said, had been planted only two hundred years ago and were not to be considered authentic. He was lecturing to the variously drunken and sober party. Sobriety was under attack. Several cold bottles of Verdicchio circulated as the single file moved up the path and toward the first beautifully decorated wall.

"It is no accident that this group should visit this particular villa."

"Tell 'em kid," Becker muttered.

With Mr. Becker's encouragement, Cody proceeds. "Old Hadrian was a man of taste and refinement and he bought the land on which we stand with his wife's money. Observe the sources of my analogy. Artistic judgment combined with the judicious use of other people's money, the mixture seasoned with a pinch of nepotism: the ideal movie executive."

Karol walked among the strange shapes of ruins, perfect

head lowered, listening to something Kim was saying. His eyes floated along the waters of the long pools; a bemused Narcissus.

Becker called out to Ezra, "Hey, listen to the Schvartzer, he's good!" His cigar gleamed in swift arc under colossal cypresses. To Ezra's drunken eyes it was like some cipher inscribed on the night air. The smallest things seemed charged with meaning.

"Even more," Cody continued. "Hadrian built all this as a gigantic memory machine—a revisiting, a re-creating of the places he'd loved and sometimes conquered in his travels, in his youth. An idea worthy of a Louis B. Mayer."

Max took Ezra's arm. They mounted stone steps. "What does he know about Mayer? I knew him; I did special jobs for him. The man was a giant."

You shouldn't have come along," Ezra said. "You must be exhausted."

"Yeah—that over-the-pole flight is murder." He climbed exuberantly over random rubble. They passed sheared-off columns, bits and pieces of mosaic, here and there a tall, unbroken column straight and unreal in the moonlight.

"Hey, Cody," Becker was uncorking another bottle of Verdicchio. "Didn't he hate the Jews, Hadrian?"

"Jews and Christians both," Cody replied. "He loved the Greeks, mainly. Jews and Christians were hung up on morals—Hadrian was looking for beauty. And the Greeks had it." From up ahead the sounds of a Schubert song underscored the echoing conversation. It stopped abruptly and was replaced by the sound of Karol's Sony being rewound.

"The villa was a kind of publicity program for the ideas of his youth. We here should all understand about publicity." Cody had a knack for turning his words against the people he talked to. Ezra found it irritating. He searched among the shadows for Kim, but couldn't find her. A car jarred to a stop somewhere nearby; a door slammed. Karol's little music machine filled the ensuing silence with liquid notes from a song Ezra had never heard before; it sounded vaguely like Tchaikovsky—sweet, surreal under the hazy black sky, under the amber flow of wine. Then he saw her: she had climbed higher than the others, was climbing still higher on the ruined wall flanking and looming above the long rectangular pool—the Stoa Poikile, fish pond, centuries without fish. Ezra caught her and turned her around to face him. There was enough moonlight in the air for him to see that her face was flushed. One of the green, elongated bottles of wine sat securely between two rocks at her feet.

"Did you know that my daddy drank wine all the time. And quoted Whitman when under the influence?"

"I knew your father drank. I didn't know about the Whitman."

"In spite of the good gray poet being on the wrong side in the Civil War, he was a big man in my house. Did you know that we were going to get so deeply into all that?" She gestured below.

A car had arrived—some kind of European station wagon that Ezra could not identify—from which descended Michael Maurice and Sordino. The old director seemed to be lingering, as if he had no destination; had merely found himself by chance at Hadrian's Villa at 11 p.m. Michael Maurice, however, lost no time in finding Karol. Something was in the air. Something that made Ezra want to stay where he was—above it all with Kim.

"Nobody could predict it would get so wild," he said.

"And nobody could predict I'd like him so much. Him and his Schubert lieder. Robbie asked me if I could have the painting finished by the end of this week."

"Can you?"

"Maybe. Why is it so important?"

Ezra pointed below. "Can't you guess." He reached down for the wine bottle.

"You're drinking a bit." Kim said. She swayed, eyes closed.

"Only a bit, only tonight. I've got a lot on my mind."

"Oh, don't I know *that*? Much, much on your mind. You're passing through something and something is passing through you. I can see light and energy coming out of you, right here in the dark."

Ezra tipped the curved wine bottle back and finished it off. She reached for it and shook it sadly, then investigated the bottom of the bottle, finding it not quite dry.

"I have to explain to you," she said. "About my vision back there in your house."

"Oh, no. You do not have to explain that at all."

"It wasn't fair, and I do have to tell it. Because my vision has expanded. I woke up one night last week, and I had the big Whitman vision of what I was talking about. You know —'I hear America singing, the varied carols I hear.' "

It was funny hearing Whitman in her increasingly Southern diction. "Ah hear...."

"And ah am caught up in it, and the whole country is caught up in it, and ah am drunk enough to present it to you in its beautiful wholeness. Slightly drunk but whole." A hand brushed Ezra's cheek: tender, uncharacteristic. "Heah me, Ezra, it's not only you and Robinson. It's all these carefully trained composers studying their Gregorian chants and their Brahms and twelve-tone rows and then writing music for *Tom and Jerry* cartoons ... or imitation Mahler climaxes for imitation love scenes ... the painters I know who studied Titian and the Bauhaus and then do layout designs for magazine spreads featuring Ann-Margret. That's why ah hear America *not* singing. It's a damn pity, that's all, a damn pity.... And ah'm talking to you because you're in it, now, aren't you? It's happened, whatever was going to happen, isn't that right, Ezra? She stood, poised on the wall, one arm raised in drunken benediction, forgetting that it was

Italy not America over which she waved her disappointed hand; a woman/Whitman who had not heard the song she wished to hear. Then she was leaning against the rock wall, half sitting, half-lying, and asleep.

Ezra walked down a few steps standing in the wine-sway of the reddish moonlight. Below him he saw Sordino, scarf-swathed, gleaming next to Cody's blackness and Becker's whiteness and Michael Maurice's insistent presence. Kim was right. She had somehow heard that tiny click in his mind at the Hostaria dell'Orso, that final click that said he was in it all the way. There would no longer be a question of what he wanted or what he would do. He would map his plans—like the schemers all around him—and win or lose his battles. He would try to win and to stay victorious. And if someone asked him—as he had asked Nick—who he was with in case of showdown, *he* would be prepared.

The third bottle of wine precipitated the decision; but he doubted if it was the cause. The time was right; events were pressing; and choices would have had to be made swiftly about many things. It would be so much easier to make each individual decision, knowing that what he wanted, for as long as it might last, and for whatever it might bring him in the way of money and control over his own destiny, was: Power. No great actual power, to be sure. A papier-mâché Hadrian with limousines and jobs and money at his disposal—not actual lives or legions. Still, he felt it rush in his blood with pleasure. He would play with it, would enjoy it, would build a great new office in the studio tradition, as soon as he had Nick Bohm's job . . . would fire in great blood baths and hire in great magnanimity. . . . Max would do "special jobs" for him—with all their unstated promise of sensuality and power.

He was drunk with single-mindedness. There were only two kinds of people in the world. Those with single-souls and those with double-souls. For that one instant it all seemed perfectly clear. The single-souls, like Kim, were the blessed ones. The double-souls, like himself, were damned. (Endlessly circling some eternal airport in some eternal New York/Boston, New York/Washington Shuttle.) More than anything else at that moment, he wanted to be allowed into the company of the single-souled, the directed, the ruthless. He would do whatever had to be done to force his way in. Illusory or real: market research plans, psychoeconomics, stock-market struggles, nothing was too ambitious for his consideration. He would sweep Kleinholz from his wheelchair of power and proceed to tape and control the world.

From the moonlit pit below there drifted the sounds of a Schumann song. A stiff and sober Michael Maurice spoke under it, his hand on Karol's shoulder. A few steps away Sordino stood and watched, his face in shadow.

Ezra could not make out precisely who was pushing whom, but suddenly there was a certain amount of scuffling going on. Then the sound of Karol's machine was turned up into a distorted blare. A beat later an arm was flung up, then down; the sound stopped.

The tumult woke Kim. She jumped up and seemed, even in her groggy state, to understand what was going on. Ezra heard her mutter, "Oh God, what are they doing to him. . . ."

There was the sound of raised voices and of Kim's feet scrabbling in the stones as she started to run and then to fall. Ezra had never moved so swiftly in his life. He was reaching out to grab Kim just before he was under her. Even so, she twisted her leg and fell before he could get proper hold of her. He was able to stop her from tumbling down the steep hill into the fish pond, or onto some of the great boulders that they had passed on the way up.

He got her down to the side of the fish pond himself and

enlisted Max's aid. Between them they moved her toward
the entrance, beyond which the limousine was parked. At
the entrance, Sordino was holding forth in Italian, angrily,
to a sullen Michael Maurice. Karol stood nearby, that perfect face wet with tears. When he saw Kim he threw himself
at her, ignoring her disability. She moaned: the pain of her
ankle and her concern. "Hey," she murmured. "Hey, all
right, honey, hey."

It was quite clear that everyone was suddenly sober.
Max muttered, "We're trying to make him a knight—and he
acts like a fucking queen."

The Spy Driver started the car and followed Sordino's
limousine out, past the dark pond, past the vague ruins,
finally picking up speed beneath the long alley of stiff,
formal cypresses. Karol was in the other car. Ezra had been
unable to prevent that.

"Worse," Becker murmured from the front seat. "It's
going to get worse before it gets worse."

Cody closed his eyes and slept. Kim, too, slept, the
heavy-breathing sleep of fatigue and wine. Becker kept his
counsel for the moment. The Spy Driver drove and listened
to the silence.

Ezra planned.

16

"You remember, Marks?" Sordino smiled at Ezra as if
they were old friends having breakfast. The public embarrassment of the evening before had brought them a little
closer, had modified the director's usual austerity. "You remember what I said to you about the sexual life?"

"That it doesn't work."

Sordino shifted awkwardly in his chair. "I had not thought to demonstrate the truth of it so quickly," he said. Behind the makeshift table on which bitter Italian coffee and *brioches* and jams were spread out, a sweating crew struggled to move a crane into place. It was 5:30 a.m. A man in dungarees and a T shirt squirted smoke from a canister around them until Sordino waved him away. He explained that the morning's scene—Karol's final one—took place on a winter evening. The smoke was a winter effect. Ezra must forgive the bad odor it made.

"How's the picture going? On schedule?" Ezra asked.

"You must ask Robinson. He is the producer. I concern myself only scene by scene."

"The boy . . . ?"

"Magnificent! A great success. If only—" The old man gazed out at the deserted street, pocked by studio cars and limousines and the wardrobe trailers. The heavy-lidded eyes turned back. Ezra could see he was worried about how far to go.

The air was close and already hot. Ezra could hear himself breathe. All the while, waiting for Sordino to complete his thought, spreading strawberry jam, he wondered why Sordino had asked him to breakfast. (He wondered, too, how Kim's foot was and if Nick had his promotion film and if he could safely get Karol alone to convince him to leave at once—without bringing in his secret weapon. He had a lot to wonder about.)

"Have you ever read our Italian poet, Leopardi?"

"Shelley was my poet."

"Still you understand the self-destructive element in romantic love."

"Yes."

"And you know how difficult it is for Michael."

"What I know is: Karol has to leave as soon as possible."

Sordino smiled. He was patient. "I was hoping," he said,

"that you could do whatever it is that you have to do—and still save whatever part of you that loves the poetry of Shelley."

On impulse Ezra said, "You've been in this business for many years. Do you have any advice as to how to do that?"

He did. Sordino told of his mother. Remote, difficult, queenly, she ruled over the Sordino family—Communists, anarchists, dukes and duchesses—as an absolute monarch. A loving and powerful woman, she was a natural target when the Nazis came to Italy, and to Naples, where the Sordinos had been aristocracy for centuries. Shrewd and practical, she knew that coexistence was her only choice. Yet there was some part of her she had to save. It came down to something as simple as: she would not shake hands with a Nazi. They could confiscate her lands, occupy her house, drink her wines, and drain her money. All that was involuntary. Shaking hands was a voluntary acceptance of the unacceptable.

"So," Sordino said, "one morning she rose early, before the rest of the family, took a hammer, and broke her right arm in two places."

"My God...."

"Yes—the gesture was extraordinary. And in my mind it is always that second blow that has the heroism. One break would heal quickly enough, perhaps. Two—it lasted until the Allied Armies arrived. She never had to shake hands with a German until she died at the age of ninety-six. She died quietly in her own bed. That was before they took you to hospitals and tied you to a bed with tubes pushed into every possible place...." Irritably he pulled at his scarf and changed the subject. "It is too bad you could not have known Michael fifteen years ago."

"I saw his movies, then."

"He was gentle and beautiful—*dolce*."

In the ensuing pause the hot, windless morning seemed

to congeal around them: sounds floated and finally descended—men calling to each other in an Italian mixture of impatience and gentleness.

"I do not think he means the young man any harm," Sordino said. "He believes he is caught up in a passion—*gigantesca*—"

"And all poor Karol wants is to sing Schubert lieder."

"Everybody wants something very much. Your friend Robinson—what he wants is to do another picture with me. Balzac's *Lost Illusions*. With the boy to play the young writer, Lucien de Rubempré."

"Will you do it?"

"Tell me," Sordino did not even field the question; he merely let it slide away. "Will *Festival* be a great success?"

"If we ever get a final cut."

"Tell Mitch Stone I would like to see the film. In spite of everything." He was talking around the reason for the breakfast. Ezra broke into that vagueness and said, "Is there anything I can do to help you, Signor Sordino?"

Sordino stretched out his hands immediately, not imploring, simply in a gesture of frankness. The hands looked older than the man; without the vitality that informed the crags of cheeks and brow, they seemed closer to death.

"Yes," he said. "I turn to you to be of help to Michael. Do not punish him for his behavior with the boy."

"I don't punish . . ." Ezra began, but the hands waved him into silence.

"If there is a chance for a knighthood—I want Michael to have that chance."

"We're trying—Nick told me yesterday. . . ."

"About the promotion film for the Queen's staff?"

"Yes."

"You have not heard?"

"What?"

Ezra was probably the last film person in Rome to know.

Nick's daughter had arrived, as per plan, with the can of film in her luggage. They made it past customs into the city, into the hotel, opened the can, and out slithered a greeting card from Mitch Stone: a baby rattlesnake presently residing at the Rome Zoological Society.

"So you see, other measures will have to be taken on Michael's behalf."

"The poor girl," Ezra said.

Sordino shrugged. He said, "Perhaps you will send Nick to London with some film I will give you, to show Michael's performance—to achieve, perhaps, the Royal premiere, in time?" Ezra was more startled than at the snake story. Send Nick to London, to anywhere?

"I can't send Nick anywhere."

The look from Sordino made clear how much Ezra could do that he would not admit to. Paranoia, negative and positive, set in at once. Perhaps Robinson had given the impression that Ezra was taking over from Nick: that Kleinholz's distant promise was a reality.

The expectant look on Sordino's face, the upturn of pressure on the broad brow, the widening of the shrewd eyes; he could not tell what it was that pushed him, at the last, but he spoke with an easy confidence, "I'll do everything I can. You can count on me."

If words and their tone meant anything, he had taken command. Sordino leaned back in his chair and dropped his nervous hands from his scarf. "*Va bene,*" he said. And told Ezra of the land he owned in Sicily and that he and Nick and Karol must be his guests when all this was over. They would see the Greek ruins that were not far from his family's house; Ezra had never seen such reds and browns in the earth and trees and rocks. Sordino's smile had some vitality now, his movements an energy that had been missing; an authority, a confidence that was put into use as Michael Maurice and his entourage approached the sidewalk set.

Ezra had witnessed a moment of felicity; a backward glance and a plea for clemency by an old lover. The lights blasted on and off, experimentally, and in the inching of chaos toward order he saw Nick Bohm approaching, a curl of gray hair over one eye, squinting and shimmering in the yellow light.

17

"I spent an awful lot of my life in hotel rooms," Max Miranda said. He leaned back on the sofa, absorbed by it like a pudgy doll in an artificial setting. He was trying to appear relaxed. That lasted about thirty seconds. Then, more typically, he perched himself on the edge of a cushion. "I'm sorry it's so late," he said.

It was 1 a.m. Ezra was tired, and Max must have read his eyes correctly. Max had made a career of reading the eyes of his superiors.

"I have an early date, so this is the only time I've got. It's all right. Are you enjoying Rome?" Ezra said.

Max shrugged that off. "It's all the same to me, boss. I got a job to do. I don't know from places, cities."

So much for the capitals of the world. A thick silence filled the room. Behind the round cheeks, the chewing pale lips, the squinting eyes, some inarticulate suffering was taking place.

Ezra spoke first, out of mercy. "What's up, Max?"

Max pounded his knee; sudden violence in the quiet room. "I can make it with you." He repeated, "With *you*," as if Ezra might have mistaken whom he had in mind.

"Make it ... ?"

"It's my job, it's my life."

"Yes?"

"I'd never steer you wrong."

"I'm sure of that."

As if reassured by this arcane exchange, Max relaxed enough to allow himself a smile. If smiles could be dark, it was a dark smile.

"I checked you out," he said. "I made a few phone calls and I found out."

Max, the bearer of tidings, was about to reveal the past Ezra to the present Ezra.

"You take care of yourself pretty good in the clinches. I heard."

It was good to know one had been formidable, but hard to hear of it without laughing. With a delicate *amour-propre* like Max, you didn't laugh. "But what do you mean, you can make it with me?"

Astonishment! "I've been with the studio all my life. Well, first with Metro and I went back and forth to Goldwyn in the Fifties, but mostly all my life. If you're going to be the man—then I can promise you absolute loyalty. If you're the man, I'm *your* man!"

Ezra turned away in embarrassment. A sudden shrewdness gripped Max's discourse. "I know, I know, a man like you takes loyalty for granted. But I also *know*! Not slick, like Nick, but I *know*! I told Kleinholz fifteen years ago he should've put everything he could spare into a record company and a TV operation. He didn't listen. So he did—too little and too late—and he tells me, 'Max, you know you were right. Warner's has the music money and Universal has the TV and we're just making movies for people who don't want to go out to the movies any more.' " Max paused to wipe his forehead with a monogrammed handkerchief.

Ezra allowed the silence, not quite knowing what was being offered outside of a short, plump bundle of nerves, loyalty, and experience.

"If you'll only let me, I can show you a lot."

"Everything's up in the air, but I'm still working for Nick."

"Example," Max rushed on. "The European market. Over sixty per cent of the gross comes from over here. I know everybody, I could take you. We have fantastic people —an army all over Europe."

The click came again. And with it a sense of pleasure. Who could refuse command of an army?

"Okay," Ezra said. "Don't plan on going back to L.A. just yet. Stay loose, and I'll let you know what the next step is. Don't say a word to anybody. Good night, Max."

When he was alone, Ezra thought: If we are to be defined by what others say or think of us . . . What was he? A Washington wonder boy come to save the movie business (*pace* Jack Valenti), a man who takes pretty good care of himself in the clinches (what forgotten aggressions were in the memory of Max's informant?). He searched for a moment for some incident of spectacular toughness, of ruthlessness. Whether he was innocent or not, his memory was. For the moment, he was content to be a character in the imagination of Max Miranda. It gave aesthetic pleasure.

It might even have practical value.

18

"It's a perfect time to be laid up in bed," Kim said.

"You're just avoiding guilt at getting falling-down drunk."

"Karol is shooting, so he can't sit for me, anyway. And I can draw and draw. Besides, I just slipped."

"No pain?"

"The swelling's down. *Il dottore* says I can walk on it as soon as it doesn't hurt."

"I could have told you that. My God, how many sketches are you doing?"

"Thousands. He's a wonderful subject. Nick says they're going to do a book of them to promote the film."

"Oh, has Nick been up here?"

"Here" was a great bed in the middle of a bedroom swamped with pieces of paper: finished and unfinished drawings of Karol. The almost completed painting had been brought into the room and was leaning against a mirror facing the bed. Kim lay in a welter of drawings, drawing still more on a large pad, wearing a pink robe and an Ace bandage on her injured ankle.

"Don't be jealous. Successful men have no time for jealousy."

"I'm not successful yet. Everything's still in question. First, I've got to organize some very fancy research and change the way movies have been tested for decades."

"Oh . . . ?"

"Is that scientific stuff all a mystery to you artists?"

"I'll tell you what mystifies me most. Nick, Nick, what makes him tick?"

"I thought you saw him clearly. Doing what he was born to do—that old publicity magic. Not like the the rest of we technocrats of the world, buying and selling what should only be taught or given."

She carefully ignored the reference.

"He's like wind," she said. "He's there but not there; he moves with style but no purpose—and afterward you see there was purpose—but you don't know if he knew it then or if it developed as he moved or if style *is* purpose in his territory."

"Listen," he said. "My visit is not without purpose. Not purely a sick-room call." Her supine position in the mass of papers and tangled sheets gave the remark a passing sexual tension. If there would ever be a moment to reopen that issue, this was not it. Ezra added, quickly, "I have a favor to ask you."

"Ask."

"Everybody wants Karol to leave before the weekend."

"Not quite everybody."

"Will you help? Karol will do anything you say."

"I don't know about that. But . . ."

She leaned toward him. "I don't want him to have any trouble. And these people can be only ugly trouble."

"Then you'll see him out of here?"

"Yes—the poor child." She picked up a few drawings and said, "I don't think Sordino has anything to do with this, you know."

"No," he said. "He's in love with the image of a young English actor he loved some years ago. The difference between that and the present reality is killing him."

"Where are you going?"

"Lunch with Nick Bohm."

Slyly, she said, "How can you lunch with a cloud?"

19

It is a different Nick who orders lunch at the Piazza Navona. He begins cordially enough by telling Ezra about this most lovely of all Roman piazzas. Ezra learns that it was once under water in the summers, hence the name, Navona, of the Navy. The tourism lasts only a few minutes. Then, the usually vague Nick Bohm begins to spread a concrete sense of rage.

"You heard about Mitch Stone and the trick he pulled on my kid?"

Ezra had heard.

"He'll get what's coming to him for that. Son-of-a-bitch with his snakes. And that miserable little cockteaser ..."

It took a moment before Ezra realized he meant Karol. In the professional conciliatory tone that came naturally to him—Robbie had once called him the Henry Clay of government—Ezra suggested that Nick was only being defensive about his friend Sordino.

"Karol's just an inexperienced kid. It's Michael Maurice who's spreading pain around—on the old man and everyone else."

Nick stared over Ezra's shoulder, down at the floor, everywhere except into his eyes, as the conversation turned to publicity matters. Nick had apparently spoken to Sordino. He raised the question of someone being sent to London with sample film for the Royal Equerry.

"I know what Sordino asked you to do. To send me—and I know there's a lot of shifting around going on." With a great effort, he made eye contact with Ezra. "You don't send me anywhere."

"You'll notice I didn't try."

Nick scored one. He pressed further. "And I want you to head back to L.A. tomorrow. Get moving on the record promotion for *Festival*—just in case we should ever have a picture to release."

"No," Ezra said. "I've been thinking. If we can manage to get *Festival* shown at Cannes, and if it does well, Becker's going to want to release it in key cities, fast. Pick up revenue. To look good for the company meeting. I'm taking Max with me for a little whirlwind trip: Paris, London, maybe Frankfurt."

Nick Bohm shifted his chair back from the table; glasses tilted, a few drops of wine spilled. Ezra waited. If Bohm's next words were in the form of a question it meant Ezra had won this skirmish. If a statement ...

188

"How about taking care of that snake-research job you started?" Nick asked.

"That's launched. I'll get the first flash report today or tomorrow from this fellow, Marcus, in New York."

"Christ," Nick said, "It'll be good to get back to doing twenty or thirty pictures a year, instead of being bogged down in these two. Three or four more weeks—and we can get moving again."

Tacitly, it was settled. Neither would send the other anywhere with marching or operating orders—at least until after the company meeting. Like competitive officers in the same army, facing a battle, their rank would not be finally determined until one or the other fell in action.

20

It was too early to call the studio. L.A. was nine hours earlier than Rome time. Instead, Ezra called Marcus, the research man in New York, to see if there were any flash results regarding snakes on film, to report to the Old King.

When deciphered, the results implied that snakes on film had a negative effect on over 50 per cent of the people interviewed. That could be bad news if Ezra was to solidify his position as peacemaker between Stone and Kleinholz. By careful questioning of the figures, however, he managed to find a slight skewing in favor of youth who did *not* react negatively. He then found some figures proving that older people had less "want-to-see," that is less interest in *Festival* as a future moviegoing possibility, than people under thirty. Thus, a case *could* be made to show that the dislike for snakes-on-film involved only people who would probably *not* be potential ticket-buyers. It was specious, since no one could calculate the effect of good reviews and word of mouth on people over thirty, but it gave him enough ammunition for his call to Kleinholz.

"Shit!"

"No, Lothar: facts."

"Shit. I don't believe in research."

"Stockholders do." The mention of stockholders gave Kleinholz transatlantic pause. Ezra drove on. "I'll have all the data worked up for you when I get back. I'm stopping off in Paris and London to set up publicity on *Festival.*" Ezra wondered why Kleinholz did not pick up the fact that he was improvising a role, inventing himself and his job on the spot.

But all that came back at him over the phone was a quick series of questions: About holding the budget down on the picture, about how the dailies looked. And, heaviest question of all: Was the kid making more trouble? By now, such questions were easy for Ezra to field. He disposed of them with the authority of a man who knows he is inventing himself; with the power of belief any creator has in his own creation.

21

It took Ezra a half-hour rummaging in the mess of memory until he found the name of the man he wanted: Jack Sydell, from Amherst. Cynical, charming, stuffed with scientific honors by the time he was twenty-four. He hated statistics and research, hated sociology (that paradiscipline, as he called it), and had become famous and successful by renting them out to government and business. Jack Sydell slept with computers and was just the man who would give

Ezra a pseudo-plan to show, if the real plan could not be delivered in time.

Sydell did not seem surprised to hear from Ezra via the transatlantic telephone.

"The CBS computers are the big boys," he murmured, as if he was in a faculty committee meeting, discussing tenure for a $12,000-a-year professor. "I'm not sure it could apply to a business with *your* variables. . . . But it's worth a try. More than that—my instinct tells me you can do something. What you really want is a prediction as to whether an imaginary person will go to see a certain film, based on demographics, geographics, and psychographics—in relation to a given set of data . . . in this case, story line, stars, et cetera. It will cost a fortune—to set up a control group the size you need. . . ."

"But compared to the cost of one single film that dies— say three million dollars—it's nothing," Ezra said.

The voice of academic reason came across the wires: "For three million dollars, Marks, we can set up a control group that will control the world. As a matter of fact, ten per cent of that will do it."

It was arranged to get a preliminary report in ten days.

Ezra called Max at Giannini's office.

"What's the name of that young man in the department —horn-rimmed glasses, bright. . . . He made some remarks once about how there should be a better way to test pictures than the old ways. He mentioned computers . . . had some training in them."

"One of *our* guys?"

"We had a meeting right after I joined the company. Everybody was 'yessing' the hell out of me except him. He was quiet except when he told me I was wrong about something."

"Oh, *him*! That's Joe Centilever. A trainee."

"That's the one. Have him call me as soon as you can."

On he went, pressed and pleased. When the call came, he told Centilever how his casual remark had never left his mind; he told him how Kleinholz, Nick Bohm, and he, Ezra, were all counting on him to help save the studio. (Having noticed "save the studio" was the operative phrase; and realizing he'd need the invocation of more powerful names than his own.) He sketched out what he needed and told Centilever to call Sydell in Amherst, told him to live with Sydell for the next ten days if necessary, but to get that report. Centilever was grateful and excited. He would bird-dog the project; Ezra could count on him.

When he hung up, Ezra's shirt was soaking wet in spite of the excellent air conditioning provided by the Excelsior.

As if to test his newfound persuasiveness, he put in a call to Mitch Stone, left a message, doubting that he would call back, changed his soaking clothes, and packed a bag. He tried to get Robbie, but he was at the location shooting. Just as Ezra was leaving the room, the phone rang. It was a sullen Mitch Stone, nervous at the war with the studio, apprehensive about the Cannes Festival. Ezra offered his services. He could, he stated (part of him watching in amazement), use his influence with Sordino to have him persuade the Cannes officials to exhibit *Festival*—with or without Kleinholz's approval or final cut. Mitch Stone was either cautiously interested or stoned—or both. Ezra left it for Mitch to think over. They would speak again in a few days, when he would be in L.A. Could it be, he wondered, that Mitch Stone wanted to be rich as well as authentic?

The strategy, in any case, would be: to play off the imaginary influence on Michael Maurice's career, expressed by Sordino at breakfast, against the imaginary influence with Sordino he had just claimed to Stone. It was all a lovely Roman festival of the imagination. It might even come true. Ezra felt as a stockbroker must feel when he buys and sells a stock he's never actually seen, paid for, verbally, with a promise of money to follow, mentally banking the imaginary difference as profit. He remembered reading somewhere: "everything begins in mystique and ends in politics."

22

The face of the boy appeared on the screen, loomed larger, moved forward as the camera moved in on it. It was a presence brooding over Robinson and Ezra as they sat whispering in the screening room, saying good-by, watching the first dailies flown back from London, where they were developed each day.

"How's it coming?

"It's begun. I'll let you know more after I get back to New York."

"When you get to New York, go to the Warwick Hotel, Room 1407."

"What's there?"

"The war room."

Karol was playing a love scene adolescent-style, with a young girl, while Michael Maurice hovered at the periphery. Sordino had cut in some dummy music from a Schumann symphony behind the sce e, for mood.

"Beautiful," Robinson said. "Don't be thrown by the war. It's no stranger than the peace. I'm glad you've been here. I need all the friendship and sanity I can get these days."

The brooding face was a stunning presence in the room. The high cheekbones, the slowly opening, softly closing eyes dominated the screen; the mood was intense. The smoky winter of 1912, the embroidered tablecloths in the dining room of the Albergo Appia, the children in linen and

lace, the gentlemen in evening dress, the distant sounds of
the trio playing in the lobby. Over it all that head with the
white bloom of fine marble, etched over with serious brows,
was poised like a strange flower in exquisite sensibility: it
was the loveliness that exists in a young human being just
before the moment it finally chooses its own sexuality. Sordino had made this magic as simply as all great things are
made; as if by one seamless action of his hands. The boy was
his creation.

Robinson laughed, then sighed. "Isn't that amazing? We
are present, dear friend, at greatness, not an everyday happening."

The screen went white, and they adjourned for a drink
to the little bar at the Hotel Inghilterra, at the bottom of the
Piazza di Spagna. Robbie liked it because it was very un-
Veneto, no suffocating goldfish-bowl movie-biz atmosphere
as at the Excelsior. It was a little "literary" hotel, frequented
by people like Moravia and Giorgio Bassani, when he was in
town. Or so the bartender informed them.

"Okay," Robinson said. "It looks as if we have two masterpieces of a kind to work with. *Festival*, and what Sordino
is doing with this kid. Listen, don't jump and shiver when I
say *us*. You and I don't need Becker to bind us together. It's
just a crazy development, a couple of bright boys with all
the advantages getting into the movie business at the top."

"I was wondering," Ezra said, "if you were still capable
of some irony."

"Don't be patronizing. The reason I wanted to see you
before you took off . . . Every day gets better. More people,
more projects, more stock and proxies pledged . . . Do you
realize," Robinson said, as genuinely amazed as if he had
just become aware of an eternal truth, "that this is the only
major with no real head of production. Just Kleinholz. It's
crazy."

"You haven't gotten to the reason. . . ."

"I have to know about you—about how much I can depend on you."

"How about thut auld-lang-syne speech you just made?"

"What have you done to make sure the boy will be out of here as soon as humanly possible?"

"I've taken care of it."

"You damned well have *not*."

"He's crazy about Kim. I got her to promise that she'd talk to him, explain. . . ."

"That's what I mean, for God's sake."

"Keep your voice down. This is not Trastévere. Everyone understands English here."

Robbie drank and ordered again. When he spoke his voice was modulated, controlled: "Ezra, I'm going to teach you something that can only be taught once. If you want to be sure something has been taken care of, in this business, *take care of it yourself.* Don't trust it to Kim, or to anybody. Only yourself. End of lesson. Almost. Karol's a lovely and unusual boy. And I yield to no man in my admiration for Schubert lieder. But Michael Maurice is going to have him —or he's going to kill him. Or kill himself. And the studio can't stand either possibility at this point."

Robbie's tired eyes told Ezra that he still was not sleeping well—they were red at the rims, shot with blood-streaks. His smile was nervous, strained. One small addendum to Robbie's lesson for the day: trying to get back in at the top might be as tough as holding on in the middle, or starting at the bottom.

23

Karol was unexpectedly helpful. Ezra need not trouble himself. The boy knew he was to get out, to go back to his familiar, safer life. The departure would take place before the weekend. He would stay one day after the completion of shooting, for the presentation of Kim's painting to the international press. He would answer the silly questions, would pose for the appropriate photographs next to the painting, next to his adored Kim, next to MM and Sordino, he knew all this. Oh, he knew everything. The lusts of older men did not surprise him. Unfortunately, Ezra sensed, they provoked in him a certain play, a certain capriciousness that shone in the spaces between his smiles and his frowns.

Ezra had found the only spare moment to be alone with him: a quick wardrobe session with an uncomprehending designer kneeling on the floor, mouth full of pins. The Sony spilled out Hugo Wolf. Karol stepped off the wooden platform and swirled around to show off a white linen sailor suit. Something in the narcissistic splash of white and the accompanying laugh worried Ezra. They talked of music and poetry, and Ezra told Karol that when he was Karol's age he had written a song based on a poem by Shelley:

> O world! O life! O time!
> On whose last steps I climb. . . .

They laughed, and Ezra said that sixteen was a metaphysically ambitious age.

Karol said, "I like Kim and you the best."

"You hardly know me," Ezra said.

He wondered what it was about Karol that touched him, outside of that immensely touching physical beauty . . . some memory of boyhood; no, too many differences between him and this swan of a gentile Hungarian boy . . . he all outward grace and assurance, while Ezra had stumbled gracelessly through boyhood.

"I have a girl friend," Karol said. "A Jewish girl who plays the piano when I sing. She invites me to dinner and I learned how to say the blessing for bread and for wine."

And, surreal surprise, he stands there, one arm in his jacket and one arm out, and sings, beautifully, the blessing for wine that Ezra had not heard sung for years.

24

Phantasmagoria! Dictionary definition: a changing incoherent series of apparitions, appearances or fantasms, as in a dream; a fantastical stereopticon exhibition. Witness: phantasmagoria of the days between leaving Rome and arriving back in Los Angeles. Phantasmagoria is not too loose a word, too fanciful for that jumble of wild hours. Ezra had the good fortune to take Max with him to Paris for the first lap of the trip.

On the plane, papers riffled between them, they sat side by side. Interspersed with tales; Max's Hollywood had lived in anecdotes, not ordinary days and nights like the rest of mankind.

First, they work.

COMING:

Vogue magazine—six-page layout, photos and text covering new Bill Blass designs based on *Lion* wardrobe. *Playboy* magazine—photo layout on Karol. *International Fashion Digest* (new periodical aimed at dep't.-store and fashion-industry executives: circulation 12,000) first issue —report on *Lion* as source of ideas in various fields. Newhouse Newspaper Service & Chicago Sun-Times Syndicate —round-up of photos of wardrobe in *Lion*.

MEMO FROM NICK BOHM TO EZRA MARKS (ccs to everybody from Kleinholz on down).

Activity for world premiere in London: based on likelihood and hope of Royal premiere.

Publications—*Financial Times, Guardian, Sunday Times, Evening News* and *Evening Standard* set for interviews with Sordino; *Sunday Times, Financial Times, Evening Standard, Filma* and *Filming Magazine* and *Woman Magazine* set for interviews with Michael Maurice; *Guardian, Daily Telegraph, Daily Mail, Sun, Woman Magazine, Vanity Fair* magazine and *Woman* and *Home Magazine* set for interviews with Karol. *Radio and Television*—BBC Radio shows *Arts This Week, Today,* and *World at One* set for interviews with Sordino; BBC Television shows *24 Hours* and *London This Week* set to interview Sordino and use film clips of selected scenes.

Two-hour Special on Life and Times of Michael Maurice planned in case of inclusion on Queen's Birthday Honours List.

Break for Pan-Am's Champagne Dinner and Max's mythic memories of Nick Bohm.

"Before I ever met Nick, I heard about him. When he was eighteen, Nick worked for David Selznick. Remember the big fuss about finding the right star to play Scarlett O'Hara—all that shit about an unknown and then ending up with Vivien Leigh? Well, where do you think Selznick hid her out when she came to the Coast . . . and he didn't want the papers to know it was her till just the right time? Nick's crummy little apartment on Fountain Avenue."

Max's small moon clouded over. He could express amazement, confusion, incomprehension, and mystification in a thousand different ways. He was the poet of doubt. The world never failed him: delivering new opacities to a mind that asked only lucidity but lived in a world in which it was unavailable.

"Can you believe that son-of-a-bitch?" Max was also the

poet of obscenity and could dress curses with the perfect tone desired: in this case, affectionate bewilderment. "When Dietrich comes to the Coast—maybe eighteen, twenty years ago, she's still a big star, right—nobody can get in to see her. Nick, open door and a big kiss. Ingmar Bergman comes to L.A. for the first time—can't speak a fucking word of English. But Nick Bohm—those two words he knows."

Darkly, Max brooded over his champagne. "He does things for them; that's got to be it."

"Things?"

"Things nobody else can do."

"Like what?"

In their new intimacy, Ezra is tempted to ask Max about his own tragic past—about the "awful things" secretaries whispered and Nick Bohm protected—as he did no other piece of information. But he cannot find the opening words. He abandons the notion.

Later, he opens his mail while Max watches the movie and dozes. Phantasmagorical note: the mail, delivered to Rome via the studio pouch, contains two—not one but two —scripts. One from a former dean of history at Columbia, a drinking buddy. And one from a friend of a cousin in Phila- delphia. Would Ezra please see what he could do—now that he was in the halls of Hollywood—not that there was any obligation, of course—but perhaps the time was ripe for a script that dealt with—?

Surprise!

MEMO FROM MAX MIRANDA TO EZRA MARKS (ccs to no one).

Playboy magazine story set on THE NEW BREED OF STUDIO EXECUTIVE. Feature story on Ezra Marks.

Written by Cody; scheduled for early fall, after openings of key films.

And delivered by Max like a well-polished apple.

Before Ezra could say anything, Max said, defensively, "Why the hell not? It's good for our side."

"Max, what *is* our side?"

"Come on, boss, you know." Uncomfortable Max, misunderstood Max. "*Our* side."

"Oh."

"Just leave it to me," Max said. The same Max who wondered what it was Nick Bohm did for the people who were so loyal to him. Perhaps he sensed that he and Nick did essentially the same things—but that the mystery of style was what delivered their loyalty to Nick and withheld it from himself.

As Ezra goes over some ads, he wonders at the fine actors who had trapped themselves into these embarrassments. He also wonders at his new ability to think of several schemes at once. Scheming, unlike genuine thinking, is done half with the instinct and half with the blood. Thus, as he is passing on the strength or weakness of a movie ad, he is hatching a plan to solve the "novelization" problem of *The Lion's Farewell*. They would approach someone such as James Jones or Irwin Shaw for the job. If the gods smile instead of laughing out loud and one of them agrees: success, followed by the announcement to the press (and the possibilities of a best seller would be good—without the mass secret buying of books Nick had described). Better still, perhaps they would approach some English novelist who'd known Lawrence. Did Graham Greene ever meet Lorenzo? Was all this only champagne and fatigue talking inside Ezra's head? Is there a special interior monologue that belongs to phantasmagoria?

Max, fully awake now, the picture finished, the screen down and coffee being passed, on to *Festival*. Publicity has to work on the assumption that peace will return—that there will be a film to play in the theaters. Mitch Stone interviews set up for Italian, French, and German television. Promotion film on the search for Karol also will be shown all over Western Europe and Japan. Instead of a Gounod song cycle in a concert hall seating five hundred people, approximately one hundred million people will see Karol being discovered by Sordino. The mathematics of cinema.

"Radio Luxembourg."

"Check."

"*Oggi* magazine."

"Check."

Phantasmagorical note on landing in Paris: they are met at the airport by at least three people: a Pan-Am passenger agent, the studio's man in that city, and in this case jolly old Anglo-Franco-Italo-Hollywood Archer, the agent from the travel bureau with whom they do business; and a chauffeur to handle the luggage. Travel is thus smoothed by this ancient trinity of the movie studios; francs, lire, or pounds pressed into Ezra's hand, money pressed into other hands to smooth the way, hands waved at customs people, names murmured, butter poured over the gritty floor of airports over which they slide their way into waiting limousines. Ah, Trinity, blessed percs for which no monetary equivalent exists, costing decades of investment yet having mainly emotional value.

Limousine memories: The problem of rounding up enough youngsters, the right kind of youngsters to sleep on the ground all night at Cannes; the effect desired; the religious document of the youth culture. Headbands and pot-smoking all night in the Mediterranean night air. Naïve confusion from Ezra Marks, to wit: since *Festival* is their document and they are waiting for it, anxiously, won't they show up in hordes if we just let the word out? Limousine laughter: the skepticism of years. When you think they'll show up, they don't. Perverse bastards. No, clearly this is a job for Drakmalnik.

Drakmalnik is the man without whom the wheels of publicity would have jammed fifty years ago. Drakmalnik knows where to "get things" (often at the last minute). Drakmalnik knows which cops can be bribed. Drakmalnik knows where to get sound trucks in cities you would swear had never heard of such a device. Drakmalnik knows where to get searchlights: in a Hollywood culture that lives on lights, spotlights, giant searchlights, colored lights, Drakmalnik had the biggest collection of searchlights in Hollywood. Drakmalnik was the master conjurer. No one knew where he lived. But he could always be found.

They arrive at the Plaza-Athénée Hotel on the Avenue Montaigne; where it is agreed that Drakmalnik will deliver two hundred hippies—or suitable facsimiles—to Cannes the week *Festival* is shown.

It is impossible to decide what time it is in Ezra's head, but it is still early in the evening. Thus, M. Dupont is asked to join them in Ezra's suite, with the proposed ads for *Festival*. In the improbable elegance, all exquisitely curved legs on antique chairs, deep satin on low-slung couches, and high-cradled telephones out of old Lubitsch movies, they spread the ads on the floor.

One absence strikes Ezra by its pertinence: the absence of snakes. Even across the Atlantic Kleinholz's displeasure has registered. Isn't the crucial scene a unique Indian ritual involving a rattlesnake held in Mitch Stone's mouth? Ezra asks. M. Dupont, a gentle and enthusiastic soul who has been with the King Studio for thirty-two years (like everyone else in the European company), demurs politely. Does not everyone know there is a war on? That there may be no such scenes in the picture? That there may be no picture at all?

"Is this the approach being used in all the European countries?" Ezra asked Max.

"Yes."

"How much will it cost to change them all to a new approach?"

Money had been mentioned, costs. Max's vagueness vanished. He did some quick calculations in his head, compared the numbers with M. Dupont, and said, "About forty thousand dollars."

"Do it!"

"Do what?"

He drew, from the memory of that California early morning, a rough sketch of Mitch Stone kneeling in the dust, face painted with occult symbols, the rattlesnake in his mouth. Around it he printed the letters F-E-S-T-I-V-A-L, in an arc, like a rainbow or curve of sun motes.

"Do that," Ezra said.

"In a tight finish?"

"In a tight finish! The picture may be a smash at Cannes; we have to be ready. Get the best artist you can find. Get Bernard Buffet. . . Get Dubuffet. . . ." He laughed. (It was phantasmagoria, wasn't it?) And said, "Max—easy come, easy go."

With one move, he has bet that there will be a picture, that the final cut will be Mitch Stone's, not Kleinholz's; he has also bet, by implication, that he may dance, independently of Nick Bohm, to tunes of $40,000 and more.

25

Supper at Chez René, a bistro in the Saint Germain. Umberto Rossi appears. There is suddenly a large table at the rear, with M. Dupont and his staff, all of them seeing

Max off to Rome and Archer off to London. There ensues an orgy of eating *choucroute garnie* and drinking Beaujolais and a clear brandy called *marc.*

Flushed with wine, drowsy in the aftermath of new determination, Ezra smiled when Umberto Rossi suggested to the waiter, "*la bouteille avec la serviette pour notre ami américain.*" To which Dupont added, solemnly: "*Mon patron, le chef de la publicité du monde entier.*"

The waiter brought a bottle wrapped in a white napkin and poured. There were small nervous giggles from Dupont's secretary, a slender, previously solemn young woman. Ezra thought he caught the word *serpent*, but someone sssshhed. They drank the *marc*. It was strong, bracing, and bitter. But why was it wrapped in a concealing napkin, why the giggles and the secrecy? Ezra reached over and unwrapped the mystery. Within the clear liquid lay coiled a snake. He felt dizzy, but he'd been dizzy earlier. Umberto Rossi told him the snake *marc* was the specialty of this bistro. Not everyone could take it.

"The snake is immersed, alive, in the alcohol," he smiled an Assyrian smile. "Its last gift, before it dies, is a spurt of the venom." His gold cuff links winked brightly.

Ezra was bathed in a brandy-sweat.

Outside, Paris floated in a haze of heat. Umberto Rossi and he walked ahead of the others. Ezra must have seemed sad because Rossi plunged an elbow into his side and said, "Cheer up, Marks. After all, tonight you drank the venom of a snake."

"I seem to be haunted by snakes."

"And I flew to Paris just to walk these streets with you. So smile and let us talk."

"Just to walk with me?"

"At the suggestion of a friend."

In the aftermath of Ezra's surprise, they drifted into talk of many things, including, it seemed, riches and poverty. Umberto Rossi had his own theories, which included the belief that only the dirt-poor rise to great wealth. Middle-poor becomes middle-rich. It was an interesting algebra of ambition, connected, somehow, to where one had slept as a child. Rossi himself, had slept on a rope hammock suspended between two trees, in earlier days.

They stopped for more brandy, then continued on. The others had apparently departed for airplanes and beds. On a bridge leading from the left bank to the Ile St. Louis Ezra learned that Kleinholz had been so poor that he'd slept in the kitchen on a board over the bathtub.

"*That's* poor," Umberto Rossi said in triumph. "And the truly poor also reach for the greatest power. It is no original insight. But I have observed it. It is a certain variety of sickness I have never understood. Sex is good and money is good—and sometimes they meet and sometimes they don't. I am very rich and well supplied with women of all sorts." He leaned against the railing of the bridge, sweat beads covering his forehead and said, "I want to be still richer, always still richer, money in real estate, in films, in very fast custom-made cars, in bank accounts, and stocks everywhere. I wish also to perform even more perverse pleasures with women and girls of many ages and styles, alone and in combinations. But—" he waved his hand in a delicate gesture; Ezra became aware of how small and compact he was, dark face intent, white teeth hidden by a serious mouth. He did not seem or sound drunk; he was. Behind him Ezra saw the magestic filigree of Notre Dame against a darker sky.

"—But," Rossi said, "I think a man *has* to want all these things. The one thing I have never understood is to want the power. The desire to make another man do what you want him to do, *that* is the sickness. Not the fucking, or the scrambling for more and more money. I have been in the movie business all my life—I have been lucky and I own theaters all over Italy—and I even have color-printing

plants to make movie posters. And Nick Bohm and Becker
and I ... Well, never mind, I have been lucky.

"And I will be lucky again, with the help of Becker and
Robinson and perhaps you. But the one pleasure that ought
to be forbidden is the one pleasure that will never be forbidden, because I think it is maybe at the center of the
world. And that is the desire to exercise power over another
man or woman. Bad," he said, this Assyrian moralist of the
movies. "Bad." He leaned on the bridge wall and spat down
into the water. It seemed somehow fastidious rather than
vulgar. He turned back to Ezra. "I have seen so much of
that terrible desire. Mr. Robert Robinson is a clear-thinking
man; a rational man. And I think you are his friend and his
colleague and you are such a man, too. We are both a little
cloudy with alcohol at the moment. But perhaps it is time
for the power to end and the intelligence to begin."

It became clear that Max and Archer had not gone, because suddenly Max was on the bridge. How much had he
heard of the theory of power versus greed? And what impact would it have on that perfectly conditioned studio
mind? A certain brandied benevolence swept over Ezra for
the roly-poly purist of survival. Max was saying good night
and handing over some papers Ezra had asked him for,
apologizing profusely for forgetting, earlier.

"That's all right," Ezra said. "I've got London and then
the long ride to New York; plenty of reading time. And you,
old Max ... ?"

Old Max was heading back to Rome to help Nick Bohm
run the press party for Kim's painting and the boy. Tell
Nick, Ezra reminds Max, that the boy *must* be out of there
by the weekend. Otherwise they are all—he gestured to the
murky Seine. Max replied with the equivalent of "Don't
worry, boss." Ezra was too murky, himself, to bother to rep-
rimand him about that ugly, imprecise word: boss. Because
it was growing less ugly? Potentially·more accurate?

"Pssst," Max said, as if a secret were possible at that point. "I got you Umberto, tonight. Chalk one up for Max." The evening ended in an assault on the Ile St. Louis home of James Jones. Ezra had told Umberto Rossi his plan.

"I know Jimmy Jones," Rossi said. "It's Sunday night— and every Sunday night Jim has a poker game at home. I think when you ask him to extend a story by D. H. Lawrence, he will tell you to go fuck yourself—but every man must make his own mistakes." They ended by ringing a bell and shouting, ineffectually, outside of the house. Ezra dragged Umberto Rossi away as the inevitable concierge appeared. It was only then that they realized it was Wednesday, not Sunday.

26

Jotting down his expense-account notes on the plane to London, Ezra learns that Archer, too, has a store of Nick Bohm anecdotes. The scene: a hotel room in Iowa City, where a world premiere of a rustic musical is being held. The boys: Max, Archer, and others, are sitting around trying to work out their expense accounts—what dinners, lunches, and drinks, using the usual real people in the usual fictitious situations to declare as reasons for the expenditures. This man and that woman is being proposed and discussed. Nick Bohm enters: grabs a telephone book tears it in four equal parts, and hands one part to each of the publicity men, "Max," he said, "you take A to F. . . . Archer, you take G to M." Super-Nick, unfazed by reality, so long as the money flowed.

The scene: a yacht in Boston Harbor that belongs to Serge Semenenko of the First National Bank of Boston, the big backer of films. Max and Nick are there instead of at the

Boston airport meeting a star. Max is worried about Kleinholz. Nick puts in a call to the studio and while he talks, Archer and Max make airplane noises in the background. The Rover Boys in Hollywood; the expense accounts were all part of the laughs.

"But," Archer sighs, "the laughs are getting a bit few and far between."

Witness the papers Max had handed Ezra. Proposed ad for the *New York Times*, the *Wall Street Journal*, and other appropriate media:

Headline: MR. KLEINHOLZ MAKES ONE STATE-MENT TO THE PRESS AND THE BOARD OF DIRECTORS MAKES A DIFFERENT STATEMENT TO YOU.

Body copy: On March 17, 1970, according to an article in the *New York Times*, Mr. Kleinholz stated as part of his solution to the continuing problems that have plagued King Studio, that he was setting a $2,000,000 (two-million dollar) limit on the budget of all new King Studio movies.

On that same day a letter went out to the stockholders stating that Sordino's production of D.H. Lawrence's *The Lion's Farewell* would be budgeted at $4,500,000. This is typical of the management that brought you after-tax losses of $36,800,000 in 1969. And is moving toward a potential after-tax loss of $77,344,000 for 1970.

WHEN A COMPANY LOSES OVER 60% OF ITS STOCKHOLDERS' EQUITY IN ONE YEAR, WE THINK THE STOCKHOLDERS ARE ENTITLED TO SOME PROTECTION. WE, THEREFORE, ANNOUNCE THE FORMATION OF THE KING STUDIO STOCKHOLDER'S PROTECTION COMMITTEE . . . TO SOLICIT YOUR PROXIES AS A MANDATE FOR INTELLIGENT, MODERN MANAGEMENT IN THE FILM BUSINESS . . . AND FOR KING STUDIO.

A note was appended. "Ezra: What do you think of the committee title and the ad copy? Please let me know as soon as possible. Robbie."

He wrote and rewrote the ad all the way to London. In a London ancient-looking in its classic mist of rain, he forced himself to stay awake and review publicity plans for *Festival* with Archer's staff, and to interview a proposed new advertising agency for King Studio in the U.K.

Then he slept, naked on the bed, alternately sweating and shivering in the air-conditioned suite at The Dorchester. He awoke and called Kim in Rome. He was told she had just left for a press party.

27

Second wind hits—in its wake Ezra hits New York, ready for anything, for everything. Sends cables in all directions at once: first, one to Robinson containing revised copy for the ad; tougher language, clearer. Cable to Nick Bohm about changes in European *Festival* ads, plus details of mad novelization scheme. Overriding purpose: to generate the sense of Ezra Marks's activity in the company, as deadline days approach.

More practically, a cable to Sydell in Amherst; sitting in Nick Bohm's office on the forty-fourth floor, ordering a limousine to bring Sydell and Centilever to New York from Amherst, Massachusetts, ordering tickets for L.A. Quick lunch and visit to the War Room: Room 1407, Hotel Warwick. A long green table in the center. On the wall, maps indicating relative strength of stockholders: loyal and disloyal.

Eastern-style attorneys directing dozens of girls calling every one who owns ten shares of stock or more, asking their vote against Kleinholz. Vote for the Committee for the Protection et cetera. Ezra now apparently an important part of that et cetera. Greeted enthusiastically by Eastern-style executives ("Empty Suits," Robinson had called them. "But we need them to solicit the big Exchange firms.")

One of the Empty Suits asks if Ezra will be available for special presentations to Hornblower & Weeks (controlling 220,000 shares) and Lehman Brothers (400,000 shares). The Empty Suits have heard talk of research results, uniquely developed and held by King Studio—that is by the Committee for the et cetera. Yes, Ezra will present the research plan and anything else needed—but not until he gets back to New York from the Coast. A new New York for him: Corporate New York, all formal style, well-tailored suits, money implied in handshakes, power implied in smiles. All recorded in cables condensed as poems, transportation provided by limousines, black and stark as symbols.

28

"The deeper I go into this thing, the more I think it can work," Sydell said.

"It has to," Ezra said.

"If the screening process is followed all the way, and the demographics prove out, we may have the only way to pre-test for successful movies." This was Centilever, the thin, edgy young man who'd first mentioned the idea. He was exhausted and very excited.

"Hold it," Sydell said. "What you *may* have is at least a way to cut your losses to the bone, early in the process."

"But that's where all the losses go," Centilever said. "Chasing the dogs. Not backing the winners. Anybody can do that."

"Have the election computers ever been wrong?" Ezra asked.

"No," Sydell said. "Hey, how'd you get into this racket, Ezra?"

"Just lucky," Ezra said. "Look, I'm on a morning plane

to Los Angeles. I don't care how late we stay up, but by the time I get on that plane I will fully understand everything about this research model. Food and sleep will be sent in. Nobody leaves."

29

He'd decided not to tell Honey he was coming back; something suggested that perhaps that was over, that its rightness, if it had ever existed, belonged to a certain starting time: apprenticeship. If they were together now, Ezra had the sense that he would probe into motivations, into origins that could be trouble to everyone.

It was noon Los Angeles time, 3 p.m. New York time, and some unfathomable half-Paris-half-Rome-half-N.Y.L.A. time in Ezra's head. The driver who met him at the gate was the same one he'd had the day he'd arrived at the studio; ex-stunt man with a hole in his cheek.

"Welcome back, Mr. Marks."

"Thanks."

"Marty. You remember me, Mr. Marks?"

"Sure."

"Home? Or the studio?"

"The studio."

"Some doings," Marty said. "Snakes everywhere. Crazy business." Ezra remembered Robbie's warning: Spy/Drivers at the studio, too. He grunted something unintelligible. As he did so, he realized that he had absolutely nothing to hide. The spy system, the gossip system, worked so well that everyone knew everything.

"How's the Sordino picture going?" Marty asked.

"Trouble," Ezra said. "Lots of trouble."

211   *director's cut*

Serenely, Marty replied: "Yeah, that's what I hear. That's some kid."

And having proven Ezra's theory of universal knowledge, he headed across Caheunga under the crisscrossed shadows of palm trees.

It begins smoothly; small talk. Kleinholz is gracious, tossing questions about Ezra's secretary, satisfactory? about Ezra building himself a new and bigger office—see Ape, see Max, see . . .

But circling can go on for just so long: finally, one must land. Ezra lands on the Marcus research report. Complicated data fills the pages Ezra holds, but wheelchairs breed impatience. Snakes, his impatient whirling head asks, yes or no? No for older people, yes for younger people. But— younger people are the big market for the film, so the answer is, in effect, yes. Stone has won the snake war on paper. Kleinholz is furious. Rage on wheels.

"Lothar, let him have his cut."

"I'll let him have *this*." Fist on table.

"We have less than three weeks to . . ."

Ezra is interrupted by a barrage of tapeyears. Flinging open a cabinet, Kleinholz extracts tapes, muttering dates and data.

"Look here, Forty-eight, when I turned down Harry Cohn on a merger. . . ." Tape is slammed on spool and spun; voices which could have been anyone but which the purity of Kleinholz's recording obsession guaranteed authentic. "I should buckle to these kids when I stood up to the toughest . . . ! Forty-nine. . . . Television was killing me . . . but . . . Ah, listen to this. . . ." Another tape bears witness, "Here— Fifty-one. Un-American Activities Committee—killers. Listen to that. . . ."

It was an insane *bruitage* played by a Krapp gone crippled instead of merely aged and addled. Ezra is dazed with sound, with history.

Toughness yielded to snobbery and status: The Prince of Wales on a studio tour, pronouncing the name Kleinholz exquisitely. Tapes fell from his angry hands and were left lying while the old man searched for the right moment in the right year to demonstrate his right to absolute control over his studio, his films. "Lewis Milestone . . . hah . . . little better director than that punk. . . . Listen to this, after the Academy Awards. . . ." A pause to wipe his face, red and perspired. And in that pause Ezra heard Kleinholz's voice, saying, "I don't care how or what you do. The picture can ruin us or save us. . . . Get it under control. . . ." And a voice that sounded like Nick Bohm's—or does it—replies, "He's just a kid. . . ."

KLEINHOLZ: "I don't give a damn. . . ."
OTHER VOICE (NICK'S): "I'll do what I c-c-c-an."
KLEINHOLZ: "You'll do what you *have* to."

It was Nick's characteristic stammer under pressure. Kleinholz wheeled ferociously back toward the table, muttering, "Wrong goddamned tape in that box—kill that Ape. *Ape!*"

Blocked by the long table, the wheelchair not responding quickly enough, hearing the voices continuing when he wanted them stopped at once, Kleinholz saw the wire on the floor near his chair and pulled it: silence.

30

"I told you what would happen," Mitch Stone said. "That night on the pier in Santa Monica." He looked even more exhausted and at least five pounds lighter. "I told you

Kleinholz believed he was still in charge." Mitch lay flat on the floor and closed his eyes. "When people who are. no longer in charge behave as if they still are . . ."

Somewhere a button was pressed, sound flooded ears: the track from *Festival* being endlessly edited, amplified. Ezra drowned, dizzied, in the sound. First Kleinholz, now this: attacked by sound.

MONTAGE: FLASH-FORWARD

Nick Bohm pressed a button in a screening room in London: Archer yawned in his seat next to a fat official of the Queen. (*"We're trying to make him a knight—and he acts like a fucking queen."* Per Max Miranda.)

Kim sits on a bench in the hospital. Half-asleep, numb, waiting for the bad news, she remarks that hospitals, like airports, like dreams, have a universal look and feel. The nausea she has felt for six hours recedes; she sleeps, her neck stiff and awkward-looking. A nurse passes, notices this, but decides not to disturb the sleeping woman.

"What's for dinner?" Max asks the stewardess. She looks tired. Max wonders if she is menstruating. He knows her from other flights, but has forgotten her name.

"You know," she says.

"But I like to have you tell me," Max says.

"I don't want to be in the movies," she says. "I love flying, my boy friend is a gangster. So pick anything—as long as it's steak."

"Joker," Max says. Tiring of the game, he orders the steak, eats and drinks in moody silence.

In the living room of his house outside of Rome, Sordino holds Michael Maurice by the shoulders. Maurice is trembling. Sordino has been weeping, but that is over now.

"How about a compromise cut?" Ezra said. He was full of the exhilaration of action; but his voice sounded calm, authoritative. "Take out the big snake ritual—the scene when those people started screaming—and just find some other snake material to give the ritual touch you want."

"You're not suggesting castration," Mitch Stone said. "All you want is a circumcision."

"Wrong," the savior of the motion-picture industry said. "A little cosmetic surgery. Nobody ever dies from cosmetic surgery."

He had offered a compromise to each of the opposing forces. It was unimportant which one yielded. Either way there would be a film to sell, and more control for Ezra. He thinks: I am becoming a Kleinholz character, flat, at last.

31

Ezra ran into Cody at Musso-Frank's that evening. It was a nice, seedy, long-wooden-bar-and-booths, old-Hollywood kind of place, mentioned in all the memoirs of New York expatriates of the Thirties and Forties. Just the kind of place he was in the mood for: a quiet dinner alone, then home to his house and his turtle. The larger purpose was not to call and see Honey. It was strangely important *not* to see Honey. Cody saw him and detached himself from a crowd of rock-music types. "Hello," he said, "have you heard the news?"

Ezra misunderstood. "Max told me a couple of days ago."

"A couple of days?"

"That you're going to make me famous."

"Oh, you mean the *Playboy* piece. I meant the other news," Cody said. He stood very close, his face unsmiling, heavy lids almost concealing his eyes. "It's about Karol. . . ."

"What about him? What happened?"

"He's dead. Somebody murdered him. Last night, when they had the big press party."

"Last night . . ." Ezra repeated, stupid with shock.

"They found him this morning. The police must be having some serious talks with Maurice and Sordino. Remember that funny business at . . ."

But Ezra was not sitting still for Cody to complete his reminiscences. Like a hundred scenes in bad movies, he threw some bills on the table and left. He did not want to hear from Cody what Karol being murdered meant. It didn't have to mean anything at all, for a moment, except that that amazingly beautiful face was no longer beautiful, that the voice would not sing, that someone had put a stop to the drama by killing him. He'd never known anyone who'd been murdered. There had been a friend who'd committed suicide, an alcoholic journalist who'd been fired from a dying magazine; he'd hanged himself, which was violent. But it did not have the same sound and feel that murder had: violence, unexpected, from the outside.

By the time he'd driven up Laurel Canyon and back and then up the Freeway, toward Santa Monica, then back to the Hollywood Hills, where Honey lived, Ezra was in a rage.

There is no such thing as real thought at such moments. Rather, a black cloud of disgust, remembered fragments of conversation, all those discussions about what to do with the boy. And all those conversations about what would happen if no way were found to handle the situation. Someone had found out what to do. The situation had been handled.

When Honey opened the door, Ezra burst past her like a blast of wind. He had not stopped to phone; she wore a nightgown and a quilted pink robe. On her face were the remnants of cold cream. She was astonished to see him; pleased, too. All around the living room were scattered brochures, four-color pamphlets. Honey was considering some important purchase. He had interrupted a quiet evening of decision.

She kissed him. "Welcome home," she said.

"That's what the driver at the studio said." It was just as well to make it clear from the start that she was with a man in an irrational rage. "Tell me—did Nick send you up to my room that first time?"

"What?"

"Don't 'what' me! I want to know."

"What do you want to know?"

"I want to know how much pimping and whoring I've actually been in the middle of all this time."

"Go to hell!"

They were still holding each other, in the middle of this exchange. She was too startled to pull away. He wanted to keep hold of her for control and he pulled off her pink robe. "No," she said. But the protest was only verbal. Ezra was in control; the push and pull of her muscles under his hands told him that. It gave him no pleasure. He needed something more than acquiescence to appease his crazy anger. He found what he needed in a a pushing, grabbing, slamming embrace. They ended up in the doorway between the living room and the kitchen, his head bumping into some big piece of wood, his hands, as they groped for Honey's neck and shoulders, hitting smaller pieces of wood also. He didn't want to hurt Honey; he just wanted to obliterate her along with his own consciousness, with the wildest thrusts and plunges he could muster. She accepted it on some simple level, far below questions of hostility or humiliation or violence. Her response was without value judgment; sex without tenderness, without play, was also sex. It was an insensible, destructive, savage screwing in which they both were drowning different things: his disgust and anger, her surprise and fear at Ezra's sudden furious appearance.

Afterward, he saw they were lying in a debris of wooden fragments.

"What is all this?" he asked.

"I'm building a doghouse. Nick is buying me a dog: a Lhasa apso. The I Ching says I should put my trust in animals. I didn't expect to make love on the floor."

"Is that what that was? Making love?"

"In a half-built doghouse." Honey laughed, groping in the sawdust for a cigarette. She stopped laughing when he told her what had happened, when it became clear that he was leaving.

"Who did it? How was he killed? Why?"

"I don't know."

"Don't go, Ezra."

Honey was upset now, weepy and frightened at news of murder, coming after a kind of assault. She clung; she was willing to discuss his opening questions about Nick and the first time. But Ezra was no longer interested. She stared at him bleary-eyed, crazy-looking. He was taken, suddenly, by a wild nervous fit of sneezing and drove away from there drained and shaken—as if it were he who had been taken in rough sexual violence. He imagined the chaos of Kim's feelings, the anarchy of Robinson's situation, the terror of Michael Maurice and Sordino.

> how do you like your blueeyed boy
> Mister Death

book three

final cut

1

The Rome of Karol's death was held in a heat wave.

"I'm sorry," Max said, as if he were afraid Ezra would blame him for the furnace into which they walked at the airport. "The worse heat since 1950. I was here then."

"Where's Nick?"

"Everywhere. Where's Nick! The police, the newspapers, the telephone. The funeral is this afternoon."

Just the few steps from baggage claim to the sidewalk where the limousine waited were enough to leave Ezra soaked and breathless.

"He was so young," Max shook his head as if the mystery lay in the boy's youth as much as his murder.

"What do you think, Max? Who killed him?"

"I live in the back, boss." Max turned his pudgy hands outward; the timeless gesture of total innocence by the partially responsible. Max's reluctance to commit himself to theory did not extend to information. He told Ezra much that he would have guessed and much that he would never have thought of. That Sordino and Michael Maurice were the prime suspects; that the murder had taken place at the press party. It had been moved, at the last minute, from the French Academy—the old Villa Medici at the top of the Spanish Steps—to Hadrian's Villa. The Temple of Antinoüs to be exact.

"Were you there?"

"I was working. Was I there! Everybody was there. We got fantastic coverage from the world press."

"Whose idea was it to move the party?"

"Nick's. It turns out Antinoüs was some kid."

"Yes. I know. How's Kim? I couldn't get her on the phone."

"She'll be at the funeral."

2

Captain Calamandrei, tall, darkly handsome, and gently aromatic of garlic, questioned Ezra about how well he knew Karol. Ezra found himself telling a strange police officer that he'd come to like Karol more than he'd realized. The boy had a great deal of charm. To which Captain Calamandrei added, "And physical beauty." He asked if Ezra had witnessed the fight between Signor Michael Maurice and Karol at Hadrian's Villa on the night of May ninth? Ezra told the truth and learned more than he taught the Captain. He learned that Karol had died at about 11 p.m.; that both Sordino and Maurice had left Hadrian's Villa by that time— assuming that Karol was with the publicity people; that Nick Bohm seemed to be innocent because he had been with the American woman who painted Karol's picture, for most of that night. . . .

3

It was a hot, crowded, scandalously noisy funeral; unpleasantly lit by flashbulbs outside of the church and even inside, at one point.

Sitting in the steaming church, scanning the crowd for Kim, Ezra thought there must be something wrong with him. Everyone was preoccupied with the question of who had murdered Karol. To Ezra, the fact of his death was so overwhelmingly concrete, so inevitable and horribly true, that questions of alibi, of motive, of the homosexual rivalry with which they had been living, all seemed irrelevant. The exotic elements did not escape him; the hats and capes of the dozen or more carabinieri outside; the plainclothesmen in dark, heavy-looking suits standing in their sweat, looking from horizon to horizon like programed scanning machines gathering data for Captain Calamandrei. They were simply not as real as the body in the coffin at the front of the church.

Ezra caught a glimpse of Kim sitting with Robinson near the front. She wore a white dress and stared straight ahead. Robbie's face was expressionless, formal; all plans suspended. Ezra thought about the implications of Nick Bohm's alibi. If it was accurate, it was bad news for Ezra. If Kim or Nick was lying, it was bad news for Nick Bohm. Stop thought at the edges, right there, go on to observing entrances—Giannini and his group, Becker, an uneasy half-smile on his face, too carefully shaven and powdered. Finally, after the church was stuffed, after it was barely possible to draw a breath, Kleinholz entered, imperious on canes. Ape, at his elbow, made a path.

"Like something out of *The Song of Bernadette*," Max whispered.

"Don't expect a miracle," Ezra said.

"I always do," Max said gloomily. "Why should today be any different?"

There was a banal speech by Karol's family priest flown in for the purpose. Phrases like: ". . . threshold of stardom . . ." and "a soul as beautiful as his face . . ." An elderly man no one knew, fainted from the heat and was taken away for questioning by the police. There was, however, the beauty of the Catholic mass, and Michael Maurice suddenly rediscovering the dignity of poise and control. And Sordino looking very old, his throat wrapped in one of the scarves he'd been wearing since Ezra had met him. Sweat moved in Ezra's shoes and socks. His back was stuck to his shirt. The corners of his eyes were forced into tears by perspiration; vision blurred. Several vague figures moved forward and picked up the coffin as an even vaguer figure followed them, swinging a censer and chanting in a monotone. The family group assembled, stiffly, and followed the slow steps of the pallbearers.

The church emptied itself in a hot, jostling uneven flow. There was a small knot of celebrities. Ezra saw Sophia Loren, Mastroianni, Silvana Mangano, Kirk Douglas, Olivier—whom he knew was making a film in Rome—most of them there in silent sympathy with Sordino or Michael Maurice. Afterward, it was impossible to tell how the trouble started. Certain people in the crowd outside seemed to surge toward the celebrity group. Someone cried out. Flashbulbs burst like artillery shells. People all around Ezra began to push and run. Police shoved those nearest them. Urgency cracked the sultry air. Ezra's eye registered Ape curving a protective arc over a bent Kleinholz. The dark, oval face of Umberto Rossi slipped into view, bearing a frozen smile packed with white teeth, a glint of gold, then slipped away. Ezra's sense of what was real and what was not slipped away with him. He had been looking for Kim, but that was now clearly hopeless. The last image that pressed in on his vision and his consciousness was startling: Sordino had got caught up in the crush and was pressed against the right wall of the outside of the church; gargoyles winked above his frightened face. His mouth moved as if he were speaking. His guardian angel, Nick Bohm, was for the moment unavailable. Beyond and above him the pallbearers struggled with the coffin, the steep steps, and the turmoil.

But what Ezra saw and registered with the force of an image that explains so much—as after a dream when one remembers suddenly both the dream and an association that explains it in an instant—was that, for the first time, Sordino's throat was bare. The omnipresent scarf dangled, a blue and red ribbon revealing a bull-neck through which ran a long, L-shaped, ragged-edged surgeon's scar; a great section of throat had been carved away in an attempt to save the whole man.

4

"How far down does it go?"

"Four more floors. Keep going."

"For God's sake, how many churches is this?"

"Four in one. It's all in the guidebook. Upstairs was the nineteenth-century Catholic church. This is the Early Christian church. Everyone says you can't leave Rome without a visit to San Clemente. Even Stendhal says so. Maybe it'll be cooler down below. Follow me."

"Look at that fresco. Those colors!"

"Did you see Sordino's throat?"

"No."

"Cancer, I think. Somebody ripped away that scarf he always wears and I saw the scar. Awful."

"Oh, Ezra, it's all awful."

"You remember that turtle you drew at my house?"

"Yes. That's right, distract me. . . ."

"It's gone. Vanished. I looked everywhere, the night I heard Karol was dead. We haven't discussed who did it, have we?"

"I didn't do it."

"Poor Kim. Did I tell you he sang a Hebrew prayer for me the last time I saw him? Hold my arm, these steps are tricky."

"Dank and damp—it's more like a dungeon more than a church."

"This must be the oldest Christian church. Down below there's supposed to be a pagan temple. You know, they say Nick Bohm once beat up somebody for Kleinholz, years ago."

"What does that mean? Who is 'they'?"

"Robbie, Max. Everybody wanted Karol away. Maybe—"

"It wasn't Nick."

"Did you tell that to Captain Calamandrei?"

"Yes, I told him."

Ezra shied away. He was not quite ready yet. He felt suspended as in fluid; had felt that way, more or less, since leaving Los Angeles the day before.

"I think it was probably Michael Maurice," she said. "I hate him and his fake Oscar Wilde pose. Bastard!"

"His alibi holds up."

"I don't care. Maybe their timing is off. Or maybe I'm wrong. Christ, do we have to go down to the lower level. It's getting scary; so dark and bare. Tell me, old Ezra, tell me," she turned a blinding smile at him in her Southern, unpredictable way. "You disappeared so suddenly. How *are* you?"

"I was having a marvelous time spending thousands of dollars on impulse." He told her of the snake-in-the-bottle and of rich, powerful Umberto Rossi and his aversion to power. He told her of anything he could think about, as they walked around, the only visitors at the bottom of the strangest church in Rome.

But finally he said, "The Captain told me Nick's alibi is you. That you were spending the night together. Is that true?"

"Yes."

They were in a corner composed of a dozen small cells, possibly for prayer, with two rectangular stone tablets, possibly for some kind of sacrifice, human or animal.

"What did you expect me to say?"

"I have no idea."

"I think I wanted to find out what was behind all that smoke," Kim said. "Fire, maybe? I can't be sure now. I was a little drunk. But that's no alibi . . . if I need one. We left before the party was finished. Old reliable Max was taking care of everything."

"Not quite everything."

"Don't give me that bitter sound. I'm free to do whatever the hell I want. The painting was finished and you were off

somewhere spending lots of money. It was a safe, uncomplicated evening of fucking. With you it might have been very
unsafe, and very complicated."

The clear vision of Kim and Nick in bed together was
liberating. He'd been holding his breath, since Karol's death.
But the drive set in motion could not be stopped, apparently, not even by a murder. And he had been waiting for
some igniting principle to get going again. That principle
was irrational, but it worked. It was, simply, the notion of
Kim and Nick making the beast with two backs. Kim owed
him nothing, technically, and Nick owed him nothing at all.
(There was also the matter of Honey, which he chose to
ignore—being human and self-forgiving.) It was an excuse,
no more; but it sufficed to blot out the image of Karol, perhaps purple-faced, perhaps with neck askew. (All those visions came from movie murder mysteries; the coffin at the
church had been mercifully closed.) After all, he had not
known Karol very well, a touching figure while alive, and
touching in his premature violent death. But meanwhile,
whatever change events had created in Ezra felt ireversible.
It drove him from that chilly pagan temple, up through four
levels of history, through five thousand years of blind belief,
toward where he had to go.

The post-murder meeting. Everyone significant was present. Most of them held plane reservations out of Rome on
the night flight. Ezra was early and observed, curiously, that
no one shook hands as they arrived: nods, smiles, even jokes
and waves, but no handshakes.

Press releases were presented by Nick and reviewed by
Kleinholz. It was reported that Drakmalnik had delivered

one hundred and ten youngsters to France and that the
Royal premiere had been canceled that morning by telegram. Nick looked pale, fuzzy around the edges. Nick Bohm
was having public and private troubles. Public troubles:
Kleinholz did not look at him. All communication was handled indirectly: no eye contact.

Becker had one thing on his mind. "Let's drop the picture. It's tagged with an unsolved murder. Christ, let's just
write off the dollars we've spent so far."

Kleinholz seemed to feel Becker was being a touch cava-
lier with his money. Becker, facing his daily danger of public humiliation, shrugged and said he didn't really give a
shit, they could just as well finish the picture; sometimes
these things backfire and the public beats down the doors
because the kid star has been killed. Thirty years of bending
with prevailing winds had given him a flexible spine.

Kleinholz said, "I say we close down. We're in for two
million, but we'll save three on the rest of production and
advertising and publicity."

Nick murmured something about the necessity of Sordino's presence if they were going to talk about shutting
down; but it was a measure of his public trouble that no one
listened to him, no one paid him the courtesy of replying. It
was a measure of his private trouble that he would make
such a quixotic suggestion: that the victim be present at the
determination of his fate.

Robinson objected to closing down. When he spoke, the
quality of attention and authority in the air wavered. No
one, as yet, could be sure precisely where Robinson fitted.

When Umberto Rossi spoke, immediately afterward, the
atmosphere condensed around his words. No ambiguity
here.

"We are fortunate enough to have a marketing man
here; a public-opinion man. Let's hear from him."

For a second the buzz of central air conditioning was the

dominant sound. Then Ezra spoke. From somewhere he
found a quiet eloquence. They were all speaking in the ab-
stract. He, Ezra, had seen the dailies. They were magnificent. A masterpiece was being made here. It is impossible to
keep news of a masterpiece from the public.

Furthermore, stockholders are cynical, not puritanical.
Whoever killed Karol had moved the picture from the entertainment page to the front page. Neither Sordino nor Maurice was in jail or under active suspicion—this was not exactly what Captain Calamandrei would say, but it was close
enough. The picture should be finished, too, because a di-
vided management under attack from outside groups and
from within the company cannot afford to cancel a major
production for any reason. (A Machiavellian inventiveness,
unexpected, spontaneous, kept arguments flowing.) If it was
to survive, the company should, in fact, be contracting for
new properties, with all kinds of film-makers. Mutterings
and murmurs around the room approved, affirmed. Robinson inclined his head, the prophet accepting his recognition.

Ezra went on to describe the international publicity coverage set up for *The Lion's Farewell.* True, much of it was
to have featured the boy. But they could promote the tragic
absence as well as the presence. Kim's painting was now
worth far more than they'd paid for it. Then, sudden shift in
emphasis. This was a small picture, after all. The studio's
real hopes were on *Festival* anyway. (Serious danger of
pushing Kleinholz too far, here.) The mood in the room had
shifted in favor of saving the picture.

Kleinholz concluded—after a suitable pause for change
of tapes—Sordino would finish the film! The meeting was
over. They would allow the old man his last masterpiece.
Nick dashed from the room, undoubtedly to tell Sordino the
news. A warm and relaxed sensation centering around the
stomach told Ezra that he had won something: if nothing
more, a claim on Sordino's gratitude.

Just outside the door, in a temporary pocket of privacy, Robinson and Ezra held their own meeting.

"Have you got anything for me?" Robbie asked. "We're getting down to the wire."

"I think we may have Rossi."

"I mean the project."

"I'll know after New York. A few days. What happened in there with Nick?"

"Kleinholz has him marked rotten for two reasons. One, he holds him responsible for not protecting the boy—not getting him out of town. Two, he thinks Nick may be in with Mitch Stone, because of the snake in the can of film his daughter brought from L.A."

"That part is crazy."

"I'm just reporting facts. I didn't promise they'd be rational. I owe you one for that performance in there. If the picture was dead, I'd be dead."

"Let's not keep books, old friend," Ezra said. "I'll call you from New York as soon as I've got something."

The newspapers at the airport were full of parallels between Karol's murder and the murder of Antinoüs. Nick was explaining the similarity to Ezra. But Sordino had done it a few hours before. Antinoüs had been a beautiful young boy from Bythinia whom Hadrian had loved—or was rumored to have loved. Pagan antiquity is full of such ambiguities. Unlike modern, Catholic Rome—in which everyone had decided that the boy had been sleeping with both Michael Maurice and Sordino and had paid the price for it. The mystery of the death of Antinoüs had never been solved. Fished out of the Nile while Hardrian wept—a rare sight, considering the glib gift for murder he developed in his later years—Antinoüs was memorialized in the Temple of Canopus. Several thousand years later, in the Sala Rotunda, Karol was photographed by the cameras of twelve countries, next to the bust of Antinoüs. And journalists wrote sweetened words about the rebirth of the cult of Antinoüs, whose original cult, some said, had been the first breath of romantic obsession in the ancient world.

It had all been Nick's idea. Ezra imagined Max shaking his head over it: "How does *he* know all that stuff? From where? Why?" Much might have come from Sordino, Ezra assumed. He'd had a brief meeting with Sordino before leaving for the airport. He'd asked the old man for the favor he needed. A good word for Mitch Stone with the powers of Cannes. Sordino had granted it. Nick had told him of Ezra's speech at the meeting and he was grateful. Not that it really mattered, he added with a shadow of his old disdain. He could always get the money to finish the picture elsewhere. Italian sources were available, as well as the majors. Nevertheless . . .

"I will speak to Favre LeBret at Cannes. But you must ask Stone to come here with a print and screen it for me. It is not enough that you tell me he studies the book on my films. Not enough."

"I'll ask him. There won't be any problem."

"I cannot guarantee . . ."

"Also, no problem."

"No, he must come and take back the requiem mass he preached over my grave. He must come and after I have seen his picture I will show him my picture. I will show him what can be done with one camera instead of thirty. With the imagination instead of reality."

That was when Sordino had told him about Antinoüs. His large eyes had grown distant and he'd fiddled with his knotted scarf. He was sitting in front of the Movieola, having apologized to Ezra for receiving him there; apologized in a proud way, pointing out that he always cut his films as he shot; always had a rough cut ready by the end of shooting. The theatrical opening could always take place six months—at the latest—after the start of principal photography.

The image of Karol was frozen in the Movieola: an insolent smile on his delicate lips. Using the picture as his theme, Sordino denied the parallel to Antinoüs. "That look was not typical," he said. "He was a gentle boy. There was play in him, but not bad—to say—evil. Not that anyone knows what Antinoüs was truly like."

"No," Ezra said. "I think of him more like those Schubert songs he played all the time."

Sordino smiled miserably. "Yes," he'd said. "Like 'Auf der Bruck'; he was like that. Simple, but full of strange feelings." And bowed a leonine head on his arms and wept.

"I *did* love him," Sordino had said. His wrinkled hands opened and closed helplessly. "I would not tell this to Captain Calamandrei. But I *did* love Karol. But not in any way to use him, . . . or to harm him . . . or to degrade the friendship. I have not loved women for many years.Though" —a momentary roguish break in his sorrow— "there was a time when I made much trouble in that sphere." The smile faded quickly. "But for many years, no. Still, a boy like Karol, in his way, at his time . . . there could only be . . . what there was. Only, good." No mention, either defensive or hostile, of Michael Maurice. Only a last remark that perhaps Karol's murder, like that of Antinoüs, would remain unsolved.

The parade of King Studio executives to the gate distracted Nick and Ezra from their guarded conversation. Nick had just mentioned how dumb he thought Ezra's ideas about the novelization of the screenplay of *The Lion's Fare-*

well, how tricky it had been to use the snake motif in the advertising for *Festival,* without checking with him; the authorization of $40,000 which had, magically, turned into $70,000. The moment was about to turn ugly.

Just as tags were being fixed to Nick's baggage, Max, the studio troubador, Max the bringer of truth and lies, Max the singer of studio songs, brought the news that Giannini and the Spy Driver had been arrested: suspicion of murder. Nick grabbed his bags from the platform and careened toward the main exit.

"Look at him go," Max marveled, despairing. "What is he going to do? What's in his mind? What does he know? Where is he going? Why is he running? Who is he going to save?"

7

By chance, there was no one in first class but the King Studio executives. The night flight from Rome was always light on passengers, even in summer. The morning flight was more popular. Not everyone was in as much of a hurry as this group of men, on their way to prepare for a company meeting in New York: their beginning or their end. They deserved a plane to themselves. There could not be many such corporate moments.

Max's last chanted questions rang in Ezra's head: question-bells that could, as well, ring for all of them. "Where were they going? What did they hope to save? How?" Ezra gazed out at the black sky. Below them, Captain Calamandrei might be questioning Giannini and the Spy Driver. Or was he perhaps past that—the testimony all taken, the confession obtained, the conviction wrapped up?

During most of the flight back, Becker played gin rummy with one of the men in sales, alternating it with endless dictation into a cassette recorder. The cabin was full of small talk, the embarrassed jokes, everyone concerned: How did the arrest of two studio employees involve them? No one speculated as to motive . . . too dangerous . . . once begun there was no stopping that line of thought . . . a long thread of gunpowder from old movies leading to an inevitable explosion.

The familiar landscape of the nighttime traveler: the plane's darkened aisles . . . engines steady soporific hum . . . some passengers dozing . . . one staring blankly out of the window at a sky that stares blankly back . . . a stewardess bending over a seat, coffee cup in hand . . . the light on over the lavatory: OCCUPIED. . . . The ordered, daytime way of receiving and recording experience breaks down, like sentences collapsing into ellipses. . . .

Kleinholz summons Ezra. . . . Ape brings the command . . . in that half-light, the jump-suited Ape looks as if he's ready to parachute from the plane. . . . Ezra stifles a yawn . . . follows him to the seat next to Kleinholz, who sits enfolded in papers and tapes . . . still sleepy, Ezra hears the offer he has thought might be coming soon . . . or never . . . three-year contract . . . encased in glorious numbers . . . $2000 a week . . . to begin . . . stock options . . . ten thousand shares . . . spaced appropriately . . . glorious titles abound as well . . . vice president of advertising and publicity, world-wide . . . ah, world-wide . . . *du monde entier* . . . the words come also impelled by gusts of foul breath . . . whether from exhaustion or poorly digested food . . . and triggers some surprise hesitation in Ezra . . . he will think it over . . . flattered and pleased . . . will give Kleinholz his answer in New York . . . no surprise from behind the bad breath . . . think—naturally . . . consult your lawyer . . . of course . . . unmentioned is the apparently replaceable Nick Bohm. . . . Ezra is to be prepared to address the company meeting. Ah, yes, he is new marketing blood. . . . Then back to his seat to stare at the sky-shrouded window in blind, exultant confusion.

8

Fresh, innocent words spoken by the two secretaries who guarded Nick's office in New York.

"They got Giannini at last, that old thief." Thus Luisa, an Italian girl whose father had been a distinguished director back in the distinguished days. Luisa had been at the studio and in the New York offices. She longed to be reassigned to the Coast.

"And his driver," Gerry said. Gerry was the second girl in the office. Both of them had spent their entire secretarial careers in the service of King Studio. They gossiped a sort of operatic duet. "Giannini steals from the advertising, from the printing of the color posters, from the transportation. . . ."

"Splits it with Umberto Rossi."

"Who splits it with Becker."

"Who . . ."

Ezra entered the anteroom; there was an embarrassed pause. "Don't stop," Ezra said and laughed. "I'm too new to be in on the splits."

"Well, you know, Mr. Marks," Luisa said, "that's just business, that's the way it goes."

Nick's office, which Ezra had been instructed to use for the remainder of this New York stay, was the size of a small gymnasium. A Louis XIII desk was placed cater-cornered to a broad window overlooking Fifth Avenue. A long conference table and chairs, and a lovely beige couch completed the arrangements. Fresh flowers were placed in a vase on the table every morning by Luisa or Gerry. Ah, Luisa and Gerry, what an anthology of further "splits" could you compile, had we but world enough and . . . Fresh flowers daily, and splits—while the studio loses 67 per cent of its equity in one year.

The girls were complex. Gerry wept in the ladies' room because Giannini had given her a Dior scarf for Christmas and now might die for the crime of murder.

"Life in L.A. is so much nicer, Mr. Marks," Luisa said, handing him the morning's batch of cables. "You can play tennis at lunchtime without leaving the lot."

A cable from Archer in Cannes: KIDS POURING INTO FRANCE. HARD TO HANDLE STOP NO ANSWER YET ON FESTIVAL SCREENING. Corporate poems, these daily cables. Ezra particularly liked the hidden rhyme between France and the first syllable of answer. You took your amusements in whatever disguise they came. Amazement too: a memo from Kleinholz to Ezra, ccs to no one—no one listed, that is. One could assume the usual number of "blind" copies. Short and pointed: King Studio would now compromise on a cut with Mitchell Stone. They needed the picture too badly to be stubborn. This would be the first order of business when they returned to the Coast. In the meantime, Ezra was to continue his approaches to Stone on the compromise and report back to Kleinholz.

There was a thin line of untraceable mystery, the mystery of how far people could be pushed, the mystery of when Kleinholz's ego suddenly eased up on him, long enough for him to change his mind. . . .

Ezra remembered Stone, lying on the floor in his castle, laying all the troubles of the modern world to the reluctance of those who were no longer in control of things to admit

that loss of power. And Nick Bohm's prematurely tri-
umphant stammer had been answered. ("Ssshhow t-t-them
who's in ch-ch-arge.")

Tape-memories:
KLEINHOLZ: I don't care how or what you do. . . . Get it
under control.
NICK BOHM: He's just a kid. . . .
KLEINHOLZ: I don't give a damn.
NICK BOHM: I'll do what I c-c-c-can.
KLEINHOLZ: You'll do what you have to do.

In the great expanse of the empty office, in the dim blue-
black of the early New York evening, it seemed even more
sinister than it had sounded in Kleinholz's office on the lot.
It was impossible for Ezra to take in. People one knew were
not murdered. In the course of a robbery or a street crime,
perhaps. But not a genuine, secret, and unsolved murder.
People one knew did not commit murder. Either the tape or
Kim was misleading. And Giannini . . . in Max's words, an
ordinary ganef? Nothing made sense.

Except for the research report. It would take at least
$300,000, maybe more. And at least six months. But at the
end of that time, they might have a discipline with which
the success or failure of films could be predicted or controlled. Many millions of dollars could be saved, and Ezra
Marks would be, if not the savior of the film business, then
at least the Saint Paul. Such are the fantasies of benign role-
playing in business. Stuff the report into the attaché case
and swing down the hall lined with stills from forty years of
King Studio productions. Smile at secretaries, a stern look at
a minor executive in sales who waves—one can only assume
he has heard the news. Down the elevator into the yellow
and blue summer night. Walk to the hotel for a brief rest
(we at the top need more rest than others), then a drink and

dinner at the Russian Tea Room, thinking all the while of tomorrow's meetings and next week's meeting. And do it all as if you've been a movie executive for years instead of months.

Memo: *Don't dial Kim's New York number!*

9

"Sorry to disturb you, Mr. Marks."

"That's all right, Lieutenant."

"We'll only take a few moments of your time. I'd like to check over this list of some of the employees in your department."

"Who gave you the list?"

"Well, we're cooperating with the Italian police, and they are with us. In fact, everybody's cooperating."

"I see," Ezra said.

"Umberto Rossi."

"He's not my employee. He's an executive in an Italian affiliated company. Who *did* give you that list?"

"How about Archer?"

"Yes, he's in the department."

"What's your impression— did he have it in for the victim?"

Ezra thought, They really say "the victim."

"Not at all. I can't imagine he could have been involved."

"Why are you so sure, Mr. Marks?"

"I don't quite know. Archer is—he's—well, the complete functionary. He would never do anything as independent as murdering someone. If he did, he might have my job. Is Archer a suspect?

"Not really. We're just trying to see if there's some kind

of chain." There was apparently no way of gaining information by asking questions of the police.

"Does Nick Bohm work for you?"

"That's hard to say." How explain the changing balances
of studio life? "Anyway, Captain Calamandrei told me his
alibi is established."

"I can't go into that. Did Mr. Bohm ever express feelings
of violence toward the victim?"

Many times, many times, Ezra thought. But those are
just expressions. The term: "I'd like to kill that cocksucker,"
is merely daily verbal coinage in a volatile industry. Impossible for the man playing the role of executive to explain it
to the man playing the role of detective.

"Not that I recall. Some anger, yes."

"Why?"

"Everyone was eager for the boy to leave town. There
was a bad situation developing."

"A homo–sexual situation, you mean?" He broke up the
word so that it sounded like a zoological definition.

"Yes. Tell me, what did you mean by 'some kind of
chain'?"

"Well, if, as you say, everyone was eager to get rid of the
boy, maybe everyone was involved. The Italian police have
narrowed down the suspects to a few . . . maybe to one."

"Then you don't mean everyone. . . ."

"No, but that's what we mean by a chain."

"Tell me," Ezra said, "Exactly how did Karol die?"

"A broken neck. He was struck or thrown pretty hard;
pieces of bone were sticking out through the skin. Now, I
only have a few more of your employees to discuss. Who is
Kimberly Cross, Rafaello Giannini, Max Miranda, Lothar
Kleinholz. . . ."

"Lieutenant, I'd give anything to know where you got
that list."

10

Ezra was finishing dinner at the Russian Tea Room, wavering between coffee and work at the hotel, or Sanka and sleep, when Max walked in. It was surprising that he got past the headwaiter. He wore blue slacks and a seersucker jacket that looked as if he had slept in it for nights. Max wore no tie; his eyes were too wide open, as if afraid he might stumble and fall if he did not watch the area around him carefully. His left hand was jammed into the pocket of his jacket. His right hand waved over the expanse of the restaurant, a divining rod searching.

"Sit down, Max," Ezra said. "Before you fall down."

"I've been looking for you, Ezra," he said.

"You look awful. Where the hell have you been?"

"Around. They told me at the office you were here."

"Want something to eat?"

"No. I want a drink."

"How about some food. You look as if you could use some."

"A Black Russian, that's what I want, need."

"What's a Black Russian?"

"Vodka and Kahlua."

He drank one quickly and ordered another.

"All those jokes about being the boss," he said, "and now you *are* the boss!"

"It's only a department, Max. Kleinholz is the boss."

"Is he?"

He was hunched over in his chair, curled around that second Black Russian, one hand on the glass, the other crushed into his pocket. The skin of his flushed cheeks was tight across his face.

"What's going to happen to Nick?" he asked.

"Nick is a way of life unto himself," Ezra said. "I don't

know what's going to happen to him. What's wrong, Max? What is it?"

Max's eyes blinked, quickly. Sensitive to Ezra's stare he said, "I took some pills. One of Mitch Stone's kids gave them to me. 'Ups' he called them. I figure that's better than 'downs.' Right?"

"Not necessarily."

"Everything's changing. Next week's the big meeting." Nick's always telling me how he's seen those things come and go and none of it touches him."

"That's Nick. Not me. Everything touches me. Nothing touches Nick. I'd like another one of these."

"Without me," Ezra said. "I've got a big day tomorrow."

"Who was Antinoüs?" Max asked.

"Look," Ezra said. "I was visited by the police in my hotel just before coming here. They were trying to find out who killed our Antinoüs. I don't know who did. And I have a confused idea of who he was, in the original. But if you're going to drink yourself even sicker than you obviously are, you'll have to do it without me." He stood up and touched his arm. "Max, if you've taken pills, whatever the hell 'ups' they gave you, you shouldn't drink. It's been a bad time but don't knock yourself out like this. I'm going. Just sign my name to the check, will you?"

"Please don't do that," Max said.

"Don't do what?"

"Don't start to go away, now. I want to talk to you."

Something in Max's tone told Ezra to leave at once, or else something sticky would be coming up. Max's ragged look promised trouble. It reminded Ezra that people— Archer, Nick Bohm, and others—had spoken in passing of Max's bad personal life, long in the past. Undrawn pictures of torments that might be reappearing, in some visible form, tonight. It was best not to confront it directly. He was start-

ing to move away, preparing some banal remark about fatigue and the next day's work when Max said:

"If you'll look at my pocket you'll see that I haven't
taken my hand out of it since I came in here. I don't want to
sound crazy but you can figure out what I'm talking
about."

"Oh, shit, Max. How drunk are you?" Ezra sat down
opposite him again.

"These are the first two I've had."

"Then it's those 'ups.' Why don't you just call it a night?"
Walking wounded, he thought; that was his first misty impression, and it was getting clearer.

"Because I have something important to tell you. And I
don't think you should be running away before I tell you—
or even afterward." A small laugh, from the back of his
throat, hoarse. "Most of all not afterward."

Ezra looked at him, this ridiculous figure, hopeless in
any bid to be taken seriously, even for a moment. In that
one moment Ezra took him quite seriously at last.

"My God, Max," he said. "What is it?"

Max nodded as if to say he understood that Ezra knew,
already, what it was, and Ezra half-nodded back. They were
like two caricatures of old men wearily nodding their
knowledge of awful, unchangeable evil. As if to say it hardly
has to be told, the terrible things people can do, the terrible
thing that Max had to tell him, the terrible thing he had
done.

They had come a long way; a long way from that first
day and the golf cart ride around the studio lot, Max giving
pertinent and impertinent data about the executives, the
stars, calling him boss and chief in his limitless anxiety; a
long way from Max's yearnings for studio status, from his
bewildered continuing chronicling of Nick Bohm's mysterious career, a long way from the innocence of petty studio
graft and gossip to the simple flatness of: "It was me."

In spite of what Ezra already knew, had almost known since Max sat down, he needed a more direct statement.

"What do you mean, Max? Did you kill the boy?"

Max grew unexpectedly agitated. The free hand waved in the air. "Listen," he said, "don't expect me to say anything about killing. That's not the point. But it was not Giannini or anybody else, it was me. That's what I have to tell you."

They sat there looking at each other. Ezra tried not to look at that ridiculous pocket with a hand and perhaps something more dangerous hidden in it. He didn't believe that Max had murdered Karol. What was probably true was some chain of causation in which he was involved.

Ezra said, "Tell me, Max."

"Oh, yes. Don't worry." His face became a circle furrowed on top in seriousness. "You see, I thought maybe nobody would be arrested. I read somewhere that eighty per cent of all murders stay unsolved. Why couldn't I be in that eighty per cent, hah?" He shook his head in Max-like disappointment at his usual bad luck—passed over for promotions, raises, a murder discovered when it might so easily have been forever undiscovered. Bad luck stuck to some people all the way.

"With Giannini arrested—when they did that—I knew I had to come and talk to you."

"Why me?"

Max smiled; a wraith of a smile hovering over bleary eyes and trembling mouth. "We have an appointment. I was going to take you to the prop department on the lot and pick out some fantastic stuff for your new office, remember?"

"Come on, Max. Why *me*?"

"But I'm not going to get to the lot now. So we'll do it here."

"Where?"

Ezra glanced down at the bulge in his pocket, silly but

menacing; some pastiche of a gesture picked up from scenes watched in screening rooms for years. Ezra took a breath and said with an assurance he did not feel, "Let's go, Max. Let's go to the police."

Max shook his head with more sadness than anger. Ezra waited for him to say something, but he just kept shaking his head from side to side as if he would never stop.

The magic of the unseen. The pocketful of Max's hand and whatever else made Ezra obey. For the moment there was no mystery about who was in charge.

11

They stopped on the corner of Fifty-seventh Street and Eighth Avenue to buy a fifth of vodka for Max. Five minutes later they were walking through a warehouse on Ninth Avenue packed with the detritus of Max's life and mind. It was Drakmalnik's legendary collection. Nick had promised Ezra a glimpse of it. Archer had suggested a visit someday; here it was at night. Max switched on lights for various sections, leaving others in darkness.

Anchored in dust and surrounded by long-unused packing crates and mottled coils of rope, the integers of the Drakmalnik equation presented themselves. A World War II tank hulked grandly in a distant corner. A great searchlight half covered in canvas slept nearby. A jumble of the furniture and clothing of a hundred eras covered the floor: long couches on which were draped togas, pseudo-Elizabethan costumes, evening gowns of the ante-bellum Southern period, sequins and guns from the Roaring Twenties. A towering pile of ten-gallon cowboy hats rested on an exquisite *escritoire* of one Louis or another . . . a giant crystal chandelier overhead and one resting on the floor, missing

pieces of glass like missing teeth . . . next to it a gigantic pile
of eyeglasses, every style and period . . . near that a slag
heap of shoes suitable for wearing by George Arliss, George
the Third or George Raft. . . . It was the accumulated dreck
of a whole world. Drakmalnik's cemetery—where all good
"things" go to die after being photographed for the movies;
thence to be resurrected from time to time for special publicity photography, for television commercials, to be com-
mandeered for the offices of new studio executives.

With its mountains of shoes, hats, and eyeglasses, it
resembled concentration-camp terrain. Max wandered
through the debris, poking here and there, like some *Gau-
leiter* of Ninth Avenue, of the studio. . . .

"Look at this, Ezra." He was a revivified Max, jabbing
right and left with his available hand. "You should have this
couch in your new office. It was in the living-room set of
Rebecca. The first picture I ever worked on. Figure that—
1940! Two years after I came to this country."

News! He'd had no idea Max was an immigrant, even at
an early age. There was no trace of an accent.

"Worked on! I was a gopher. Go for coffee, for cigarettes."

It was an odd barnlike roof with eaves and objects Ezra
couldn't make out slung over them. As they moved forward,
Max always carefully behind him and a few feet away, they
passed several pieces of Egyptian statuary, World War I
posters on the wall, a coffin standing on end. Max seemed to
breathe easier here. Ezra had removed the cap of the bottle
of vodka for him. Max sipped from it, as from a bottle of
Coke.

"This is the unofficial prop department for the East
Coast," he confided. "Drakmalnik has a deal—Nick and I
arranged it—and when the studio doesn't need something,
Drakmalnik rents it out for TV commercials, industrial
films; he doesn't breathe without turning over a dollar, that

man." Max spoke with great admiration. It occurred to Ezra that he was a man given to powerful, loyal attachments; that the machinery of those attachments had broken down somewhere; that because of that breakdown something much worse than an evening of charades might come of it. He had been letting Max lead, not knowing what else he could do. Now he began to plan.

Max was still in the depths of his admiration for Drakmalnik. "He's got stuff here the prop department at the studio could never find. And I've stood here with him—in this craziness—and he just raises a hand and points, and whatever you need is right there." A wheelchair appeared from under a pile of Indian blankets. "Hah," Max said. "The best years of our lives."

"What?"

His repetition made it clear it was not a comment but a title: *The Best Years of Our Lives*. Nick and I worked publicity on that together. He worked for Goldwyn full time then, but I was free lance."

Ezra vaguely remembered the picture: a returned veteran, an artificial limb—with or without wheelchair. Max might be doing as much free associating as remembering. He was in that kind of state. Anyway, whether the wheelchair was actual or metaphorical did not matter. It served.

Max sat on a stuffed velvet chair. He waved the vodka bottle expansively in a cloud of dust. Some instinct prompted Ezra to ask about his wife. There was always a veil of unspeakability around that theme. The unspeakable might open something up: make Max vulnerable to reason and close down the show at last. The track was obviously the right one. Max stopped being expansive. His face grew cloudy and he slumped in the chair. He said nothing, eyes staring, chips of stars enclosed in a moon. Afraid at what he might have done, Ezra kept talking. He asked about the press party at Hadrian's Villa. Nobody, not even Captain

Calamandrei or Kim, had told him the way it had actually been that night.

"The funny thing is, there's nothing to tell," Max said. "I swear to you." And proceeded to tell about the arrival of the press at Hadrian's Villa, the roped areas set up for V.I.P.s; everything flooded with light from searchlights trucked in from Rome; photographers sipping champagne and taking set-up shots of Karol. Nick had had a long talk with Michael Maurice about the progress of his knighthood—the waspish old star was on his good behavior. Sordino in a fine mood gave interviews and posed next to Kim's painting. A feast of mutual cooperation. All those hatchets that had been so active were, that evening, buried in the soil of Tivoli.

Finally, as the evening was dissolving, people singing out good-bys, floods winking off one by one, limousines heading back to Rome, only one detail remained. Max was to find Karol and give him his instructions, details, tickets.

He found Karol in the rear of the Temple of Canopus, surrounded by pillars, rocks, rubble—having just said good-by—*au revoir?*—to Michael Maurice. The boy appeared nervous, but Max decided to ignore it and just do his job. Mechanically, he told Karol he'd been terrific, that he was leaving in the morning on Pan American Flight 603 for Budapest. He had even written it down on a slip of paper which he handed to Karol, telling him the tickets were with the concierge's desk at the Excelsior.

"It was simple, right? Like I said, nothing to tell."

But Karol laughed. That was an important point. He laughed at that precise moment.

" 'What's funny kid?' " Max asked.

"Karol replied that it was funny the way studio people assumed that whatever they want to be done *will* be done."

Max said, " 'Be reasonable. Your part is finished. You know what kind of trouble you can get into hanging around here.' "

Max's ears were alert to sounds from behind: cars rolling up, doors slamming, and the cars buzzing down the hill.

Max said: " 'Look you're teasing me to make me feel bad, right? You've got that piece of paper, pick up your tickets. My advice is: don't be in Rome after tomorrow morning.' " Max's gifts were not verbal. What followed was his attempt at eloquence. " 'We've got terrific stuff lined up for you in London and then in America; you can go to the Far East, even. Everybody says you're going to be very big. Just help us get through these next few weeks okay, and we're all home free.'

"And then he looked at me and laughed and said, 'I don't want any of that. . . .' "

Unthinkable statement, by Max's lights. But how to explain the choice of Schubert, Schumann, Hugo Wolf?

"And he said a whole lot of other things which I don't remember because I was thinking it's not right that one kid should kill everything for so many people . . . for a whole studio . . . like those other kids, those freaks of Mitch Stone's that are killing everything for so many people . . . and I didn't know what to do . . . and I felt weak and then I remembered all of a sudden what you said to me in Paris and it made me feel better. . . ."

"What?"

"On the bridge, late at night, with Rossi and I forget who else. . . ."

"What did I say to you, Max?"

"Hey, Ezra, come on. . . ."

"I'm asking you, what did I tell you?"

"You don't remember?"

"It was late. I was beat and full of brandy."

"You said: 'We've got till the weekend. Get rid of him, or he'll get rid of us.' Something like that. And I remember you pointed down to the river—like the kid was going to drown us all."

Ezra said nothing. Then he repeated, "It was late. . . . I don't know what the hell you're talking about."

Max's bleary eyes looked at Ezra in contempt.

"When I couldn't take it for another second, I picked up that kid and threw him against the stone wall. I was tired and I was full of booze. He didn't move from the minute he fell; I could tell from the sound it was going to be bad, very bad. Oh, Jesus, boss, what am I going to do, what am I ever going to do?"

"You'll be okay, Max," Ezra said. "Come with me now and let's tell them the whole story. You didn't plan a damn thing, you're not a murderer, for God's sake. You did something wild on impulse."

Max said, almost inaudibly so that Ezra had to lean forward to hear, "It's not your fault, but you got to believe me . . . the last thing I thought of before I picked that kid up . . . weak, old Max Miranda picking that kid up like that . . . that last thing I thought of that I can remember clearly was what you said to me on the bridge. That, all mixed up with a feeling, a terrible wish that everything could be the way it used to be . . . the whole thing a going concern. . . . You don't know what it was like when we had forty pictures a year going—the lot buzzing like crazy, Max Miranda running the publicity, stars and directors and producers, everybody knew where he stood in the scheme of things. . . . You know? There was a kind of order that you bitched about, like the Army. . . . I only put in six months because of a punctured eardrum. . . . In fact everybody hated the system a lot . . . *but it was the system!* You knew it was there. You knew what to hate if you wanted to hate. If you were a Communist you could hate it for that reason. If you were a writer you could want control of your script . . . an actor wanted better parts, more dough . . . if you were a director you could want final cut. Hah! That's one thing Kleinholz would never give. And Mitch Stone can hold his breath till he chokes and vomits snakes, he's never going to get his cut out of the old man. . . ."

The Ezra who had been driving from situation to situation, from project to project, was stilled by Max's tale of not-so-accidental death. Max had given him a "down"; perhaps a final "down." Where tomorrow had been in his mind—the entire space occupied by presentations, reports, Kleinholz's contract, the balancing of Becker and Robinson against that offer, the upcoming meeting: that space was now blank. He had been observing the effects of a young boy's life being stopped; now it seemed he had been present at the event, had played a part, no matter how small, in the murderer's mind. . . . (In some corner of his own blanked-out mind he noted the difference between manslaughter and murder; Max had been correct. There was no question of murder here. Someone had struck someone else in anger. The result had been death. But in whose name had the blow been struck?)

He felt choked in, asthmatic; a combination of Drakmalnik's dust and a disgust that stuck in the chest and got confused with the actual mechanism of breathing. It grew into rage at being confined in Max's house of memory. Max had misunderstood his words, misused them as certainly as if he'd spoken in French on that French bridge. Was this why he'd chosen Ezra to search out? His boss and captive audience—because in his imagination they were partners in the terrible event?

Ezra couldn't bear to be Max's partner (real or imagined), Max's boss, Max's spiritual guide, Max's victim, Max's executioner or the recipient of Max's yearnings for a lost world of order and value. All he wanted was to be away from there.

If Ezra was "down," Max was still partially "up." He said, "I never did anything with violence in my life. There's a famous story about Nick once working somebody over—

but I have never touched—not until . . ." It all seemed to be getting out of his control. Then, with a nervous smile (as if afraid he might be thought mad) :

"You know, I was going to hijack a plane with you. That was my first idea. This is the year to do that, right? Everybody's doing it. All these Third World cats. Well, I could be a Fourth World hijacker. I could represent all the people who do what they're told year after year—until suddenly, one day, nobody knows who's giving the orders, really, or who they should obey, or what they should do any more. There must be a hell of a lot of people in that spot, right? Maybe enough for a Fourth World. But where would we take the plane? We—that's you and me. I was going to take you as a hostage. You need a hostage these days; very important. But where—where would we go?"

Ezra moved in. "You couldn't do anything like that," he said. "You're not a violent man—and you've seen too many terrible things—too close to you."

Ezra began to work on his freedom gradually, probing—oh so gently—with suggestions—oh so sympathetic—that Max might have been treated badly by fate. (He seemed to recall someone using the word tragedy in speaking of Max's past, but he wasn't sure so he walked around that word.) Drawing him out, Ezra assured him that the authorities would understand what had happened with Karol.

Max softened. Did his hand shift from his pocket? No, he was eternally one-handed, but he closed the distance between them more often in his wanderings. Did he turn his back? No. But he covered his face with his hand long enough, perhaps, for Ezra to cover much of the distance to the door. He was unwilling to risk running for it.

Ezra led him from his first jobs through his first dates with his wife, troubled lady that she was, through his first fears that he was getting in over his head. The time she disappeared for a week and could not account for where she

had been, what she had done. The sudden depressions and
the half-hearted suicide attempt. The days when she did not
tend to her hair, looking like a Raggedy-Ann doll some child
had forgotten to care for; the weak bladder leading to the
puddle on the screening-room floor.

By this time he had the feeling that if Max let him
through the gates of the past he would emerge free. Finally
it came out. Banal, it had the distance and strangeness of
the familiar. That *Daily News*, New York *Enquirer* world of
domestic tragedy and scandal that is as near as the corner
newsstand or the tenement down the block, but as distant as
the slightness of its essential claim on our attention, our
credibility.

When it finally came out he told it distractedly, twisting,
even turning his back. But at that point all Ezra had to do
was listen: not run or strike Max down, just listen.

"They don't tell you what it could be like . . . they don't
tell you in the books or the movies about what it's like when
you walk in—when you see the bodies twisted in some kind
of jigsaw puzzle. They don't tell you about the smell—it
couldn't have been more than a few hours, but they were
both stiff—I don't know how many times I've heard the
guys—all my friends at the police department—if you're in
publicity long enough they all get to be your friends down
there—they always call them 'stiffs.' And then the shock to
find out that's what they really are. Only they're *yours*! She
used to get so depressed and there was nothing I could do
about it. She was an angry woman. And she was afraid of
everything! Listen, she wasn't so crazy. There's a lot to be
scared of. . . . I'd been away on a publicity trip, a junket—
Honolulu. People to smell like that . . . I forget what picture.
But can you imagine what it's like to kill your own child—
Jesus Christ, I mean can you imagine for one minute what
goes through the mind of somebody who kills their own
child, deliberately? Who thinks about it and then does it?

to feel the life you put in them go out . . . with your fingers . . . I mean there can't be anything worse than that. . . . Especially a gifted child like that, my little Susan . . . she was the smartest five-year-old you ever saw . . . used to make clay sculptures and exhibit them on the hill in Bel-Air. . . . And now I've killed a kid, too. . . . But I couldn't kill a kid, not after that, but what I can't stand is that even though I couldn't kill him, he's dead. He came up from the ground so easy, like we were going to dance, and I was so mad, and I threw him down just like I didn't want to have anything more to do with him, because I was just doing my job and he wouldn't let me do it, that was all, not to make him stop living, I could never make anybody stop living. . . . I didn't want anybody dead but somebody *is* dead. Nobody wanted death . . . nobody you know ever wants anybody dead, but somehow people are dead . . . and I did the same thing my poor, crazy wife Ellen did, I killed a kid . . . only I didn't feel like I'd really done it—she knew what she did, planned it, made it work. . . . I just went to do a job and ended up with a body on the ground. . . . In a funny way if you think about it like a movie, all of us wanting him out of there and then him ending up on the ground not moving, it doesn't seem so peculiar, it seems like you could see it as the ending of a picture. . . . Listen, I don't feel so good, Ezra I feel sick. . . ."

Ezra watched Max's pocket, a seersucker bulge, and the instant before the liberating movement he was waiting for, he saw something else: a seep of blood—red slowly creeping down the striped fabric.

It was all over, he could see that; and all he could say was, "Max, what did you do . . . ?" like some mother in a story, that was all he could say, and he said it at least three times. . . .

Then Ezra reached over, as gently as he could to disengage the sticky, bloody hand from the cloth stuck to it. But

Max pulled it out, violently, just to get his poor wounded hand to his weeping eyes. The blood mingled with tears in an awful ritual that must have soothed, because he kept the hands there, the whole one and the torn one; the one whose wrist he had tried to hack to ribbons to stop whatever film was playing in his mind that had to be stopped, ragged red strips of skin hanging from the wrist, like used Band-Aids. His round face was the face of a blood-soiled cherub when he was finished.

"Please," Max said. "Please tell me what I should do, tell me what to do, please, boss, tell me, tell me, tell me. . . ."

12

Our beginnings never know our ends. . . .

Ezra arrived at the New York Hilton an hour before the stockholders' meeting was to begin. Sixth Avenue was being torn up for a new subway extension. A long line of taxis waited in front of the hotel; cabbies sat in their sweat and impatience, while out-of-towners and stockholders coming to the King Studio annual meeting entered in a sunny drizzle.

Robinson was alone, finishing breakfast in his suite. He was dressed in a gray tropical suit, shoes off for temporary comfort, gray silk socks, and gray slippers. Since their last meeting he had become a comic-strip character: Grayman —capable of taking over entire companies in a single bound. Grayman with a murderous cold; Dristan and Contac, handkerchiefs and inhalers shared surface space with papers, cups, and saucers. Robinson smiled from behind angry-red eyes and a wet nose.

"Stress," he said. "My doctor says I get allergic in stress

situations. Well, it's my choice. I choose to go through life with teary eyes and dripping nose—all for ambition." A respiratory disaster, he wheezed and coughed an invitation to have some breakfast. "At least those spots that wandered in front of my eyes are gone. Remember those spots? I was a mess."

"Just coffee," Ezra said. "I had breakfast on the plane."

"Where the hell were you?"

"I just got on a plane to get me out of New York. Anywhere. It turned out to be New Mexico."

"What did you do all those days?"

"I was a tourist, Indian pueblos, that kind of a thing. And I met a nice kid who wants to go into the movies. And an old director named Russell James. I slept a lot. Convalescing. I was trying to put my head back together. After Max took it apart."

"Mr. Hoffman at Hornblower & Weeks, and Mr. Theodore at Lehman Brothers are still waiting for you to show up."

"Sorry."

"It was a little embarrassing to the committee."

"My apologies to the committee. Kleinholz managed to find out where I was. He sent me a telegram."

"I heard he made you an offer."

"Right. On the plane going back to New York."

"That just shows how strong we were getting. He's covering all his bets."

"Anyway, I couldn't stay in New York for one more minute. Actually, I started out for L.A. after depositing Max with the police, and calling the lawyers—but I seem to have ended up in Santa Fe."

"Hot this time of year. That's what I need." He blew his nose and stared into the handkerchief as if to decipher the results. "Listen, how are you? Everybody was worried."

"Could I have a list of 'everybody'?"

"Start with me."

"I'm okay. I went to the D. H. Lawrence shrine. Did you know that Frieda was buried outside the tomb?"

There were papers strewn all over the coffee table between the dirty dishes and ashtrays. This was not the morning to discuss the terms of D. H. Lawrence's will.

"Crazy that it should be Max," Robinson said.

"Is it?"

"I heard he had you under a gun or something for hours. . . ." A new Hollywood legend was being born.

"He had me under a bleeding hand in an empty pocket for hours. Robbie, I don't know how to just go on as usual."

"What are you talking about? Karol laughed at Max at the wrong moment—and he got very mad, a lot of pressure everybody was under—and the rest was basically an accidental death."

"Accidental?"

"He shoved him. He didn't try to kill him."

"He picked him up and threw him down so that he would somehow just not be there any more."

Then he told Max's little tale of words spoken on the bridge in Paris. One of those nice little odds and ends that wouldn't convict anyone in a court of law, but if the court of law was inside your head, were bad enough.

Robinson stood up; he loomed over Ezra and sniffled impatiently. "If you want to romanticize it and deal yourself in on the responsibility, that's your business. But it's foolishness. Of course everybody concerned, even slightly, in chains of events like these, is responsible to some degree. But for that very reason—because everybody is a little involved by implication—the less any one individual is to blame. Except the poor fool who lets himself be pushed to the point of doing something rough. Do you understand what I'm talking about?" He closed his rheumy eyes for an instant.

Ezra listened, ice-cold, and said, "Yes. You're talking about something called psychoeconomics."

"Oh, shit, Ezra. Don't play so innocent. I didn't lie to you when I told you about the studio and the movie business. It's very American. The profit motive in one of its strangest incarnations. It only horrifies someone like you because art gets mixed up in it. And where there's art you expect some kind of special humanity in the mixture. But exactly the opposite seems to happen. When art gets mixed up with business it leads the way to the worst kind of corruption of both processes. Except, now and then, when you get lucky, and the art comes out clean. The people and the business part never do."

"Thanks for the absolution. I forgot you went to law school."

"You *should* thank me. You've been connected with a couple of extraordinary movies. You've been offered more money than most people ever get near—plus a little pleasant power. I haven't done so badly for you, old friend."

He sipped Robbie's coffee and picked up his tone. "Old friend," Ezra said. "While you were worrying about me, I was out in the wilds of the Southwest thinking about you, about our green days; about your funny apologetic attitude at Cambridge about teaching something called communications, while I laughed at my own little monster: demographics. The pseudosciences. It was over a drink at the Ritz Bar on Boston Common. And on the way out we laughed at the sign over one of the doors: Not an Accredited Egress Door."

"For God's sake, Ezra. . . ."

"You owe me a minute. You brought me into this to be of some help to you. If that's not the way it's turning out, you still owe me at least a minute."

Robinson lowered his head. "Take your minute," he said.

"That was the day I told you about my father and the

compulsion he had that things should mean something. He called it his own little sickness, but that was just his way of being unpompous. Because that logophilia of his, that's something that people like you and me used to take for granted. We might quarrel over what something meant. But not about the central idea. We were not people who would ever line up with the barbarians, to whom survival is the only thing that means anything. Not Ezra and Robbie. And we didn't stick around when things got really ugly in D.C. Not us. Kim says the difference between men and dogs is dogs never bite the hand that feeds them. Don't you remember the contempt we had for the string of Administration people under Johnson—most of them hated the war—who quit 'for reasons of health.' And can't you see that one of the reasons things went bad here is that nobody knows who's in charge any more? People are acting out of loyalty ... to nothing!"

Robinson loomed large over Ezra. He frowned, as if determined to take his accusations with gravity. "We missed the days when everybody knew who ran everything. Not just Hollywood; everywhere. Or maybe people always think in the good old days everybody knew who was handing out the orders—or who had the right to hand them out."

He came closer so that Ezra had to look up into his face. "I know you're shaken up by this Max thing," Robbie said. "But remember me in the garden of the Beverly Hills Hotel. All that fuss of being thrown out because somebody who *seemed* to be in charge was fighting me over the budget of Sordino's picture. *I'm never going to be that powerless again.* I think it stinks that a nice boy like Karol is dead. But there's nothing I can do about it, and it's not really what we're talking about." He could barely wheeze out the last few words. He then proceeded to further hoarse emblems of friendship by warning that Ezra could expect a change in the atmosphere surrounding his research report.

Robinson was relieved to get to practical matters, under the guise of warning a friend. The "hit" fever was in the air. The sober concerns of running a tighter ship, of scientifically managing the business did not weigh so heavily any more. Ezra was not to be surprised if people blinked when he spoke about the danger of betting millions of dollars on hunches, on manipulated preview screenings. Those were concerns of harder times.

"You set it up yourself," Robbie allowed himself an asthmatic laugh. "You got Sordino together with Stone; you got him the special screening at Cannes. You changed everything. I've never seen such a response. They tore up the seats. You couldn't fake that. With that kind of response nobody cares about the engineering of consent."

The cautious Grayman added a cautionary note. The committee still wanted Ezra with them. His speech on the research proposal would be helpful. The outcome of today's meeting would not be known for several weeks; not until the proxies were counted and the SEC could make its evaluation and statement.

"If your speech goes over big, Kleinholz will claim you, we'll claim you, you'll be everybody's boy."

"But essentially my ace in the hole doesn't mean much any more."

"Ezra, you should have been there. They carried Mitch Stone on their shoulders. He could have been a war hero."

"I've never liked war heroes much," Ezra said. He went to the door. Robbie stood next to him. There was something unspoken, still, between them. On a hunch, Ezra asked him about Sordino and the Balzac picture, *Lost Illusions*.

Robinson said, "I'm doing the picture. But not with Sordino."

"I thought it was all set."

"Nothing's ever all set. Don't you know that yet? I *can't* go ahead with Sordino."

Ezra did not want to hear the answer, but he had to ask.

"He's not a well man. I can't take the chance." Sordino's scarf had finally unwound.

"Who's going to do it?"

"Mitch Stone is crazy about the project. And it's a picture about youth, a young man from the provinces conquering Paris. Perfect!"

"You're burying Sordino."

Robinson's face went blank; no expression at all. It must have been his way of expressing rage, one Ezra had missed over the years. Or else a learned response, a way of surviving in his new habitat. Breath whistled in his chest.

"There's a four-hundred-million-dollar company up for grabs in that stupid grand ballroom, and Sordino is going to die of cancer—and I'm going to die when the time comes of whatever I'm going to die of. Mitch is going to do the picture. Not Sordino."

Ezra was tenacious, not because he had nothing to lose but because he now suspected he had nothing to win.

"Mitch can do another picture."

"This is the one he wants to do. And it's the right one. It's for the same audience as *Festival*."

"I can't believe it, Robbie. That's the Great Ape Trick. You were going to give movies back to the film-makers." For a moment a steady eye contact threatened a change in the power balance between the two old friends. If either one had turned away, the other one would have felt victorious, no matter what was finally won or lost.

But something stranger happened. Without blinking, Robinson said, "Maybe I was wrong. Maybe movies always have to—and *will* always have to—play the imitate-the-last-great-success-game. Because in American life if youth is in the air then, dammit, youth is the great success. If nostalgia is in the air then that's the great success. Maybe we have to stop apologizing for running in streaks, in cycles. Maybe that's the name of our game. If the next cycle is American history then—to hell with it—we'll make a great movie about Thomas Jefferson using the latest hot-shot film-maker and star of the moment. And if we're smart enough to get out just before the cycle ends—more power to us. If not— tough shit! Somebody else will." The reversal was so complete it had its logic. Compromise is usually suspect. Conversion is convincing. Ezra made a last try at manipulation: "If you want me to work with you and the committee, then think this one through, again."

The very weakness of Ezra's position eased Robbie's rage. Color came back to his face, some tone, a musical inflection to his voice. He invoked his old friend's name twice, the way relatives do.

"Ezra, Ezra," he said. "You have nothing left to bargain with."

"How about Rossi. You need him. He wants to work with me. The way we'd planned."

"Umberto sat next to me at Cannes when the kids went insane with excitement."

"Drakmalnik's kids."

"No, everybody. I was there. Even me. So, whoever wins this throw of the dice for the company, has the picture . . . and a monster world gross. Research? A better way of knowing what you can spend, what you have? That can come, maybe, some day. Whoever wins is just going to go for between fifty and seventy-five million, right now. So, what you're asking, really, is a favor, for Sordino."

"For auld lang syne. For Robinson and Marks, I can ask you not to scuttle an artist because he has a throat full of cancer."

Over the landscape of that room—the dirty dishes, the

spread papers on the coffee table, over the thick pile carpet that cushioned their steps—there passed a distance between Robbie and himself, an infinity of empty space so great that it was as if they were no longer in the same room or the same city. There was no need to wait for an answer, no need to wait for anything. Robbie's sneeze was like the period after a sentence. Ezra's question had been too deliberately naïve. Not even Nick Bohm with his passionate loyalty to Sordino would have asked what he had asked. If you can ask questions like that you've come to the end.

13

Company Meeting: The wooden chairs being set up in the grand ballroom, the distant sound of hammering as Kleinholz sits on his wheelchair throne. Ape supervises the setting of the stereo system—for replay as well as taping, this time: the score of *Festival* will be played for the stockholders at a crucial point in the proceedings. *Image*: on a purple curtain next to the dais is a painted blow-up of Mitch Stone kneeling on the ground holding a snake in his mouth. Many years before, Ezra had walked up Fifth Avenue and had watched some Japanese store hang out a flag emblazoned with the Rising Sun. He'd felt, for a moment, the foolishness of passionate ideological combat: sooner or later you will be hanging the flag of the one who is now the very Devil over your streets, in the name of passing time, of convenience, most likely in the name of commerce.

Kleinholz stared lovingly at the picture, turned his attention to Ezra: "I know what's happened"—he adopts a momentary somber expression"—but don't think you're the only one who cares about Max. . . . Worked for me for years

. . . I'll stand by him. The best lawyers. Complicated case,
anyway. No question of death penalty; Italian law, American citizen, all being sifted, but don't worry."

In the meantime, Ezra is fourth on the program.

Testing Robbie's thesis, Ezra told Kleinholz he had his
research speech nicely laid out.

"Fine, fine. Just remember that we have the biggest
youth picture of a decade devoted to youth. Never mind
research—this is a hundred-million-dollar picture." (The
ante grows.) "The *Gone with the Wind* of the young. That
kind of thing." A blare of rock music burst from the loudspeakers and as swiftly stopped. Testing, one, two three.
Ezra was not to talk too long—and not to worry about questions. There will be no baiting; the word is out about *Festival*. Stone and Leggatt will be present for glamour and
interviews.

"Lothar," he asked, "whose cut did you screen at
Cannes?"

From the wheelchair came an impatient wave of the
hand. Cut? Why must one be bothered with irrelevancies?
"The compromise cut. The snake business didn't seem to
bother anybody. Your idea, I know. Compromise is your
specialty. I get that loud and clear. One reason why you've
got a future here."

The score from *Festival* blasted into the room. Then,
past the figure of Becker standing in the doorway, two
workmen carried in Kim's portrait of Karol. Young Antinoüs
in the last of his glory; mockingly beautiful, shimmering in
the thickly textured paint, proclaiming such youth as could
not fade, such life in spirit—shining through clear blue eyes
—as could never die.

264

14

Stockholders, attorneys, members of the press, employees of the studio, both American and foreign, directors who owned stock or had projects pending with King Studio, agents, a few stars brought in by Nick Bohm for glamour, or because they were his friends, and several amiable eccentrics who haunted annual meetings for obscure reasons of their own: almost eight hundred strong. They crowded into the Grand Ballroom and were fed coffee, doughnuts, and Sacred Publicity Texts. These were dispensed by Nick and his staff from the publicity department command post at the rear of the ballroom.

Bustle and tension are common to such occasions. On this particular morning it was intensified by the sense of impending conflict. The troubles and internal struggles of the studio were not news to these people. They had come for varying reasons of their own. But few of them were without anxiety, bitterness, or at least a concern for self-defense.

At precisely 10 a.m. the officers of the company filed onto the dais. Ezra was seated between Becker and Graham, the treasurer. Graham was a white-haired, quiet man who kept his eyes fixed unswervingly on Kleinholz.

"Mr. Chairman . . ." a voice called out from the floor. Kleinholz stood behind the podium. He was supported by two canes. There was no wheelchair in sight. It was not a moment for wheelchairs.

"Mr. Chairman . . ."

"The meeting is now open. Good morning," Kleinholz said. "I hope you will all feel free to say anything complimentary about the manner in which my colleagues and I have been running your company." An opening joke has always been obligatory, from Demosthenes to Kleinholz.

The ripple of laughter was brief. A hand was waved on

the floor. "Mr. Chairman." Without waiting to be recognized, a squat, red-faced man stood up. "Is it true that the
budget for *The Lion's Farewell* is already in excess by over
two million dollars? Is that how ... ?"

Kleinholz gaveled the man's mouth shut. "That will be
covered during the report on current production, at which
time questions will be entertained from the floor."

Ezra registered a new Kleinholz: the parliamentarian.

"If you'll check your printed agenda, you will see that
we have a report on the extraordinary response given our
big new feature film, *Festival.* We also have a special report
on a new research program which will help us run this company in a more profitable and scientific fashion, in the future."

Another maverick refused to wait for the agenda to run
its course. This time, a middle-aged woman in a red dress.

"Point of order, Mr. Chairman."

The Chairman recognized the claim of a point of order.

"Why are we, the stockholders, paying Mr. Kleinholz a
salary larger than that of the President of the United
States?"

"That is not a point of order. But I will answer the question, anyway. One reason: in spite of our fiscal problems,
our debt is smaller than the country's. I earn every penny of
that salary."

This time the laughter was more widespread.

A moment later Kleinholz introduced Graham for the
Treasurer's Report. Just at the end of a string of percent-
ages, dollar and equity losses, cents per share, none of which
Ezra was in any condition to take in and sort out, the squat
man who had begun the questioning earlier, stood up with
angry questions about the financial gutting of the company,
the destruction of the value of his stock, the secrecy behind
the soliciting of proxies, allegations of a deal between the
Committee for the Protection of the Stockholders and the

present administration of the studio. . . . He refused to be
silenced by Kleinholz's gavel. Other voices were added.

Kleinholz gave a signal and the room was filled with a
blast of music from *Festival*. The lights faded, and a screen
descended in the front of the auditorium. Five minutes of
Festival footage were shown. It included a snippet of the
snake scene, a few bits of elegantly cut nudity and sexual
play, and some wild musical moments. When the lights
went up the applause was enthusiastic. The squat man and
the lady were, for the moment, silent. Everyone present had
read the *New York Times* that morning. They had learned
over their coffee, of the reception given to *Festival* at
Cannes. It was Nick Bohm's annual coup, and he'd pulled it
off at just the right moment.

During Becker's recital of current production, including
a progress report on *The Lion's Farewell*, Ezra kept waiting
for some mention of Karol's death. Nothing from Becker,
and nothing from the floor. Not that there was any context
in which it could be introduced without stopping the machinery completely. Death, manslaughter, had no place at
annual meetings. Becker droned on.

Ezra was next on the program. He took a quick internal
temperature test. Still ice-cold, still blank. Which speech to
make? The research presentation was ready but it felt inert
on his lap, in his mind. A dramatic denunciation of studio
life, followed by a public resignation? An elegy for Karol;
a small moment of remembrance for a casualty of the studio
wars, with a second or two tacked on for Max Miranda? A
quixotic announcement that Sordino *would* direct *Lost Illusions*—in spite of sickness and death? No. None of them
were aesthetically right. And it had, at the last, become an
aesthetic question. The important part was to feel right in
the mind and in the gut, for just one moment.

Practical considerations no longer existed. There was to
be no $2000 a week, no vice-presidential title, no power,

papier-mâché or other. All that was his now was one public
moment—and flight!

Suddenly, Ezra found himself, as in a hundred dreams,
standing behind the lectern. He had an extraordinary sensation of freedom. All bridges burned, or about to be. In that
long pause as his eyes moved slowly from left to right he
realized he was even free to change his mind. He could open
the folder, describe his plan, make some kind of deal with
whoever won control.

A small restlessness before him and on the dais behind
him told Ezra he had waited a second too long for comfort.
But comfort, too, was now irrelevant.

He only had to wait a few seconds more to realize what
he wanted to say. Just once, since joining the studio, he
would like to make a simple statement of truth as it appeared to him. The most important and simple truth he
could think of, without regard for consequences. The exact
opposite of publicity language, that thief of truth whose
thefts could hardly be measured any more.

"Ladies and gentlemen," Ezra began. The audience settled down. The delay had made them anxious, but the opening salutation promised familiarity. "A young man has been
killed by an employee of the studio." (And thought: And we
are all somehow implicated. But the statement of the fact
was the important part, not the unstated opinion.)

It was as simple as that. The words had come to him
with a rush of joy. He had absolutely no idea what he was
going to do or say next; or what anyone else would do. The
very openness of the moment was pleasing to him.

The shock that struck the audience was represented first
by a long silence. It was total—not a murmur. All faces
turned toward Ezra to hear what he would say next. But
that was all he had to say. It was a true statement. Therefore someone should say it, and he had said it. Yet, Ezra was
held to the spot where he stood. At least a full moment

passed. There was a stirring of standing bodies at the rear of the ballroom. As if in response, Ezra repeated the portion of the statement that was objective, undeniable, and, this morning, ignored. *"A young man has been killed. . . . "* he said once again.

There was a restless rustling, a confusion as to what was expected. Someone was at Ezra's side. It was Robinson. He placed a hand on Ezra's arm and tugged gently. Ezra ignored him. The time had come, finally, to ignore Robinson. Then Robinson was gone. Ezra had no idea how long he'd stood there. Yet he could not leave. As sudden as a thunderstorm there was a sense of menace in the air. Chairs scraped. At the side of the room he saw an impromptu conference between Nick and some hired hands. He wondered, idly, if an executive had ever been hustled from a dais by force? People were standing up in the audience, now. Someone called out something, but Ezra could not make it out. It was time for the third and last repetition. From some region of his lungs he did not know existed he found the air, the strength to call out, again:

"A young man has been killed. . . ."

It was finished for Ezra. But other things were just beginning. The floor was in total confusion. A uniform presented itself to Ezra's eye. Some practical sense returned to him. He couldn't believe they would want the scandal of calling in the police. Then he saw it was his old friend Watkins, the studio cop. Watkins of the Watkins-wink, who once had done Ezra's absolute bidding.

He was running down the center aisle, Nick Bohm behind him. The loudspeakers began to blare music again. Could one be arrested for telling a simple truth in public? Watkins jumped onto the stage. Nick clambered up behind him. Others were following. The music pounded, maniacally loud.

"Please, Mr. Marks, sir," Watkins said. An executive still

received executive courtesy, even one who had turned rogue. His grip on Ezra's arm was iron. People were milling around the front of the auditorium; the meeting was a shambles. Ezra had made his statement. He was finished. Still, there was Nick's ambiguous face, that face of twenty years of Hollywood Public Relations. He lunged at it with clenched fists, aware that it might only be revenge for certain Private Relations. Nick's face twisted in surprise; a fist landed on the side of his nose, releasing a spurt of blood. It splashed out in an arc, brilliantly red. Then Watkins grasped one of Ezra's arms behind him, wrenchingly high. From nowhere the face of Mitch Stone appeared, behind him, Leggatt and Cody: faces from a dream. Cody made a V for Victory sign and Mitch Stone yelled out, "Zap, man, Zap!" over the wild music into the chaos of the morning.

15

By the time Watkins got Ezra out of the ballroom his shoulder was fired with pain and his arm hung limp from its socket.

In a small room with green plush walls, behind the stage, the chaos reduced itself to waiting for a doctor in the midst of milling people. He recognized none of them: Nick's resident flacks, Empty Suits from law firms. In the distance he could hear sounds of the meeting progressing. At least order had been restored, somewhere. His shoulder rested in a nest of pain.

He saw Nick Bohm sitting on a couch along the far wall. Nick was holding a handkerchief against his nose. His yellow shirt was a mess. It was the second time he'd seen Nick with a bloody nose. The first was that long-ago morning at the snake ceremony. He wondered how many other times there had been? How many people had felt the frustration of dealing with that figure of vague shape—had substituted the impact of fist on face for the understanding they could not have?

Suddenly, in the delirium of pain and the confusion of that crazy morning, he wanted a crack at the inside of Nick Bohm as much as he'd wanted that other bloodier crack.

They faced off—Ezra's injured arm dangling, the flow of blood from Nick's nose for the moment stanched.

Nick spoke first. "Listen . . . l-listen, the trouble with you is . . ."

"Yes. You tell me that, Nick."

Nick Bohm stood directly in front of him his head craning off in odd movement, as if he were looking at himself in a barely visible mirror, rather than at Ezra.

"The t-t—trouble with you is—you keep looking for somebody to blame."

"For what?"

"For everything! What everybody in the studio—everybody in the whole w-w-orld has to do to get through the day. Right now it's the kid. Jeezus, that's no reason to break up a company meeting a lot of people are counting on!"

"I didn't break it up. You and Watkins did that."

"You know what I mean. You come in here. Your buddy brings you in to cover for him. And you start sitting in judgment on everybody else."

"You mean Max?"

"Max was just trying to do his job, under a hell of a lot of pressure."

Ezra swung his injured arm lightly, hoping to ease pain; it hurt more so he grabbed it and held it still with his good hand.

"Yes," Nick said. "It got out of control, but the intention is what counts. Hey, Ezra, even in the courts, the intention is what counts, right?"

"My intentions are no cleaner than yours, not lately anyway. . . . It's what you *do* that adds up at the end."

"But there is no end," Nick Bohm said. "You think in ends because you can't go all the way. Max didn't think in ends. He just wanted Karol on his way and the picture finished." Nick brushed a finger of hair from his eyes. He was as impassioned as Ezra had ever seen him; irony was lost. He was making his claim, for whatever it was worth. "Don't you see the kind of p-p-p-" He struggled so over the next word that Ezra was in an excruciating agony along with him, to get it out. His mouth twisted, he stamped his foot hard, and it came out. "*Purity*. Don't you see the purity in that? Nobody can think in ends. What are you, God?"

"What do *you* think in," Ezra shouted. "Where do you live?"

Nick Bohm threw his head back, sniffing up whatever blood still trickled at the back of his nose. They had both been wounded in the course of Ezra's denunciation. But more than dripping blood and dislocated bones bound them together. Ezra had made love to Nick's future wife, and Nick had slept with Kim. Ezra had flirted with becoming Nick Bohm, but why was it that he felt so responsible and Nick so innocent?

"Ah," Nick waved a confused or contemptuous arm. "You guys—you come in here—I've seen you before—you come in here with your fancy education . . . with your built-in crap about the movie business . . . about the corruption . . . what makes Sammy run . . . all that shit . . . and what you don't get is: we're innocent because we're you, we're everybody else, on a sunny wave length. Same program, different station, Ezra." He smiled, all charm again; an unexpected, light, and assured instant in the midst of a storm. "We're on our own side, trying to take care of ourselves, that's all. But, for God's sake, that's what people are supposed to do. *Not hurt anybody, if possible, but just take care of yourself.*"

It was too much. Ezra was outclassed by the intensity of self-forgiveness. *Same program, different station.* Who could answer that? Outside the room the struggle was being controlled by Kleinholz. Inside, it was Ezra who stammered, not Nick Bohm. He had no doubt that he was in the presence of a kind of evil; perhaps one of the significant species. But he had discovered a truth that had teased him for months: it was the absolute innocence of evil. Not only banal—though it was that, of course. Not only motiveless, as with Iago's steady drive to topple his black man, though certainly that, too. But most of all, it seemed to share, along with the rest of the human animals, the perfect conviction of its innocence. Perhaps smelling his impending victory, Nick Bohm moved closer. Ezra caught an acrid odor; it could have been sweat from either one of them.

It was a marvelous Darwinism-brought-up-to-date. Not the survival of the fittest, but survival-as-innocence; the argument against which there was no defense. In the distance a gavel struck wood. Let the publicity program for the dead begin, Ezra thought. It was he, not Nick Bohm, who had made that speech in Rome, who had reassured the studio powers that the dead Karol could be as potent a force as the living boy. It had been partly to save Sordino's picture. But only partly. He had been eloquent; had used every trick imagination could summon up. And, worst condemnation of all, he'd won. His only solace was that he had finally lost.

But his cracked shoulder was no nobler than Nick's bloody nose.

16

Ezra took a taxi to the emergency room of New York Hospital. He asked a nurse to call Kim. By the time she arrived, the X-rays were taken and a kindly Japanese doctor put the arm in a cast and dosed him with Demerol for the pain.

Kim took him back to her studio. She distracted him for a time, showing him how she would spend the money she'd earned from Karol's painting. Push out a wall here, raise the ceiling there. She gave him space, she gave him time, she gave him coffee to fight the Demerol that was making him sleepy.

Late in the afternoon she went to buy some food and came back with the afternoon *Post*. The story was on page five. All he had to do was fill in the spaces for Kim.

"You're well out of it," she said. "You can't compete with that kind of devotion."

"For a while I thought . . ."

She laughed. "Oh, yes, I saw you going at it. Research plans, fake and real, political phone calls, balancing an obligation from one against a promise to another. Very elegant, very promising."

"A temporary aberration," he said. "It's time the games ended. I'm not a prodigy any more."

"Does that mean your youth is over?" she mocked. "You should learn a little self-forgiveness from Nick."

"Don't be too sure about it all. There was a lot of money in the air. The boy is dead and the picture goes on." His eyes closed.

"You're exhausted." She led him toward a long couch against the window. "I wish I'd been there to see you do battle."

"Well," Ezra said, "it was a moment, all right. Listen,

maybe I wasn't meant to have a lot of money; maybe I'll never do much in the great world...."

She was arranging pillows, drawing shades and draperies to cover them in darkness. "I have a lot of confidence in you . . . ex-whiz-kid, temporary vice-president *du monde entier.*"

He lay down carefully on the sofa. Kim patted a blanket over him, gently avoiding the injured arm. She put out the light and stood next to him as he drowsed in a drugged mist.

"Why?" he asked.

"I think," she said in a whisper, "that all this may have tenderized you, the way a piece of meat is tenderized, you poor bastard. You dueled with them, even if you lost. You worked on Robinson. You tried. Even hitting Nick and getting your arm busted. And saying those few words of mourning. You acted like—what's that Jewish word you're so fond of?"

"*Mensch*? More like a schmuck."

"You acted like a *Mensch*, today. You couldn't know what your final point would be until you got in it up to your neck. Nobody can. You acted human. You bit the hand that fed you." She was lying next to him. Half-sleep and distant pain and her tone gave him courage. It was not needed. She was taking off her dress while she spoke. Gently caring for his wounded wing, she rolled onto her side, kissing him lightly. It was a soft, gentle way of making love, from the first touching and separating of limbs to the slow and easy entering and rocking, cradling, all enwrapped sideways, his mouth on her breast, then her lips, then back again, her body pulling and releasing pulling and releasing.

17

Later, after more pain and more Demerol, he slid off toward sleep, hearing her say, still bent on consolation, "We know that Nick was meant for Honey and Becker was meant for Nick and Kleinholz was meant—and it's sad—for Robinson. All of them marvelously meant for each other, locked in horrible—that thing you said Robbie called it—locked in psychoeconomics, till the last movie is made and all the money is gone."

She kissed him. "Good night, Ezra." And added, "Dear Ezra," very quietly, "maybe the whole thing isn't worth doing at all. Maybe there's a life elsewhere, otherwise, different, separate. . . . Maybe there's a place where being good and singing Schubert lieder is the most importnat thing to do . . . maybe not . . . oh, what's the use . . ." Her voice was almost inaudible as she drifted away and he fell headlong into sleep.

There was a different young man working at the D. H. Lawrence shrine. He gave me Paul's address in Albuquerque. There was apparently a summer semester. When Paul got home from his class he found me having coffee with his mother, a nice lady with blue hair in evenly set waves. Paul had told her about his encounter with me. He had even showed her the newspaper accounts of the meeting. She made me welcome, asked politely about the healing of the arm encased in its cast.

After the initial surprise and excitement, Paul insisted that I stay on with them. I had been going to ask just that. I still could not fend too well for myself. The immobilized arm put me off balance: the left hand was a stranger to facility. There was no way for me to drive a car. And chauffeurs were a thing of the past. Blinking in the hot sun outside of the hotel while Paul went inside to pick up my baggage, I saw myself wandering in his wake at school. Perhaps the University of New Mexico could be my recovery room, after the operation I had just undergone.

For days I dreamed under the endless blue sky. Perhaps I would teach a course on poetry and the film. No—start more slowly, naming of things à la Sordino. The poetry of rocks, then the poetry of the Southwestern flora, then fauna; work my way back to people by the naming of simple things. But I could hang on, get an appointment. What would become of me? I would become one of those people one meets at faculty receptions for the visiting "names." Marks? Oh, he was with a movie company, once. Runs the Cinema Club here. Gives a comparative course on Blake's poetry and the cinema of Cocteau.

Driving me in to the orthopedic clinic in Albuquerque to be checked by a lean young doctor named Morris, Paul laughed me out of such self-pitying fantasies. I would be back in Hollywood slugging it out in a matter of weeks. But he also seemed to understand that more than my arm was convalescing. If I spoke about recent experiences, he listened and commented eagerly. If I avoided the personal, we talked of movies, books, about Santa Fe, where he had a girl friend, a young anthropologist whom he wanted to marry. (My paranoid vision of Russell James with his arm around Paul's shoulder receded.)

I was getting my strength back. I was looking at objects the way Sordino's camera looked at them. A glass of water, a chair. There was something wonderful about a chair, especially if you were as tired as I was. Just as there was something wonderful about the heady, bitter smell of jet fuel if you were in a hurry. Airplanes had their own excitement. But that was yesterday. Today the comforts of stasis, not the thrills of movement. Today the sense of place, brown dust, mottled black-and-brown rocks, not the geometric blur of landscapes far below.

I became aware of how little sense of landscape there had been in my King Studio season. There had been mainly hotel suites, offices, planes, waiting rooms, limousines. And —proving that landscape is a function of attention not of presence—in the background Paris bridges, Roman walls, California hills. Perceived but unregistered. Stated, but not understood. Or, in Sordino's terms, not named. One afternoon Paul brought home a book he'd found in town. It was a "novelization" of the D. H. Lawrence short story by someone I'd never heard of. King Studio field men were probably out buying them up in quantity already. Such incidents had the tone of communiqués from a distant battlefront. There were others. The newspaper report of Max Miranda pleading guilty in a pretrial hearing. The trial would be held in Italy. Louis Nizer had been engaged for the defense, in addition to Italian counsel.

Most surprising of all was the news that the Committee for the Protection of the Stockholders had joined forces with

Kleinholz and Becker to resolve the proxy struggle. *Festival* opened in New York at the Cinema I, to record grosses, and Mitch Stone had begun preproduction work on *Lost Illusions*, Robert Robinson, Executive Producer.

"Will you see this Kim Cross again?"

"I don't know."

"Will you go back to Washington?"

"I don't know."

"Will you go back to teaching?"

"I don't know."

Paul laughed. "You don't know much these days, do you, Mr. Marks."

The night before I was to go back to the orthopedic clinic to have the doctor free my arm from the cast, I woke, soaking wet, from bad dreams. I lay, bound in my wet sheets like a lunatic.

In the moment before sleep took me, one shape for my experience presented itself; formed itself into meaning, logos pursuing me still. It was simply this: in spite of all that had happened, I had been only an observer—a tourist taking pictures, making notes—in a foreign land.

Los Angeles, Paris, New York
1971–1974